Annie Knows
Everything

Annie Knows Everything

A Novel

Rachel Wood

The Dial Press
New York

The Dial Press
An imprint of Random House
A division of Penguin Random House LLC
1745 Broadway, New York, NY 10019
randomhousebooks.com
penguinrandomhouse.com

A Dial Press Trade Paperback Original

Copyright © 2026 by Rachel Wood
Dial Delights Extras copyright © 2026 by Rachel Wood

Penguin Random House values and supports copyright. Copyright fuels creativity, encourages diverse voices, promotes free speech, and creates a vibrant culture. Thank you for buying an authorized edition of this book and for complying with copyright laws by not reproducing, scanning, or distributing any part of it in any form without permission. You are supporting writers and allowing Penguin Random House to continue to publish books for every reader. Please note that no part of this book may be used or reproduced in any manner for the purpose of training artificial intelligence technologies or systems.

THE DIAL PRESS is a registered trademark and the colophon is a trademark of Penguin Random House LLC.

DIAL DELIGHTS and colophon are trademarks of
Penguin Random House LLC.

ISBN 978-0-593-97949-5
Ebook ISBN 978-0-593-97950-1

Printed in the United States of America

1st Printing

BOOK TEAM: Production editor: Cindy Berman • Managing editor: Rebecca Berlant • Production manager: Meghan O'Leary • Proofreaders: Amy J. Schneider, Karen Ninnis

Book design by Susan Turner

The authorized representative in the EU for product safety and compliance is Penguin Random House Ireland, Morrison Chambers, 32 Nassau Street, Dublin D02 YH68, Ireland. https://eu-contact.penguin.ie.

Dedicated to my parents,
who met at work

Annie Knows
Everything

One

Statistically, the most common days of the week to be fired are Monday or Friday. Which partly explains why, when I get to work—today, a Wednesday—and my keycard has been deactivated, I am very fucking surprised.

"*Oof,*" I say, when instead of gliding through the plexiglass barrier, I bounce right off it. The man behind me, too, is surprised, when he goes careening into my back. The security gates are meant to be a neat assembly line, not a five-car pileup.

I fumble, trying to swipe my card again, but by now I'm flustered—I've just made full-body contact with a middle-aged man in a charcoal suit.

"Go," he orders, slamming his fob down over the sensor, granting me the access I couldn't grant myself. I'm flushed with embarrassment, my brain frozen on the moment I felt his kneecap make contact with the back of my thigh.

Behind me, the barrier alarms go off again. Another person has been denied, and when I turn, I realize I know this person. It's Suzy, the copywriter behind the company's now infamous tagline: *Tick your to-do list off one Taskio at a time.*

The pull and release of awareness is like an elastic band

snapping against my skin. The faulty keycards aren't a coincidence. They're a ghosting.

I watch in horror while a security guard steers her away, and then I can't move fast enough. I'm clawing around the bottom of my tote bag, flicking aside dozens of crumpled receipts until I fish my phone out from the debris. It's vibrating in a short, insistent staccato before I even unlock the screen.

When I do, it's covered in notifications, each little snippet forming a picture of what's transpired in the time since I last checked it. Chief among them is a mandatory meeting invite staring at me in all caps, scheduled with HR at 8:30 A.M., and long since missed. Which begs the question: can I truly lose my job if no one can get hold of me?

I have the answer as soon as I flip into my emails. Instead of my inbox, I'm greeted with a lock screen that simply says *Contact Systems Administrator*.

Next: texts. I've been added to a new group chat, aptly titled *WHAT THE FUCK?*, and the messages are pouring in faster than I can read them, the names of my teammates appearing in rapid succession. My phone starts ringing before I finish crafting a reply. I swipe as soon as I see *work wife* on the caller ID.

"Annie, where the *hell* are you?" Carrie's voice hisses in my ear. "You were supposed to be on the phone with me fifteen minutes ago."

"I'm here. In the lobby." My hands are *so* clammy. "My keycard didn't work. Someone else let me in. Am I being laid off?"

She doesn't even bother to deny it. "Just get up here. *Don't* talk to anyone. Come straight to my office."

The line goes dead.

. . .

By the time the elevator deposits me on the twenty-fourth floor I'm half expecting a group of people to be standing by the doors with confetti, shouting *Surprise! You're unemployed!*

Do I find my job ridiculous? I work for a productivity software company, so yes, obviously. Do I want to lose my ridiculous job? I do not.

My best friend Carrie works in the HR department, her door at the end of a narrow hall. I find her in her closet-sized office, a windowless room lined with thick carpet she once admitted was installed to muffle the sound of crying.

We both started work on the same day at Jotter, the now-defunct startup that was bought out by Taskio. Over awkward chitchat with a dozen other new inductees, Carrie and I bonded for life when we realized we were both new to the city and secretly hoping to manifest our own rags-to-riches *Working Girl* storyline, complete with Harrison Ford.

That obviously did not happen—tech guys are either enormously socially awkward computer geeks or cocaine-snorting sales leads that speak in gibberish—but it didn't matter. Instead, I got Carrie, my partner in crime both during working hours and outside of them.

She's hunched over her computer, typing away furiously, the echo of her keystrokes bouncing around the compact space. Her head swivels toward me when I enter the room, like an owl. Her hands, I notice, never pause in their typing.

I close the door behind me. "What's happening?"

"Shitshow," she says, summing up my own take on the matter perfectly.

In under a minute, she puts me in possession of the facts as she knows them: the big executive meeting that took place yesterday, the list of layoffs that came in late last night.

"I don't understand. How did I not know about this?"

I usually hear all the big workplace gossip. Carrie is even more skillful. Like a pig rooting for truffles.

I eye her with suspicion. "How did *you* not know about this?"

"On my life, I had no idea," she says. "I don't even think my boss knew. It feels really sudden."

"So that's it? Goodbye, Annie, have a nice life?"

"If you had turned up on the call when you were supposed to, you'd know the answer to this! Where were you?"

"Pacing around outside, arguing with my mom. Shannon and Dan are engaged again."

I'm hard put to decide, now, which of the two calls I'd rather have been taking: the one telling me I'd lost my job, or the one telling me my sister is re-engaged to the worst man in the world.

"What, the mayor guy?" Carrie asks. "I thought you banished him."

So did I. Also, to be clear: he is *not* the mayor. Of anything.

"She wants to throw another engagement party." *She* being my mother. My sister Shannon has not deigned to discuss this—or anything else—with me in over two years.

Carrie scrunches her nose. "Ew."

"No kidding."

"Anyway, yeah," she says, returning to our original conversation. "You're laid off."

"Damn it."

The hideous prospect of interviewing for jobs even more pointless than this one appears before me. I barely repress a shudder.

"Carrie, I kind of need this job, you know, to pay rent, and have friends. And to not be a crushing disappointment to my parents."

"And I sympathize with that, absolutely," she says, squaring her shoulders. "We appreciate all your hard work during your time at Taskio. The business is experiencing difficult market conditions and is making some structural changes. Unfortunately, your role has been impacted."

I feel like I just watched in real time as a demon took control of my best friend's body. I look over my shoulder, checking we're still alone. "Are you filming this for YouTube?"

She ignores my question. "Your role has been terminated, effective immediately. In recognition of the contributions you've made to Taskio, we're able to offer you a generous compensation package to help you transition to the next stage of your career. You'll need to return any company property in your possession, and as a reminder of your contract, commercially sensitive information cannot be shared during or after your employment at Taskio."

I wave my hand in front of her face. "Seriously, Carrie, are you in there? If you can hear me, blink twice."

"I have to read you the script. Legally."

"OK, well, that was horrifying. Is there more?"

"That's basically it," she admits. "How did I do?"

"Um . . . fine."

"Did you feel like your distress was taken seriously?"

"Sure."

"Was my delivery a bit robotic?"

"Kind of."

"Damn it," she mutters.

This day is so weird. "Not that I have anything to compare it to, but for what it's worth, that felt like a textbook firing to me."

She perks up. "Really?"

"Definitely. Now can we please focus on the fact that I just *lost my fucking job*?"

"Right, sorry," she says, snapping back into action.

"Isn't there somebody else you could lay off instead? You know, besides me?"

She shakes her head, her blond hair ruffling against her shoulders. "I tried that already. It didn't work. However, I may have a solution."

She turns back toward the computer, clicking open the Careers page on the company website. I shift impatiently while she scrolls.

"When the business does layoffs like this," she explains, turning back to me, "they always freeze hiring. It's against employment laws, or something."

"Isn't it, like, literally in your job description to know this stuff?"

"Zip it," she orders. "The particulars don't matter. Bottom line, they can't make any external hires for a while, so any open job listings need to be filled internally. The only thing is, if I reassign you, you won't get your redundancy package."

I hesitate. "What's the package?"

"One month's pay."

Come again? "You just said it was generous."

"It is, compared with *no* package."

"I'll take the job with the paying salary, thanks."

"OK, well then, beggars can't be choosers."

"I'll do anything," I tell her. "Just please don't send me back to Canada without a job."

"Senior software engineer?"

"Anything but that."

"Junior legal counsel?"

"The 'no law degree thing' might be a problem."

She looks at me like: *you should have thought of that before you got fired.*

I squint toward the screen. "Is there nothing else in Product?"

"Oh, no way. Product got absolutely decimated."

"Figures," I mutter.

"Unless you want to take the designer intern placement, *unpaid*," she says, clicking around the job listings, "your only other option is Data Strategy."

I pause. "Am I supposed to know what that is?"

"The department head is Naomi Evans, if that helps."

"It doesn't," I tell her. "But whatever. I'll do that."

"Hmm," she says, scrolling through the job description. "I'm not sure you're qualified for this, you know."

"Carrie! Whose side are you on?"

"Yours! I'm just *saying*, they might give you a hard time. I can assign it to you, but it's still up to the department head to decide. If multiple people apply for the role, you're screwed."

"It'll be fine," I insist. "I will be very charming, and they will be desperate to have me on their team."

I mean, really. How hard can it be?

"Not sure that's how it works." Carrie drums her fingers against her lips, then types something, clicks around and says, "The thing is . . . I'm not very tech-savvy."

"Uh, OK?"

"If I *accidentally* deleted the job listing . . . " She raises her eyebrows.

I catch her meaning. "That would be a tragic, but honest, mistake."

"So tragic," she agrees.

I shake my head sadly. "I've always said it's such a shame you're not more tech-savvy, working at a place like this."

She beams.

"Yes, well, it has its upsides. This way I won't need to find a new lunch buddy."

Our heist comes together quickly after that. Carrie makes the internal transfer on the system, moving me from my old role to my new one, "accidentally" deletes the job listing from the website, and then rescues my employee profile from the digital abyss. As quickly as I was fired, I'm hired again, my inbox blinking back to life. Like my own personal Cinderella moment, I've been turned from a peasant into a princess. I now have until midnight to convince the head of strategy to let me keep the job.

"I have no idea if this will work," she cautions. "They might be interviewing someone else for it right now. And that will be your own fault! This is why I *always* check my calendar first thing."

"Again, very sorry about that. If I had known I was getting laid off this morning, I would have screened my mother's call."

"Good. Now get out. I have ten more of these meetings to do."

Two

Taskio is spread across five floors in one of the swishy new World Trade buildings, with views stretching out over Manhattan's Financial District and the Hudson River beyond.

All five floors are carbon copies of one another: enormous, open-plan squares with hundreds of workstations, the walls adorned with meaningless phrases like *follow your curious* and *break the mold* spelled out in neon lights.

The office has been designed, at great expense, to inspire creativity and productivity. We even have several fun little breakout spaces where you can go to play guitar, or secretly cry.

This place resembles a fancy high school: there's a cafeteria, an auditorium for assemblies, and desks for the thousands of employees who work here. There are cliques, and popular kids, and the department heads all feel like teachers—they're constantly giving you grades.

As a service, Taskio is brilliant in its dumbness; it's a digital version of the cork board you probably had in your family kitchen growing up. Using Taskio, you can pin up all your little digital cue cards and sort them into lists, dragging them around between columns that you might label as "to do" and "done," for example.

As the years have gone by, the software has become ever more powerful and complicated, but the basic principles are the same. You use Taskio to stay organized and productive and on top of your *tasks*, whatever they may be.

The reason Taskio has achieved global popularity isn't because it makes you more productive—in fact, exactly the opposite is true. Meticulously managing your projects using our software is like planning to make a plan; mostly, you could get the task done in the same amount of time it takes you to note down that you intend to do that task.

But by creating elaborate boards for your projects, and assigning deadlines, and tracking timelines, all that work you're doing that would otherwise be invisible—and therefore meaningless—is suddenly out in the open for everyone to see. Taskio doesn't help you *be* productive. It helps you *feel* productive. That's why we make the big bucks.

Thanks to the cookie-cutter layout of the building—and helpful overhead signs pointing you to the different departments, like a techy grocery store—it's not hard to find Data Strategy. I don't know anyone on this team, but after a hasty Google of her name, I can at least remember the department head: an extremely impressive and slightly terrifying woman called Naomi, who gives off real girlboss energy whenever she speaks at a town hall.

Even with fewer workstations on this floor than on my own, the place is deserted. There's only one guy here, ensconced behind a truly enormous pair of monitors. He's wearing headphones, and so it's not until I'm nearly right in front of him that he clocks my presence. When he does, he seems surprised, but also not, as if a total stranger approaching him out of nowhere is the sort of thing that happens to him all the time.

He pulls off his headphones as I come to a halt at the edge of his desk. I wonder, belatedly, if I should have taken the time to freshen up before I got here.

My getup today is what my roommate Sam calls "Hot Steve Jobs," which is to say a black roll neck paired with a denim maxi skirt.

I had tossed my hair into an extremely sweaty ponytail sometime after getting to Carrie's office. I itch now to take it back down, but if I did it would no longer be straight, but kinked from the haphazard way I tied it up.

For his part, he looks like every other New York normie who inhabits this city, but slightly better, like a Hollywood A-lister who's been dressed down to play the role of Average Guy.

He's in a brown knit hoodie, a beat-up pair of Levi's, and tennis shoes. He's also wearing a baseball cap, which he seems a *little* old for, and his brown hair wings out from underneath it around his neck and ears. Not a look I admire, personally, but to each their own.

His desk, I notice, is cluttered with all kinds of crap: empty coffee mugs, stacks of paper, another hat. And . . . a mini monster truck toy?

"Heyyy," I say, dragging the word out while I try and marshal my wits back into order. "I'm looking for Naomi?"

"Evans?"

"Yeah."

"I don't know why I asked that, as if there's more than one Naomi," he says, smiling. "She's still on mat leave."

Shit. I did not know that.

"Oh. Right."

"Is there something I can help with?"

"Erm," I say, my mind whirring. What now? "Do you know who the interim strategy lead is?"

"Perhaps," he says mysteriously. "May I ask what this is about?"

"Oh, um—I was just coming to introduce myself." I peer around, looking for someone, anyone else. This guy looks like he has all the time to waste in the world. I need to find a grownup. "I'm the new data strategist."

He leans back in his chair. Something about his posture calls to mind a cat playing with its kill.

"I wasn't aware we'd hired a new data strategist."

"And yet," I say, drawing an arm down the length of my body with a flourish. "Here I am."

"Strange," he muses. "I don't remember your interview."

"Probably because you weren't there."

"And neither was the department head, from the sounds of things," he says. "That's worrying. Are you sure you're in the right place?"

"Yes."

"Could you have interviewed over at CoinDot? They're on the 29th floor. Easy to get confused."

"I'm sure," I say, gritting my teeth. "I already work at Taskio. I got reassigned."

"Ah," he says. "The layoffs. I'm beginning to understand. What's your name?"

"Annie. Winstead."

"Annie Winstead," he repeats, testing it out. "Well, Annie, if you want to send a copy of your résumé, I'll make sure the department head gets it."

"Why would I do that?"

He blinks at me. "So you can apply for the role, I'm presuming."

"I don't think that will be necessary. HR already made the transfer."

"Be that as it may," he says, "I'm certain you'll still need to interview."

"Which I'd be able to do," I counter, "if you'd point me in the direction of the strategy lead."

He tilts his head like *well, you have me there.*

"Tell you what," he says, "the department head usually does the interviews up in the canteen. Why don't you head up there and I'll go find him, tell him to see you up there in five?"

"What are you, like their PA, or something?"

"Definitely 'or something.'"

I huff. I don't have time for this joker.

"Fine. I'll wait up there."

I turn on a heel and storm off without another word.

Three

Without question, the "canteen" on the twenty-fifth floor is the jewel in Taskio's proverbial crown. Designed like a restaurant and used like a meeting space, the canteen—or Scratch Kitchen, as it's officially known—is a popular watering hole for company-sanctioned socializing. In addition to the barista who's on site every day from seven until seven, there's also a salad bar that changes daily, plus an incredibly impressive array of self-service food and drink in the pantry that's available to us at all times.

To call this area a pantry is an understatement in the extreme—it's more like an enormous general store. There are rows and rows of packaged treats, all neatly arranged in wicker baskets and organized by type. I pick up my favorite (classic cheddar goldfish) and scroll while I wait, reading through my colleagues' tales of woe, and firing off a hasty missive to Carrie begging her to tell me who in the hell Naomi's mat leave replacement is.

I'm typing THAT IS FUCKING SHOCKING to a fellow fallen product manager when a chair scrapes against the concrete floor.

I look up and freeze. I should have known.

It is, of course, downstairs guy, who settles into the seat

opposite me and crosses his hands on the table between us, giving me a smile so angelic it's bordering on evil.

From this close I can see all the finer details that failed to register from farther away: his brown eyes, his very straight white teeth, the clear plastic frames that hang from his collar. His position would suggest he's at least around my age, if not older, but there's something boyish about him, too, that makes me wonder if he's actually twenty-one and just the kid brother of the CEO.

It might be the dimples.

Or the cap.

He stares at me expectantly, like *what are you going to do now?* My temper stirs in response, the ignition click on a gas stove flaring to life.

"You're the department head," I say flatly.

"Interim department head," he corrects, stretching his arm out toward me. "Connor Reid."

I decline to shake his hand. "And you couldn't have mentioned this downstairs when I specifically came over looking for you?"

"You seemed so certain it wasn't me," he says. "Who was I to correct you?"

"How could I have possibly known it was you if you didn't tell me?"

"They did send around an email about it at the time. That, and my contact details are literally in Naomi's auto-reply."

"Fine," I say. "My mistake."

"So, Annie," he continues, like this is all completely routine. "I understand you're interested in applying for a role in data strategy."

"I'm not interested in *applying* for it," I tell him. "I've already been reassigned."

"You keep saying that," he agrees. "But HR couldn't possibly have done that before we'd at least had a chance to speak to all the candidates. So far there are four. And then of course there's the skills test."

Carrie warned me, on pain of death, never to reveal how I'd tricked my way into this role, and if this guy attempts to interview me for it, it's game over.

"I think we might have some crossed wires here," I say, as diplomatically as I possibly can. "Maybe because HR knew I was the most qualified candidate, they just automatically approved it."

"Why would they do that?"

"Because of the layoffs. It's employment laws, or something," I say, parroting Carrie's non-explanation earlier this morning.

"Right." He sounds unconvinced.

"Of course," I say, trying to be gracious, "if you'd like to interview me as a formality, I completely understand."

"A formality," he repeats.

"Sure."

"Remind me—which department are you from?"

"Product."

"Seems like a fairly aggressive career shift."

"I disagree."

"Somehow that doesn't surprise me," he says dryly.

I watch him scan over me, starting at the top of my head and working down, like I'm a file that he's reading. I try to imagine what I might look like to a stranger, hoping I give off more "put-together city woman" than "annoying little sister." Several times a year I pay hundreds of dollars to turn my hair from "flat brown" to "warm, dimensional brown," a subtle, but I think significant difference, and one I hope he catalogues. He pauses when he meets my eyes, which, like his, are brown, and which my mom always says are my best feature. Though I suspect in this case, what he's noticing is the smear of mascara on my eyelid that I forgot to wipe away, and am now painfully aware of.

Assessment complete, he continues. "Well, now seems like as good a time as any, I guess. Let's begin the interview. First question: why do you want to be a data strategist?"

Jesus. We're really doing this.

"Well," I hedge, trying to find a better answer than *because I've been laid off and have no choice*. "I've always been interested in . . . data. It's so important, especially for a business like ours."

His mouth quirks at that. "That it is. And would you say you have experience with . . . data?"

"Definitely."

"I'd love for you to give me some examples." He shifts forward on his elbows. I mistrust the gleam in his eye.

"Well, obviously we're very data-led in Product," I say, stalling for time.

"Obviously."

"And, before the merger I handled most of Jotter's customer surveys, which, really, is just another form of data collection."

"I didn't think Jotter did customer surveys. They never had a user research team."

I shrug. "We weren't big enough to need one. It made more sense for someone in Product to run them, so the feedback could go to the right place."

He bobs his head, making a little humming noise like *hmm*.

The interrogation continues.

"Are you familiar with SQL?" When I say nothing, he adds, "Can you tell me what it stands for?"

Shit.

"Of course. Super . . . Quality . . . Leads."

"Uh, no," he says, but he grins, like this is the funniest thing he's heard all day. "It's 'Structured Query Language.' For the record."

I pick at a piece of imaginary lint on my sleeve. "I guess in your department it's different."

He laughs.

"Listen, Annie, you seem nice," he says, making fairly intense eye contact. "And I admire your commitment to the cause. But I think you'd hate this role. It's really technical, and if you don't have the programming languages, I'm not even sure you could do it."

Though he is one hundred percent correct in his assessment, hearing him say it—and so gently, too, like he doesn't want to hurt my feelings—puts me in a rage. My job is the one achievement I have to my name. I am not leaving here without it.

"Look," I say, impatient even to my own ears. "It's true that I haven't worked in data before, but I work *with* data every day. I have what it takes to be a great strategist. I know Taskio inside and out, and I'm a *really* fast learner. If there are gaps in my knowledge, I'll fill them. Quickly."

"I don't doubt it," he says. "But with the best will in the world, you couldn't teach yourself this stuff overnight. It's not going to work."

"Try me," I challenge. "You said there was a skills test. I'll do it."

Connor does what I'd describe as an incredulous pause.

"You want to do the skills test."

"Why not?"

"Are you good with Excel?"

"Absolutely." *Not.* Absolutely not, I hate Excel. I will admit this to him never. I will grind his stupid skills test to dust.

"Great." His tone tells me he thinks I'm full of shit. *The feeling is mutual, buddy.*

"So we're agreed? If I pass your little skills test, I can have the job?"

His mouth twitches just the slightest bit. Is he laughing? "We're agreed. Do you want me to walk you through it?"

"I think I can handle it."

"Sure." He nods, grave again. "I'll send it over, then."

"You do that."

"I will."

"Fantastic."

"Perfect."

"*Ideal.*"

We stare each other down for another minute until I blink, and the spell is broken.

By the time I'm storming out of the cafeteria, the fear of being laid off and humiliated in front of my family is all but forgotten. I have one goal only: humble this Connor Reid and become the greatest data strategist to ever walk the earth.

Four

It's been decided by the members of the WHAT THE FUCK? group chat that we'll all meet at Murphy's Tavern for a debrief. Since I have nothing to do until Connor sends over the promised skills test, I join them. If nothing else, it's probably a good opportunity for a little reconnaissance.

Murphy's has always been the de facto meeting place of the product team—the vaguely Irish pub is run-down compared to the rest of the Financial District in a way that feels almost charming. It's perpetually dark, the wood is faded, and the single decorative feature is a huge mural of signed dollar bills stapled to the wall behind the bar.

There's a real pre-vacation energy in the room when I push through the doors. Though it's barely eleven in the morning, the drinks are already flowing. And why not? We're the only people in here, and the majority of us don't have jobs anymore. You can feel it in the air: these people are here for a session.

As expected, there's a single topic up for discussion—mostly we're all saying some version of "Can you believe this?" over and over again while the shots get passed around. Usually when there's layoffs, *someone* sees them coming, rolling toward the business like a huge storm. Today's proceedings at least have some novelty. They've come as a huge shock to everyone.

• • •

Eventually, I spot Andy's disembodied head across the room and make my way toward him, his gel-glossed hair the end point on my treasure map. As another Jotter original, Andy and I go way back—he's the closest thing we have to a rock star in the product department, and for a while there, I was basically his groupie.

Andy was famous at Jotter for launching our most talked-about feature, the template library. It's exactly what it sounds like: a huge collection of pre-populated boards which teachers or marketing managers or software engineers could use to hit the ground running when they set up a new project. It was extremely successful when it launched. And eventually, one of the reasons Taskio acquired Jotter.

I already know he and the rest of his team survived the culling—they're now one of only a handful of Jotter squads left in the entire department. He's deep in discussion when I approach, talking to Leon, another product manager who, like me, also lost his job this morning.

"There she is," Andy says, looping an arm around my shoulders and squeezing me to his side like a long-lost friend.

Though my crush on Andy took a long time to die, overall, it was an instructive learning experience about the nature of workplace flirtation, which no matter what it might seem like, indicates nothing.

Making out at the Christmas party also means nothing. Equally meaningless: getting to second base in the stairwell at that same party. I cringe every time I remember that he has drunkenly touched my nipple. Or how smoothly he forgot the whole thing.

"It just seems crazy that it would happen that fast," Leon says, returning to whatever conversation they were having.

"I'm telling you," Andy insists. "*Something's* going on. And I intend to find out what it is."

"Watch out, Taskio," I tease. "Detective Andy is reporting for duty."

"You know it. I think I could pull off one of those trench coats, don't you?"

This is a classic Andy "joke"—one where he's being funny, but also not remotely kidding.

"You could certainly try," I say.

He thinks he'd look hot in a trench coat. He probably *would* look hot in a trench coat, but would ruin it with his awareness of that fact.

"Well, good luck to you, man," Leon says, slapping Andy on the back. "Can't say I'm pissed that this isn't my problem anymore."

"What will you do, Lee?" I ask.

"I've got a buddy over at TrustPilot, he's going to try and get me in. What's next for you, Annie? You moving back to Canada?"

Andy is confused. "Why would you move to Canada?"

We stare at him like he's insane.

". . . Because I'm Canadian."

He looks dumbfounded. "You are?"

For a second, I think he might be kidding. "I mean, this isn't exactly new information."

"Dude," Leon says. "How did you miss that? She literally has a bottle of maple syrup on her desk."

"I have no idea," Andy says, with a shake of his head.

I have no idea either; I've told him multiple times.

"Anyway," I say, moving the conversation swiftly along. "I'll hopefully get moved internally."

"Nice one," Leon says. "How'd you manage that?"

"Funny story. I didn't see the call invite this morning and missed it. I didn't know anything was wrong until I got here and my keycard didn't work."

Andy winces. "Ouch."

"I went up to HR and Carrie had to lay me off in person," I say, pulling a face. "But she's trying to get me moved into one of the other open roles."

"What's new with Carrie these days?" Andy asks. "Is she still seeing that guy from Merrill Lynch?"

How does *he* know about that?

"Erm, no. They broke it off a while ago."

Andy makes a little noise like *hmm,* and I get the distinct impression he's trying to look less interested in that information than he really is. Before I can go any further down that rabbit hole, his attention is caught by the arrival of his deskmate, and he moves off to go and say hello, leaving me alone with Leon.

"Question," I say to him. "Do you know anyone in Data Strategy? They sit up on twenty four."

"Data Strategy, Data Strategy," Leon muses, scratching at his chin. "No."

"The department head is Naomi Evans," I prompt.

"Oh, *them,*" Leon says. "Yes, I do, actually. Is that what they're called?"

"I guess," I say. "That's the team I'm hopefully getting transferred to."

"I think Alex did some work with them recently. Hey, Alex—" he calls across the bar, waving Alex over.

Though everyone in this room works in the product department, we all have different disciplines. Leon and I both do user research, meaning I spend (spent, rather) most of the day scheduling calls with customers who already use our software, then ask them to share their screens as they talk me through exactly how they use Taskio, and for what. Afterward, I write up a little report and email it to its final resting place, the inbox of another product manager.

Alex is a UX designer, which stands for user experience. He's somewhere between an artist and an urban planner; it's his responsibility to make sure things like the home button are in a place you can actually find.

It sounds simple, but in fact, Alex has the diplomacy skills of a hostage negotiator. He spends his days tactfully persuading the decision makers around him that no, we don't need to look different, or be jazzy—the customer likes it best when they can navigate the software without having to take a seminar first.

Alex is almost freakishly tall, and as slim as a twig, with tawny-brown hair and a nose piercing. The way he leans down over the bar calls to mind a giraffe, munching on leaves.

"What's up, guys?" he asks, pausing to sip on his morning beer.

"Al, you did some work with Data Strategy, right?" Leon asks.

"That's the team I'm hopefully being reassigned to," I tell him, craning my neck upward. "I'm trying to get some intel. What do you know about them?"

Alex knows a lot, as it turns out. From what he can tell, they're some weird shadow faction, sitting separate from the other teams, working on miscellaneous projects at the behest of the leadership team.

They sound random, honestly. They must be the only team in the business that gets asked "What do you do here?" more than the product department.

"I did a lot of work with them last year. Building out the new reporting dashboard."

"What is that?"

"Besides a disaster?" he jokes.

The reporting dashboard, it turns out, is the final phase of the Taskio/Jotter merger. If you can even call it that. Officially, Jotter was absorbed. Like when one twin vanishes the other in utero.

"All good guys, though," he assures me. "And Connor is a genius."

I try very hard not to roll my eyes.

A few other friends join us at the bar, and I survey them on whether or not they know Connor.

"The guy who's always with Brad Pincer?" one asks.

"Er, not sure," I admit. "Is he?"

"If it's who I'm thinking of, that guy is pretty much Brad's bitch."

Brad is the VP of corporate development. He is not a popular man in Product, nor, I think, anywhere. No one seems to be exactly sure what his role entails, yet Brad seems to believe his remit extends across the entire company. He crashes meetings constantly, invites you to explain things to him like he's seven, and is obsessed—and I mean obsessed—with what he calls "cross-functional initiatives." If Connor is one of his cronies, he's also probably a complete drip.

Next, my friend Martha appears, wedging her way between us and leaning heavily against the bar to order another drink. She turns back with a slurred *sorry 'bout that,* while she waves the bartender over. It strikes me as I watch her pay for her vodka soda that she is already pretty tipsy.

"Want to do another shot?" she asks, confirming my instincts.

"I'm good, thanks," I tell her. "I have to go back to the office after this."

"Now that they've paid me to leave," she says sagely, "you could not pay me to go back there."

"Wise words, Mar. Any idea what you want to do next?" I ask her.

"I think it's time for me to move to Philly," she says haltingly.

"Right." I have no idea what she means by that and don't dare probe further. Like Alex, Martha is also a designer. Maybe they're into that there?

Martha considers us. "So what are you guys talking about, anyway?"

"The Data Strategy team. Do you know them?"

"Who's the team lead?"

"Naomi Evans, but she's on mat leave. The interim is named Connor."

"Oh yeah," she says, "I think I know him." And then a second later, "Wait, Connor who?"

I actually can't remember.

I try and picture the last name on his email signature and draw a complete blank. "Hat, glasses . . . kind of looks like a grown-up version of a kid."

"Oh, Connor Reid. Yeah. I thought you meant Connor Jones and I was thinking, how do you know my old piano teacher?"

"Have you done any work with him?"

She pauses to sip the dregs of her vodka soda from two tiny cocktail straws.

"Sort of. He helped me set up A/B testing on the new homepage designs last year when I couldn't figure out how to do it. He's pretty smart. Oh, and he loves hot dogs."

"So you liked him?"

"I mean, I thought Ben was hotter but I'd definitely have sex with him, yeah."

She looks at me very pointedly when she says this, like it's actually me who's just said I'd have sex with Connor, which I would *not,* so I don't know why I'm reacting like the two of us are already secretly doing it.

"I've never met Ben," I say, feeling the heat creep up my neck.

"He's not single, so don't bother. Can you hold my drink for a sec? I need more lip gloss."

She thrusts her glass toward me, and I hold it while she pulls a tube from her pocket and lines her lips with perfect precision. The alcohol may be impairing her powers of reason but is having no impact whatsoever on her fine motor skills.

Just then my phone chimes in my pocket. Like a creature summoned from the deep, Connor's name appears beside a little envelope on my screen with the subject line **Skills Test.**

I take my sweet time with my farewells at the bar, offering up dozens of loose-limbed hugs as I make my way toward the door, begging people not to be strangers, to let me know if they need anything, or have left anything behind. I'm unexpectedly choked up at saying goodbye to so many of the people I've known since I first moved here, and the realization that even if I keep this job, I'll basically be starting all over again now that most of my friends are gone.

"Heading out?" Andy asks, as I slip through the door. He's standing out front, having a smoke.

"Yeah. It's time to audition for my new team," I say. I point at the cigarette in his hand. "What happened to quitting?"

"Today doesn't count."

Considering the events of this morning, that seems fair.

He takes a drag. "Not many of us left now," he says.

"There really isn't," I say. "It sucks."

"You and me will stick together, though, yeah?"

I chuckle at this. "Of course. You're one of my last friends here."

"Right back at you." He nods. "Good luck in there. Give your new Taskio overlords hell."

I salute him, then head on my way.

Five

Back at the office, as promised, Connor has sent through a link to complete the assessment, the lone email in my otherwise empty inbox. I click it, and scan the instruction page, noting with a sinking feeling that once I hit submit, my scores will be sent straight to him.

I knew as soon as I'd left our meeting that offering to do this skills test was a tactical error. He assumed I wouldn't be able to pass it—I know with certainty I can't. My plan, insofar as I have one, is to cheat to the best of my ability, and then hope for the best.

A wave of nausea washes over me, whether at the prospect of this quiz, or from tequila on an empty stomach, I can't be certain. After reading through his email, I have to grip the edge of my desk and breathe.

When Connor said he'd *send it over,* I thought he meant he'd email me a spreadsheet full of numbers that I would neatly color-code and send back to him. I never bargained for a third-party platform that would run me through a series of coding tasks styled as little games. I have the sinking feeling he's outsmarted me before this skills test has even begun.

The first task is a sample, and I click through the guided instructions that show me how to complete the puzzle in front of me using bits of code.

It's a surprisingly friendly little quiz. I'm toured through the dummy task by a charming green dinosaur named Brian. He's holding a butterfly net. My mission is to help Brian find the butterfly. Though I'm not stupid enough to think this will be easy, the premise is simple enough.

Any hopes I harbored of cheating are dashed the second I click *start quiz*: each of these tasks is timed, my every move tracked via the progress bar running along the top of the screen. A bright blue clock in the right-hand corner counts down from five minutes. Can a clock be ominous? This one definitely is.

Brian the dinosaur waves me good luck and then leaves me to my fate, his animated form wandering offscreen.

We cut to a screen split down the middle—on the left-hand side is a blank notepad where I'll input the code I write, and on the right, a 2D meadow that looks suspiciously like a '90s video game. A butterfly appears. My first task is to help it flap its wings three times to land on the lone flower in the foreground.

Actually, this isn't as bad as I feared. Once the task begins, the notepad populates with all the elements you need. All I need to do is put them together. It's like playing piano on the computer—I need to organize everything into an order that makes sense.

For task one, I'm presented with a function (`flap_wings`) and a short lesson on how to create a "loop." The function will make the butterfly flap its wings once. I need to use the loop to make the butterfly flap its wings three times.

This is crazy simple stuff—even I can see that—yet it still takes me multiple attempts to check the puzzle. Eventually, I get it. I settle on:

```
for i in range(3):
    flap_wings()
```

And like magic, the butterfly moves. Brian pops back up and says *great job, you got it.*

The next few tasks continue in the same vein. I successfully make the butterfly land from flower to flower, each sequence becoming progressively more complicated than the last. At any stage I can press "play" to check if the sequence I'm building is doing what I want it to. Most of the time it isn't, but I delete and adjust until I get it. If I had to come up with the code myself I'd be toast—as it is, I can barely do it by selecting from the options the assessment gives me.

Finally, Brian appears again. Any triumph I felt at seeing his little green form fades away when he cheerfully tells me it's time to use what I've learned for the butterfly hunt. I'm to use the lines of code from the previous tasks to complete this one *without any hints.*

Damn you, Brian. I thought you were my friend.

From there, the quiz melts into a haze of panic, sweat rapidly pooling under my arms as I get closer and closer to running out of time.

Brian is supportive as I try and give chase to the butterfly, but his presence feels sinister to me now, like he's spying on me, reporting my every move back to Connor, who's upstairs somewhere, laughing evilly.

I catch up to the butterfly line by line. My final action is to bring the net down before it gets away, but I can't do it. I can't find a single sequence that remotely resembles what it asks. I'm going to fail this quiz.

I'm so demoralized at the realization that I'll have to climb down off my high horse and beg Connor to give me the job that

I just stare off into space until the final ten seconds, when I type out a line of nonsense and click submit.

Brian shakes his head, forlorn, telling me what I already know: we didn't catch the butterfly.

A colleague appears over my shoulder as the *Game Over* montage rolls. "Oh wow," he says. "It's Brian! My kid loves this game."

I turn back to face him. "What do you mean?"

"*DinoCode*," he says, gesturing at my screen. "Such a great platform."

"You've seen this before?"

"Yeah. Like I said, my kid loves it. He's been learning to code since he was four."

I frown at the screen, my chagrin growing. "This is . . . for kids?"

He looks at me like I've sprouted two heads. "Yeah. This is the junior game, see? It says so right there." He is indeed correct; right along the browser bar it reads *DinoCode Junior*. I *swear* it never said that until now. "Wait till you get to the over-10s. It's a Stegosaurus named Julie. My daughter does it at school."

If he says anything else before he wanders off, I don't hear him. My insides are a kaleidoscope of mortification and rage. So this is Connor's idea of a little joke, is it? How funny. How *hilarious*.

He has no idea who he's messing with.

Six

I'm like a cartoon kettle with steam coming out of its ears as I round the corner to where Connor sits. I intended to launch right into it but stop short when I notice the desks around him—previously empty—are now occupied by three other guys, who clock my presence immediately. Somewhere in the back of my mind, a smaller, more sensible Annie is screaming at me to remember that we need this person to give us a job.

Connor pulls his headphones off. "Well, this is unexpected."

He says this in a tone that conveys it's exactly the opposite, and he has in fact been anticipating my arrival since the second he sent over the skills test. For the second time today, I have underrated my opponent.

He stretches back in his chair. "To what do I owe the honor? Or are you lost?"

I glance over at the guy sitting directly across from Connor. His eyes dart back to his screen the second our stares connect.

"Can I talk to you for a moment please, Connor? *Privately*?"

"I'm getting the impression that this is a real now or never situation," he says, swiping a lanyard off the desk. "So I guess now it is."

He follows me to the nearest meeting room I can find, a

speakeasy-themed breakout space lined with deep oak bookcases and velvet couches instead of your usual tables and chairs. It's an almost comically inappropriate setting for this discussion, but I'm far past caring. I whirl on him as soon as he closes the door.

"What the hell is wrong with you?"

"Hello to you too, Annie. Such a pleasure to keep meeting like this."

"Cut the crap," I say, pointing a finger at him. "I know all about your little skills assessment prank."

His eyes widen in a look of extremely exaggerated surprise. "I'm not sure what you're referring to."

"*DinoCode? Brian the Dinosaur?* It's a game for five-year-olds!"

"It's not *just* a game," he says, wounded. "It's also a deeply beloved educational tool."

"Is this some sort of—of—" I'm so indignant I can hardly speak. What is the *word* I'm looking for? "*Hazing?*"

"Nah. It's just earlier you were so on your high horse I couldn't resist the chance to mess with you a little bit."

"Stupid little Annie can't possibly understand the data, is that it?"

"Definitely not." He has the grace to look sheepish. "But—if I might—maybe it was: *Annie can't possibly know all there is to know about something she's never done before?*"

The blush rips across my face like wildfire. Never in my life have I been called out so neatly.

"I was actually starting to feel a little bad," he says, scratching his neck. "In fairness, I thought you'd click the link and figure it out immediately. When it took you all afternoon I started to worry."

"Clearly."

"I promise I was going to come and apologize," he says, trying to placate me. "I got stuck on a call, that's the only reason I haven't come to find you."

"Well, now that's established, I would appreciate the real assessment."

"I mean, if *DinoCode* was a challenge, I don't think you'll fare any better there."

A noise I am in no control of leaves my body, a high-pitched squeak of frustration that sounds suspiciously like *ugh!*

He laughs, then reaches for an armchair to his left, dragging it over until it's directly across from the sofa. He motions toward it.

"Can we at least sit down, please? It's very off-putting trying to have a conversation with you glaring at me like that."

I say nothing, but oblige him, dropping down on the sofa and crossing my arms for good measure. Connor takes the chair across from me, leaning toward me with his elbows resting on his knees.

"Listen, Annie, while I admire your persistence, and am genuinely a little bit in awe of how rude you're willing to be considering you're also at my mercy, it's not going to work. This isn't the role for you."

He's doing that thing again, like he was earlier. Trying to let me down gently. I hate it.

I cast around, desperate for something that might convince him to give me the job instead of throwing me out in the cold, and then remember what Alex told me back at Murphy's, about the reporting tool they can't get anyone to use. What did he call it again?

I've got it.

"What about the reporting dashboard?"

Connor's entire demeanor shifts in an instant, going from playful to reserved.

"What about it?"

"From what I hear it's not going so well."

Irritation flits across his features, his eyebrows pressing together just a fraction before smoothing back out again. "I don't know what makes you think that."

Finally, finally, I've succeeded in putting him on the back foot. I'm sure Alex told me—he did, didn't he?—that they had been working on it together *last* year. That's a long project. A big project. And until today I'd never even heard of it.

"It's an internal tool, right? To standardize reporting." I'm trying to make it sound like I know more than I do. I hope it's working. "But people aren't using it."

"People are using it," he argues, without much conviction.

"Not enough people," I say. "I can help you with that."

He snorts like, *yeah OK, sure*.

"Do you know what I think, Connor?"

"I have a feeling I'm about to find out."

"I think you need me. You don't know it yet, but you do."

He's the one leaning back now, arms crossed, his whole posture guarded. I press my advantage.

"I saw your geek squad out there. You have enough people to help you with SML—"

"SQL."

"Whatever," I say, swatting his words away. "You have enough dorks to help you with the technical stuff already. I can focus on the rollout of your dashboard. It's a match made in heaven."

"Sounds like a match made in hell."

He succeeds in winning his first smile of the day from me. I might actually have him here. This might really work.

"Give me the job," I say, confident now. "I know what the product squads are saying. I'll roll out your dashboard, and handle any of the other annoying admin eating up everyone's time so you can focus on what's important."

"I need a data strategist."

"And I am one," I counter. "I can help you with all the data you can't find on a spreadsheet. I'll be like your secret weapon."

He's staring at a point beyond my shoulder now, his fingers drumming lightly against his lips. Then it happens: he thinks of something. I watch his eyes spark to life, then sharpen directly on me.

"I guess I could," he says, like maybe there's some big loophole after all. "We *do* need help with the dashboard."

I do not trust his tone. "But . . ."

"But," he continues, "there's one thing I'll need from you. Before I can approve the transfer."

I eye him with misgiving. "What is it?"

"Just a formality, really. A box-ticking exercise, if you will." He indulges in a dramatic pause, then comes out with it. "Admit I was right you couldn't pass the skills test. And you were wrong."

I re-cross my arms. "You know that already."

"I do," he says, head bobbing. "But I'm still going to need to hear you say it."

"Surely that's not necessary."

"Humor me."

He waits expectantly. I have a feeling he would sit here all day. It's so quiet you could hear a pin drop.

"FINE," I say, sounding like a surly teenager.

He rolls his wrist like, *go on*.

I grind my jaw.

"You were . . . right."

"And?"

"And I was wrong." It comes out barely above a whisper.

He gives me a huge grin, full-wattage. His delight is palpable. I have never seen a person smile so big.

"Truly incredible to witness. I should have recorded that. I have a feeling it's the first and last apology I'll get from you."

I roll my eyes. "OK, Mr. Fancy Data Scientist. I've been working here for six years, I'm not *that* useless."

"You bombed a coding quiz for five-year-olds."

"I can't have done that badly."

"Instead of a line of code, you wrote *this is hard* on the last question."

"I . . . didn't realize you'd be able to see that."

He laughs, the sound of it pulling a reluctant smile out of me in return. "You've got to admit. It was funny."

"It wasn't funny."

"It was a little bit funny."

"Says you," I tell him. "I'm the one who failed the dino quiz."

We both stand to leave, and he holds the door open for me, saying just before I pass through, "I'm not going to lie, I pictured this going very differently. I thought there'd be a lot more of you saying things like *thank you, Connor, you're amazing*."

"Thank you, Connor, you're amazing," I deadpan.

"*I'm sorry I swore at you at the start of this meeting*," he says, obviously wanting me to repeat it. I scowl as I walk past.

"You know what, never mind," he calls from behind me. "I accept your half-smile in lieu of apology."

Seven

It's unclear whether I'm free to go for the day or whether Connor expects me to stick around, and I don't really feel like poking the bear, so I decide to split the difference and pack up my old desk.

I steal an empty cardboard box and methodically fill it with all my work-adjacent belongings, which amount to a water bottle, four tubs of Tupperware, the maple syrup, a pen jar I've become weirdly attached to, and a stolen cactus.

Besides my friends, there's not much I'll miss about working in Product, in all honesty, but one thing I will miss is my desk. I'm on the non-glamorous side of the building, the one that stares directly into an adjacent office block that's almost identical to ours, but given the choice, this is still the view I'd pick.

I love watching all the other people going about their days. There's a meeting room visible from where I sit; as long as it's not too sunny, I can sometimes read what they're writing on the whiteboard.

Maybe if Taskio sends me packing they'll take me in instead. I could add just as much value to their organization. Which is to say, none at all.

It's amazing how pathetic it feels that I can pack the entire contents of my career into a single cardboard box. After six years the total sum of my contribution to this place will be forgotten in a blink.

Someday soon someone else will take over this desk and ask, idly, who used to sit here. And the person they're talking to will squint into the distance and eventually say, *you know, I have no idea.*

It's fine. I've survived enough rounds of redundancies to know it's not even really personal—for the purposes of these layoffs I am just a number on a spreadsheet. But it's weird, knowing that if I walked out of here today and never came back, I wouldn't leave so much as a fingerprint's worth of impact on this place.

It's amid these cheerful thoughts that my phone starts ringing.

"Hello?"

"It's your mother."

As greetings go, this one is totally unnecessary. "Yeah, Mom, I know."

"How do you know?" she says, accusingly. "It could have been your father."

"I can tell the difference between your voices," I assure her, switching the phone to my other ear. "You also told me you were going to call me back later."

"Don't be smart," she tells me. "And don't roll your eyes."

She issues this command at the precise moment I roll them. She's good.

"What's up, Mom?"

"We've decided to do the engagement party this weekend. I'll need you home tomorrow to help with the setup."

I choke on an intake of breath. "Absolutely not."

"It's not a request," she says, with the authority of one who has given birth to me. "Get one of the early flights."

"You know I have a job, right? One they expect me to show up for every day?"

"Take a holiday," she says breezily.

"Now *really* isn't a good time, Mom," I tell her. "I just got . . . um, promoted. Sort of."

She's not buying it.

"All the more reason why you should take a couple of days off."

"What? No," I say.

I catch a colleague walking in my direction and pivot, leaning my shoulder against the wall, trying to make it seem like I'm on a business call. I nod as they pass. They nod back.

"You can't just order me to fly home," I argue when they're out of earshot again. "I'm a grown woman."

"Oh you are, are you? Then start acting like one. What could be more important than your sister's wedding?"

"Seeing as it's *not* her wedding, it's her engagement party, a lot of things."

"Well, those things will have to wait."

"It's not that easy. Am I even invited? I don't think Shannon wants me there."

"Of course she wants you there," my mom says, never one to give up on trying to broker peace between my sister and me. Even if it means lying through her teeth.

"OK," I reason. "Then she can call me and tell me that herself."

"She's very tied up right now," Mom says, evasive. "There's lots to get done between now and Saturday and she has a big house sale going through this week."

"Again, why not just do this another weekend, then?"

"Because it's decided. We've already invited the neighbors."

"Heaven forfend," I mutter.

"None of your attitude, young lady. I'll see you tomorrow."

"Mom—"

"Text your father your flight number," she says, cutting me off to issue her final command. Then she is gone.

I stare dumbly down at my phone, at a total loss for what to do next. I could either: call her back and refuse to attend the party; refuse to attend the party without calling her back; go back upstairs and ask my new boss for a few days off.

I can't, in this moment, think of anything less appealing than going home to gag over the pending nuptials of my beloved sister to the Worst Man in the World. And what's the big rush? Is this a shotgun wedding or something?

Oh god. Is that it? Is this a shotgun wedding? Please, please no. I can't imagine anything worse than a miniature Dan.

It takes me a while to work up the courage to talk to Connor. Even I know this is pushing my luck. I consider sending him an email but think better of it. This conversation is best had face-to-face. At least then I can see his reaction.

There's just one problem. I can't find him. Anywhere.

The first place Connor is not is at his desk. Then he's not upstairs in the canteen. I check downstairs again: still not at his desk. There are infinite places he could be: call booths, meeting rooms, miscellaneous sofas, mysteriously placed little nap pods.

I'm standing outside a row of call booths with my hands on my hips, trying to decide my next move when the one closest to me pops open. Jackpot.

Connor stops short when he sees me hovering, bringing his laptop to his chest. Like a shield.

I give him a slow wave. "Hello."

"Just checking—is running into you for the third time today a coincidence, or have you been standing out here waiting for me?"

"Well, it is sort of a coincidence," I say. Which is not a lie. "But since we've bumped into each other, there *is* something I wanted to ask you about."

"What could you possibly need now. A kidney?"

"I'm touched you'd offer," I say. "Actually, I need to take a couple of days off."

He opens his mouth. Nothing comes out.

"Are you serious?"

"Yes."

"So to be clear," he says, scratching at his eyebrow. "After bullying your way in, your first act in this new role will be to . . . take a couple of days off."

"When you say it like that it sounds bad."

"OK." He nods. "Make it sound good."

I make a cringe face. I can't.

"I know the timing is not amazing," I admit. "But my parents are throwing my sister an engagement party this weekend and they need help with all the prep."

This diverts his attention. He tilts his head. "Where is home?"

"Canada."

"Aren't Canadians supposed to be nice?"

"Oh, that's just a rumor. It was a Canadian who started it."

"How long are you proposing to be away for?"

"Maybe a week?"

I can see that this answer has not impressed him, and hastily add, "I'll work remotely for most of it. Besides, it gives you a chance to prepare my onboarding or whatever."

He raises an eyebrow. "And if I say no?"

I place a palm on my throat and cough lightly. "Now that you mention it, I think I might be coming down with something."

This has its intended effect. He laughs.

"Are you always this outrageous?"

"Mostly, yes."

He tips his head back and sighs deeply. "What have I done?" he mutters.

"Made an *amazing* decision," I tell him. "I will go home for a few days and then come back here ready to be the model employee."

"Somehow I doubt that."

"You'll see," I promise him.

"That's what I'm afraid of," he says. He mulls it over. "Fine. Take Thursday and Friday. You'll officially start Monday."

I salute. "Yes, boss."

"*Early* Monday."

"I love early mornings," I tell him.

"And I expect you back in the office by Thursday."

"I will be here. Also early."

"Fine."

"Great," I chirp back.

"And now can you please do something for me?"

"Sure," I say. Only seems fair. "What is it?"

"Go home for the day," he tells me.

Umm. "OK?"

"Seriously. Please leave the building. I have things I need to accomplish today."

"It's a sacrifice, but one I am prepared to make," I say.

"If you cause me any more trouble between now and Monday you are fired."

"It will be like I do not exist," I promise him.

"Good," he says briskly. "Then I'll speak to you on Monday."

On my way out, I make one last visit to Carrie's office, turning the handle after I hear her muffled invitation to enter.

I find her in much the same position I left her this morning, hunched over her computer and typing so violently the letters are in danger of pinging off her keyboard.

I sigh dramatically and flop into the single chair in the corner of the room, yowling when my hip makes contact with the metal armrest on my way down. God, this *day*.

"So?" she says.

"It worked."

"I'm surprised," she says.

"So am I," I say, pressing the heel of my palms into my eyes. "It was really touch and go there for a minute. The department head was not having it."

"I gathered that, when he phoned me," Carrie says in response.

"Shit, did he?"

"Yeah, this morning, after you talked to him, I guess. Asking what the hell was going on, basically."

"What did you tell him?"

"Let's just say he probably thinks I'm the stupidest human resources manager in existence. He smelled a rat. He argued the role can't be signed off without his approval, and I just said there was some sort of mix-up. I thought for sure he was going to send you packing."

"I think that was his intention, but I won him over."

Or did I wear him down? I've spent the entire day trying to stay one step ahead of Connor, and it's only now that I realize just how little sense it made to hire me. Don't get me wrong, I'm grateful—but suspicious.

"What do you think his deal is?" I ask Carrie, thinking out loud.

"No idea." Carrie shrugs. "I don't think I've ever met him. What's he look like?"

"Like a kid who ate a magic bean and got turned into a grownup." But hotter. I don't say that part out loud.

Her lips turn up into a devilish grin. "Want to look him up on the system?"

I sit up at that. "*Yes*, absolutely I want to do that."

"Let's see here," she says, pulling up some internal employee database. "Connor Reid, right?"

"Yes."

"Ta-da! Here he is."

"What does it say?"

"Wow, he's been with the company *ages*," she tells me. "Like, nine years."

"I didn't even think Taskio had been around that long."

"Me neither. OK, how old do you think he is?"

"Now that I *do* want to know." He could honestly be anywhere between twenty-one and forty.

"He's thirty-two," she says, scrolling. So I wasn't far off, then. He's only two years older than me. "Actually, his birthday is kind of soon. May 15th. And his salary is *huge*. Jesus. I am in the wrong role."

"What's the figure?"

She prims up at this. To reveal it would be a violation of the vows she made to human resources.

"More than yours," is all she'll tell me.

"What else can you see?"

"That's basically it," she says. "His emergency contact is his mom."

"You made that seem like it was going to be a lot more exciting than it was."

"Nonsense," she says. "Now we know he's single."

I squint at her. "How?"

"Because if he wasn't, his emergency contact wouldn't be his mom."

"Or maybe he was single nine years ago when he first filled in that form?"

"True," she concedes. "We'll call it inconclusive."

I catalogue everything I've learned about Connor so far. He's smart, possibly a genius, loves hot dogs, is maybe single, has a mom, is thirty-two, hangs out with creepy Brad, makes good money and has worked here since the dawn of time. Adding to that my own observations: he is infuriating, with a dangerous sense of humor lurking beneath the surface that he will unleash on you at surprising times and in surprising ways. I must proceed with caution.

I hang around chatting with Carrie for another few minutes, filling her in on the skills test and drinks at Murphy's.

"Which reminds me," I say, calling to mind a past grievance. "Andy was asking if you're still going out with the Merrill Lynch Murderer. How did he even know about that?"

She doesn't look up from the day planner she's flipping through. "Because he asked me out at the time and that's what I told him."

"Oh," I say. So Andy *does* ask people out. Just not me. Cool.

"Relax," she says, her eyes flicking up and back down again. "I said no. I know he's your super special secret work crush."

"He's really not," I promise her. Any misguided hopes I

once cherished in regard to Andy died a long time ago. "Do you want to go out with him? You can, you know."

"Like all men in this city, he is a waste of my time," she says, slamming her planner shut. "And I don't need another fuckboy to text with."

This surprises me, a little. Carrie usually loves dating, and Andy fits the profile of her type to the letter. It's not like her to sound so cynical.

"Maybe you just need to switch things up? Date someone completely different."

"Mmm. I'll keep that in mind." She nods, like I've just given her the dumbest advice in the world, which in fairness, I have.

I drop it and change the subject, but the more I think about it, the more the idea takes hold.

When was the last time Carrie went out with someone who held her interest for more than five minutes? She's gone out with more Andys than I can count. What she needs is someone nicer, a little less flashy. And I am going to make it my business to find him.

Eventually, Carrie and I run out of things to gossip about, and she still has to finish the workday, so my banker box and I make our way back home to Washington Square.

I live in a fourth-floor walk-up in Greenwich Village with my roommate Sam, a situation that came to me courtesy of a message board, and to her courtesy of an uncle who bought this outrageously beautiful apartment sometime in the late '60s and has held on to it ever since. Sam originally lived with her sister, but when she defected to D.C. for a job, Sam decided she needed a roommate. It was two years before I found out her uncle doesn't charge her to live here at all. She uses the rent I pay her to supplement her income, which supports her pursuit of life as an eccentric, working part-time at an experimental art gallery whose claim to fame is that once a month it doubles as a nightclub.

Having never lived in New York—or tried to find an apartment in it—it was a long time before I realized how ridiculously, unbelievably lucky I was to find this place. At the time, I was just happy to have a reference point to share with people back home. When you're from small-town Ontario and people say to you *so where do you live* and then you get to say *so have you seen* Friends? *Basically there* . . . your street cred goes up by a factor of about five thousand.

I shut the door and drop my keys into a little ceramic bowl we keep by the entrance, the clinking sound disturbing the kraken currently occupying the living room.

She is—as always—dressed like a goth architect. Jet-black hair, jet-black eyeliner. Silver. Never gold.

"What's up, loser?"

It speaks.

Sam is lying flat across the sofa, her arm draped artfully over her eyes.

I blink at her. "Are you . . . did you just wake up?"

"I've told you before," she says, not moving at all. "I've hacked my circadian rhythm. Your 4 P.M. is my 4 A.M."

"So you did just wake up."

"I was out late last night."

And every night, I think. "Have you eaten? I was going to make salmon."

"Do NOT," she says, sitting up quickly, her legs swinging out to the floor, "stink this place up with your weird salmon thing. Ari is coming over later."

"Ooh, that's—" I stop when I see the look on her face.

Right. In Sam's universe, relationships are strictly casual. "... not worth commenting on at all," I finish smoothly. "Totally unrelated, I've decided to freeze the salmon and eat crackers."

"Good," she says, lying prone again.

This place is actually more of a one-bedroom. Sam lives in the room at the end of the hall, where the bathroom also is. Our kitchenette is divided from the living room by a small wall, making it mostly open-plan. *My* bedroom is technically a closed-off dining room, but a very spacious one, and even when her uncle lived here, meals were rarely served in this space.

I don't have a closet, but I do have a wardrobe, and a desk, and a queen-size bed, *and* only two of those items of furniture are touching—palatial by Manhattan standards. When I first showed it to my mother she said *oh my god, how do you live in that cupboard.* Go figure.

I love this apartment. I love the sloping wood floors, the uneven walls, the washer and dryer that's not in our unit but mysteriously lives in a cupboard in the hallway directly outside our door.

My favorite thing about this place, though, is Sam. She's like a goth version of my sister Shannon. Both of them are famously mean.

Sam, for example, savagely makes fun of me for being uncool every single day, but has a zero-tolerance policy for anyone else doing the same. Once at a party, one of her hipster artist friends called me basic—something she literally calls me all the time—and she stopped dead in the middle of her conversation, turned slowly and said, with eerie calmness, *say that again and I'll skin your cat*, then carried the cat around under her arm for the rest of the night, just to really drive the point home.

Shannon, too, is occasionally known to go to extremes. In my first year of high school, I accidentally dropped a tampon in the middle of history and this jock called Brett McMichaels tossed it across the room and told the whole class I had my period. I was extremely embarrassed, mostly because I *did* have my period, and had to walk over and retrieve the tampon, which I needed. When Shannon heard this story, she found him outside his locker, dragged him over to a nearby water fountain, and held him under it until he begged for mercy.

I twinge at the memory. I want so badly to text Shannon and remind her of this story, but since I know all I'll get is a big fat nothing in response, I don't bother. I miss my sister and her bad attitude and her brutal honesty, and have no idea if I'll ever get any of that back, though now that she's engaged again, maybe she'll finally start acknowledging my existence. At least in the meantime I have Sam, who, like Shannon, will always bravely tell me when my outfit sucks, and will almost always be right about it too.

She eventually gets up to take a shower. She's all the way down the hall before I remember to tell her that I'm going home for my sister's engagement party and will be gone for a week.

"I literally don't care at all," she says, shutting the bathroom door in my face.

"Love you too, Sam!" I call out, then head toward my room.

Eight

Ah, LaGuardia. The cursed pit of nothingness. I had no idea when I first moved to New York that I'd spend so much of my time here—you never consider practicalities like that when you're daydreaming.

The weirdest thing about flying back and forth between the same two places is that you accumulate all this specific knowledge that you never have occasion to share with anyone. Who is there to talk to about the ranking of best to worst wines at Bar 212? When I count up the number of hours I've spent milling around at Gate 51 I feel physically sick. That's days of my life that will never be returned to me.

Today, I'd welcome a delayed flight—a canceled one would be even better—but lucky me, everything is right on time.

There will be no divine intervention for me this morning; I'm going to this engagement party whether I like it or not. I spend most of the flight imagining (or is it dreading?) my reunion with Shannon and what's to come. Since it's a gathering thrown in her honor, at least she won't be able to avoid me. Not the whole time, anyway.

I thought by flying in from out of town the day before the party I'd be spared most of the preparations, an assumption that is swiftly corrected when I leave the terminal and find my mother waiting for me at arrivals.

I can tell right away she means business: she's got a full face of makeup on but is head to toe in athleisure, her sunglasses perched atop her asymmetric bob. She bestows a kiss on my cheek, then rubs the residue of her lipstick away with her thumb.

"Let's go," she instructs me. "We have to get to Costco."

Her shopping list is enormous. She carries around a little clipboard while I push the shopping cart, efficiently ticking off each item as we make our way up and down the aisles.

"We'll get these for your uncle," she says, loading a bag of fat-free chips into the cart, her flip-flops smacking against her heels as she moves. "He needs to be more mindful of his cholesterol. You know they put him on those pills?"

I did not.

We go until the cart is piled so high that I can barely maneuver it. I narrowly avoid mowing down a small child when I swing it around the end of the frozen aisle.

Mom maintains a steady stream of conversational nothings as we go, filling me in on all the latest happenings with our neighbors, and then my cousins, and even a tidbit about our dentist, who's been getting *awfully close* to his new hygienist.

I feel a rush of nostalgia when we pull up to the house, a picture-perfect snapshot of suburban living with its chestnut-brown roof and rolling green lawn. For as much as I say that I hate it here, it always feels good to come home. It's tranquil in a way that living in the city simply is not.

Dad is hard at work when we park up on the driveway, wandering around with his pressure washer and spraying down the stone tiles outside our front door. He playfully douses the passenger-side window with water when Mom stops the car, a little comedy bit he's been doing since my sister and I were teenagers and first learning to drive.

His shoulders slope more than they did back then, and the bald crown on his head has gradually expanded outward, but the beat-up khaki shorts and the blue button-down he wears for housework are as they ever were. The blessing and the curse of this place has always been the same: time passes, but nothing changes.

It takes me three sweaty trips to and from the car to get all the groceries inside, and Mom graciously allows me ten minutes to shower before I have to be back downstairs to help prep the veggies.

I sit at the worn oak table, my wet hair soaking the shoulders of my faded 2004 Track and Field Stars T-shirt. At the kitchen island, Mom gathers the ingredients for her famous onion dip.

"Your sister will be here tomorrow around noon," she says, spooning the contents of the sour cream tub into the glass mixing bowl at her side.

"Great." I keep my focus firmly on the celery in front of me, chopping a stalk down the middle with a solid thwack.

"Make sure those sticks are even."

"They are."

"And I hope you'll be on your best behavior," she adds, looking up from under her brows.

I mirror the action, tilting my chin down and my eyes up. "I will."

"This is a big day for her," she says, sprinkling her spice mix over the bowl. "We don't want any . . . drama."

"I've got it, Mom. I'll be good."

"Good," she says, wiping her hands on her pink checkered apron. "Now where did I put that serving tray?"

The food prep alone takes us several hours. I catch glimpses of my dad now and then, but mostly he's consumed by yard work until well after the sun goes down.

I buzz around the house like a diligent little worker bee, performing every chore my mother assigns to me until I finally collapse into bed around midnight and fall into a dreamless sleep. It feels like seconds have passed when she flings my bedroom door open the next morning. The alarm clock beside my head blinks 6:45 A.M.

"Get moving," she tells me without so much as a good morning. "We need to finish setting up the backyard."

Forgive me for feeling less than enthused about this party, because it's the second time I'm attending it. My sister Shannon's first engagement party was a little over two years ago. That wedding was never to be.

Whether for efficiency reasons or as a result of a complete lack of creativity, our family's second attempt at hosting this gathering is a carbon copy of the first. The advantage of throwing the same party twice, I suppose, is that the setup is easy—simply do what I did last time.

Well. Minus one thing.

There have been upgrades here and there, of course. The menu now features expanded vegetarian options, for example, and the color scheme has evolved from peaches and cream to strictly black and white, as per the changing trends of the internet. Sadly, we have not updated the groom.

I'm dragging a Muskoka chair across the lawn by its huge wooden armrest when Shannon finally appears, sliding open the glass door and stepping onto the patio. She is party ready, resplendent in a white linen dress that drapes across her left shoulder and shows her (really very natural) spray tan to advantage. Her blond hair has been styled into perfect waves, brushed until they shine.

She raises a manicured hand over her eyes, surveying the scene. Closest to her, on the deck, are the food tables, and dotted around the lawn are tall cocktail tables, borrowed from the church basement and covered in white linens. There's a drinks station set up on the far right of the lawn, which is really just a table with some empty glasses on it and a neat line of coolers beside.

Dad has painstakingly strung up our Christmas lights all along the perimeter of the back fence, and when the sun goes down later, the effect will be beautiful, casting the entire lawn and the old maple trees toward the back in a perfect golden glow.

A huge painted canvas stands sentinel on the patio, near the doors, left over from last time. It reads *she said yes* in looped cursive handwriting, and then *Shannon & Dan's Engagement Party* in neat block letters below. Underneath that, if you look *really* closely, you can see the brushstrokes painting over the party's original date.

The sound of Mom's voice floats out across the lawn. I look toward it, then snap my head back down when I realize who she's talking to.

"The tables look good," I hear my sister say to her as she steps out onto the deck.

"That was Annie's idea!" Mom says triumphantly. "See how much your sister has been helping?"

Her insistence that I prep for this party is all making sense now. Mom has been trying to get the proverbial band back together ever since the last engagement party, lying on behalf of both Shannon and myself in the hopes it will help forge a truce. I know what I say about Shannon whenever she raises this topic; I can only wonder at what Shannon says about me.

"Sweetheart!" Mom calls out to me. "Your sister is here. Come and say hello!"

She scurries back inside, leaving the two of us out here alone, forced to acknowledge each other.

"I think the Muskoka chairs should be farther back," Shannon says, skipping the hellos altogether.

"Sure."

"Dan wants enough room to play Beersbee."

"Makes sense." Who wouldn't want to play Beer Frisbee at their re-engagement party?

She watches silently while I drag one Muskoka chair, then the other, toward the back fence. I rotate them, ungracefully, nudging them into place with my hip.

Once they're facing each other, I dust my hands off on my jean shorts and turn toward the house. "I'm all dirty, so I won't . . . " I say, gesturing at her white dress.

"Yeah, don't," she says, stepping aside to let me through. She awkwardly pats my shoulder as I walk past. This is the first time we've seen each other in two years.

That my sister became the great stranger of my adult life would be a surprise to my younger self. We used to be so close.

Then came Dan.

To say I hate this man with the fire of a thousand suns would be putting it mildly. I'd pay good money to never have to see him again. Unfortunately for me, they don't take credit cards in hell.

Mom takes one look at me when I come through the sliding glass doors and hustles me upstairs to make myself presentable, with explicit instructions to take my time and not to take too long.

"People will start arriving around two," she warns me. "I want you dressed and downstairs so you're here to greet them."

Considering the role I played at the original engagement party, it would definitely be saying something if I wasn't outside with the rest of the family, smiling at the guests.

It's not only Mom who will be watching closely to see whether I make another scene: something tells me that for many of the RSVPs, I'm one of the main attractions.

I keep my vow to my mother and am downstairs, ready to go, at 2 p.m. sharp. I spend ages agonizing over my outfit to officially re-enter family life, torn as to whether to go with a look that says "innocent, contrite, sweet angel" or one that says "unapologetic demon dressed to kill."

In the end, I split the difference and decide on a floral slip dress with a huge slit right up the thigh. My hair is down, my makeup simple, and my lips bright red. I have an enormous pair of dark-rimmed sunglasses on hand so that, if need be, I can avoid making eye contact with anyone all afternoon.

I scan the terrain looking for allies as I slip through the kitchen's sliding glass door. My mother is by the gate, ready to greet people as they arrive, and Dad is already fiddling around with the barbecue. Ever the life of the party, Uncle Bill is in the middle of a crowd of people, his vibrant blue Hawaiian shirt and shock of white hair visible through the gap.

I make a beeline toward my aunt Irene and a few of Mom's friends at the other end of the garden, who warmly invite me into their circle.

"There she is, our *enfant terrible*," Irene says, wrapping an arm around my shoulder. The other ladies cackle.

"And what do you have in store for us today, my dear?" our neighbor Shirley asks with mischief.

"Nothing," I tell them all solemnly. "They decided to take the entertainment in a different direction this time."

Irene lets out a guffaw, then smacks a loud kiss on my cheek. "How long are you here for, sweetheart?"

"Five days. I'm working from home."

"These kids and their computers!" Shirley says. "My Josh is just the same. Does his banking job from his bedroom."

This sends the conversation off in a fantastical new direction about whether social media will bring about the end of the world, and if so, how soon.

"I'll tell you this," Irene says, "the amount of time Jean spends on her iPad is not normal. What could she be doing?"

"Some candy thing," Shirley answers, her disdain writ large. "According to her posts, she's up to level six thousand."

"Six *thousand*," Irene says. "That shows you. That just goes to show you."

What it just goes to show you, she never reveals. Judging from a few barbed little comments, though, it seems to have something to do with Jean missing choir practice.

"Face the music, kiddo," Irene says to me when the women move on to discussing Shirley's tomato plants. "You can't hide out with me forever. It's time to speak to someone your own age."

The backyard is now full of people my own age, or more accurately, Shannon's age, who are mostly congregated in a cluster around the beer coolers. Strange to think that most of the people I know in New York aren't anywhere near being settled down yet. Here, it's a completely different story. Everyone holds either a bottle of beer, or a small child.

"Oh my god, Annie! How are you?" One of the bridesmaids rushes forward when she spots me and gives me a limp hug, both of us pretending we're more excited to see each other than we are.

The rest of the reunions take a similar format, until I've hugged or nodded at everyone and dutifully given a mock handshake to a half-dozen chubby baby hands.

Dan is mercifully circulating elsewhere, so that's at least one awkward moment I can put off a little longer, for the rest of the night, even, if I can get away with it. All I need to do is show my respect for the occasion, say hi to enough of Mom's friends that she doesn't accuse me of sneaking away early, then sneak away early.

For all I dreaded this party, it's not that bad. Most of the things people have to say about me will be said behind my back, rather than to my face, and if anything, my presence is creating a little intrigue, so at least there's that.

I'm at the coolers, trying in vain to open my beer without a bottle opener when a nasal voice says from behind me, "Allow me."

My entire body tenses in irritation on reflex, and I turn slowly, desperate to delay this moment by even just a few more seconds. Alas, my luck has run out. There he is.

"Daniel," I say, tilting the bottle toward him.

Dan is *exactly* what you'd expect someone from the suburbs called Dan to look like. The man is a walking Gap ad. I am one hundred percent convinced he could get away with murder—his composite sketch would be so nondescript it could easily match the faces of dozens of other men within a five-mile radius.

"Long time no see." There's an understatement. We haven't seen each other since the last engagement party. He flicks the cap off with his keys and hands the bottle back to me. "How's life in the big city treating you these days?"

"Just peachy." I'm trying to smile but the muscles around my cheeks feel all wrong.

"I saw something online about huge layoffs at your company this week. You didn't lose your job, did you?"

Jackass.

"Not at all," I tell him sweetly, safe in the knowledge that it's not a lie. "I've actually just moved into a new role."

"Glad to hear it." He nods. "You never know with these tech unicorns."

"Your concern is touching."

"And so good of you to make it on such short notice," he adds. "We weren't sure you'd be able to get the time off, with your fancy New York City Job and all."

"I wouldn't miss it for the world," I tell him, the corners of my smile sharpening into points.

That my entire family thinks I'm the Canadian Bill Gates is mostly my doing. I was so desperate to avoid spending time with my brainwashed sister and her insufferable fiancé that I'd use work as an excuse not to make it home for more than a couple of days at a time. Claiming to be too busy working annoyed my parents, but it *infuriated* Dan, who couldn't tolerate someone competing with him for the Most Important Job in the Family award.

"I know Shannon thought it would be easier not to tell you

about the party," he continues, like I hadn't spoken. "But I was always with your mom on that one. You're family. Who cares if people talk."

My stomach twists. So there's the explanation I've been waiting for—it wasn't a last-minute party. I was a last-minute invite.

"Speaking of talking," I say, pretending I already knew this, "will you be going up there to say a few words? I know what a fan you are of the sound of your own voice."

The nice-guy act evaporates in an instant.

"You know what," he says, but I never get to hear it. As if by magic, Mom materializes at my elbow, her silver bangles clinking like a tambourine when she moves. "*There* you are," she says to Dan.

"Here I am," he echoes, leaning forward to drop a kiss onto her cheek.

"Daniel, sweetheart, Irene was just saying she could use a hand carrying the trays in from the car. Would you be a dear?"

"Of course."

He gives me a small salute and saunters away.

"Now you go and say hello to your cousin," Mom urges. "I bet you haven't even *asked* about his fundraiser."

Not that I need any urging to spend less time with Dan, but it's humbling to realize how little faith she has in my promise not to make a scene.

I catch a streak of blue out of the corner of my eye and turn to see my uncle Bill prancing toward me like some sort of enormous leprechaun. Though my own family are blind to Dan's many flaws, my aunt and uncle, and by extension my cousins, all share my disdain.

"What do you think, can we drive him off a second time?" Bill says, nudging me in the ribs.

"Sorry, Bill, I'm retired. No hijinks on my watch."

He pulls a green note from his wallet and dangles it before me. "I'll give you twenty bucks to get up there and say a few words."

"Uncle Bill," I say with an outraged gasp, clutching my hands to my heart. "Need I remind you that you are my confirmation sponsor? You're supposed to keep me on the righteous path."

"And I am," he says with a chuckle. "This is the Lord's work."

That Uncle Bill was my confirmation sponsor is a long-running joke in our family, since as far as I'm aware he hasn't stepped inside a church either before or since. He's the resident party guy in our family, always up for trouble. He'd drop Aunt Irene off on Sunday but always skip the mass, preferring instead to prep the barbecue we'd all get together for after.

"Hey, Bill," I ask, attempting to sound as casual as possible. "When did Mom tell you about this party?"

"She's only been badgering me about it for a couple of months now," he says. "She made me move my fishing trip."

"Same," I deadpan. "I'm super sad to be missing it."

Bill hoots at this, reminding me that I can't catch a fish to save my life. The man is not wrong; he took my cousin Steve and me out on the boat with him once when we were teenagers, and I was so upset to lose the one fish I caught on the line I jumped in the lake and tried to swim after it.

"There he is, the man of the hour," Bill booms when he sees Dan crossing the lawn toward his friends. "Come over here, Daniel."

Dan is visibly reluctant. Bill and I must be his two least favorite people here.

"Bill," Dan says, shaking my uncle's hand. "How's retirement treating you?"

"Just fine," he says, patting his belly. "What's new on the council?"

Bill shoots me a naughty wink, and I cringe inwardly, praying he won't go there. Dan being elected for town council was what started this whole mess in the first place. In addition to making him insufferable, his elevated status of elected official means he's always at the center of local news.

"You'll be pleased to hear they just agreed on the date for next year's Rib Fest," Dan says. "Last weekend in July."

"Good, good," Bill says. "And what about this new subdivision over on the south end of town? That's not going ahead, is it?"

"I don't see why not," Dan says, taking on that air of superiority I hate so much. "We need the houses."

"We also need the soccer fields," Bill replies. "Build over all of them and you'll have no place to host Rib Fest."

Dan looks like he's gearing up for a lecture, his chest rising on a huge inhale. Luckily for us, Mom appears again. I swear this woman has put a tracker chip on me.

She rounds us all up and tells us to make our way toward the patio. They want to do the toasts before we eat.

"Stay with your uncle," she tells me, squeezing my arm with force.

"Ouch," I squeak, rubbing the spot above my elbow.

"Oh, enough of this," Bill says, shooing my mother away. "Go make yourself busy, Linda. She'll be just fine."

I shoot him a grateful look, and he threads my arm through

his, giving my hand a gentle pat. I can feel eyes on me from every direction as we make our way across the lawn.

To understand this engagement party, it's crucial to understand the one that came before it.

Shannon had long since dropped out of university to move home and be closer to Dan, who was now working in local government. The two of them had been living with my parents, saving up to purchase their first house.

Around this time, Dan began voicing his desire to become mayor someday, toying with the idea of running for town council. My sister was, of course, his unpaid campaign manager and First Lady-in-waiting. The two of them hit the local campaign trail with enthusiasm.

They needn't have bothered. There were ten town council seats and eleven candidates, and one of those candidates was a well-known golden eagle from the area. Seriously. It was a political statement from a local activist group, trying to protect some woodland on the edge of town. Though legally an animal can't serve on a municipal government, let it be known that Dan only beat the eagle by fifty-seven votes.

Anyway, he was elected. As an illustrious member of town council, he was now being paid to give people his opinion—a job he was previously more than happy to do for free—and just a few weeks later, the two of them were engaged.

While Dan was out most nights hobnobbing with the town's elite, Shannon was planning the wedding of the century, a job I was roped into with such regularity that I started to wonder if it was me she was marrying. Dan had many opinions on how he wanted things done but was more than happy to leave the doing of these items to someone else. As a town councilor, he had more important things to think of now.

I was home for the week to help Shannon prep for the party. By that point relations between Dan and me had been strained for several years. He thought I was an annoying brat, and I thought he was a selfish prick. The two of us could barely get through a single family function without trading insults the second Shannon's back was turned.

The day before the party I was meeting some friends for lunch, waiting at the bar for the others to arrive. Two men had parked themselves at the bar on the opposite corner from me and were catching up over a beer while waiting for their chicken wings, each filling in the other on the details of their lives and their kids' soccer schedules, until they moved on to a story that had been making the rounds through town hall this week. Had he heard that Councilwoman Howard was having an affair?

I opened my phone and started typing out the details to Shannon, who I knew would delight in this tidbit of gossip. She and I had already lost hours discussing Councilwoman Howard—the realtor Shannon worked for had sold a house to her last year, and she often attended the same events as Shannon and Dan, including a recent charity golf tournament where she got drunk and called her husband a prick in front of the entire table.

That can't be true, the second man said. It is, the other insisted. His information had come from a verified source. The affair was with another council member, on town property. They were working late together on some big planning proposal. They'd been caught in the parking lot.

The mention of the planning proposal made my blood run cold. Dan was working on a project that sounded a lot like that. And he'd been pulling quite a few late nights.

The wings arrived, and the conversation moved on, but my heart was racing. My first instinct was to reject it—Councilwoman Howard was married, and more than a decade and change older than Dan. But other details pressed on the edge of my mind, ones that felt all too relevant now. Dan had worked more late nights than I would have thought necessary for a town councilor, and recently, he'd lost all interest in the wedding, something Shannon would chalk up to the stress of his new job if anyone mentioned it at the family dinner table. But you could tell it bothered her. There was a neediness to her interactions with Dan that seemed recent to me.

I spent lunch counting down the minutes until I could leave, and then raced back to the house, hoping to find Shannon alone. I came face-to-face with Dan instead, when he walked through the front door just a few minutes after me. We were the only two people home. I asked him about his day, and then his planning project, and all the late nights he'd been pulling. He condescendingly told me they were working overtime to get everything done before the deadline. I said: *Really? I heard it's because you're fucking Councilwoman Howard.*

I knew it was true as soon as I said it out loud. His denial sounded so lame. I told him to tell Shannon before the party, or I would. The next morning, the house was buzzing with activity, everyone rushing around to get ready. It was clear Shannon knew nothing, she was too serene. I tried in vain to talk to her, but she brushed me off, flitting away for a hair appointment with her bridesmaids, then strategically arriving late to make her grand entrance.

I spent the afternoon staring daggers at Dan from across the lawn, not that he noticed—he didn't dare look in my direction.

It incensed me that he wasn't more bothered about any of it. If anything, as the day went on his confidence grew, and by the time the toasts rolled around, Councilman Dan was out in full force.

He got up in front of the crowd and made the most nauseating speech I'd ever heard, locking eyes with me when he talked about the importance of family. I checked my watch. It was 6 P.M. I'd told him he had twenty-four hours, and I meant it.

I interrupted his speech and dropped the bomb.

"Thank you so much for coming," Shannon says, calling everyone to attention with a knife against her champagne flute. Dan stands silently at her side. Muzzled for today.

"It really means so much to us that you're here this afternoon," she continues. "I can't imagine taking this next step in our lives without all of you. We had planned to do a few toasts, but the food is almost ready and it makes no sense to keep you waiting. Instead of raising a glass to us, today I'd like to raise a glass to you. To friends and family," she says, the champagne flute gliding up in front of her. Mom stands incredulous, her mouth hanging open, a confirmation that this wasn't the plan.

"To friends and family," the crowd obediently repeats, followed by a smattering of *hear hears!*

"OK, great," she says quickly, stepping forward and pulling Dan along with her. "Now let's eat."

The entire group seems to let out a collective sigh of relief. The danger has passed. The wedding is officially back on track.

Shannon point-blank refused to even speak to me after the engagement party drama. I thought she was screening my calls, but eventually I realized that she'd actually blocked my number, and all my efforts to explain myself had been in vain.

I went analogue, sending her letters and flowers and birthday cards in the hopes that she'd acknowledge me, and when she didn't, I eventually took the hint and just gave up. If Shannon didn't want to talk to me for a while, that sucked, but it was understandable. I wasn't sorry. I'd serve my time knowing I'd caused some misery to save her from a lot more, and trusted that someday she'd understand that and we could start again.

But when I heard she and Dan were back together, any remorse I felt withered and died. If she wasn't talking to me, fine. What she didn't realize was, for a while there, I also wasn't talking to *her*.

At that point, I'd been practically banished from the family, avoiding going home so I didn't further embarrass my parents and put them in the middle of our cold war. I'd naively thought that Shannon was picking up the pieces and moving forward with her life. What she was really doing was penning the plot twist in the story of Shannon and Dan. He'd made a big mistake, but they'd worked through it and come back stronger. Dan was humbled by the experience; Shannon was strengthened by it.

What a load of shit. The only thing that changed about their relationship was that Dan stopped fucking someone else on the side—and even that I can't be sure of. He, somehow, had been absolved of his crimes, while I lived on in infamy.

The rest of the afternoon unfolds without incident. The Grill Kings—my dad and our two neighbors—do an admirable job of the barbecue. Mom's many salads and sides garner much praise.

Shannon, meanwhile, is in her element, moving from group

to group, preening at the gifts and compliments being showered on her from all directions. Not for the first time, I wonder if that's what this whole getting married thing is really about for her—a second chance to be prom queen.

By nightfall the crowd has dwindled to almost nothing. Anyone with kids has left to attend to bedtime, and the party elders head off around the same time. "Also to bed," Aunt Irene says with an impish grin.

Dan and about six of his crew are still playing drinking games out on the lawn, content to let their wives and children head home without them so they can carry on the evening.

Shannon and I start with the teardown, carrying the food platters back into the kitchen. Mom has already laid out Tupperware for the leftovers. Judging by the volume of what's in front of us, I'll be eating pasta salad for the rest of the week.

"Great turnout," I say to Shannon, looking for anything less lame to talk about.

"Not bad, right," she says with pride. "Hopefully the weather is this good for the actual wedding."

"Uncle B was saying the farmer's almanac is promising a perfect summer."

She laughs. "Ah well, if the almanac says it . . ."

"Exactly. Can I help with that?" I ask, pointing to the tray in front of her.

"You can, thanks," she says, sliding it toward me.

"Mom says the new bungalow's looking really great."

"It's getting there," Shannon agrees. "The kitchen still needs some work, but the living room is pretty much done now. How long are you home for? You should come by."

The glass door slides open and the floating head of Dan

appears, haloed by the patio light behind him. "Babe, me and the boys are heading down to Shoeless for a few beers."

"We need to finish clearing up," Shannon says. Her voice is strained.

He dismisses this immediately. "It's basically done. I'll come back and finish it tomorrow."

"What about the cards? I wanted to go through them tonight."

"There's no way that's a two-man job. You just do it."

"Sure," she says flatly. If Dan notices her tone, he ignores it, reminding her to leave the garage door open before disappearing back the way he came.

The glass door seals us into the quiet kitchen, the only sound the click of the Tupperware lid as Shannon snaps it into place. I can't think of a single thing to say that isn't *that guy sucks,* and neither, apparently, can she.

"What a day!" Mom glides into the room with a triumphant grin. "And here they are! My girls, together at last." She smacks a loud kiss on my cheek, and then my sister's.

She's delightfully rumpled, the scent of sangria mingling with her perfume, her cheeks rosy from an entire afternoon of gossip with Aunt Irene and her friends. All that's left of her lipstick is a faint line around the edge of her lips.

"Did you have fun, Mom?"

"I thought it went very well," she says. "But how about our beautiful bride?"

We wait for Shannon to respond, but she's lost in thought, spooning the fruit salad back into its container.

"Shan?" I prompt.

"Hmm?"

"Did you have a good time?"

"Definitely," she says, in the least convincing performance

I've ever seen. Mom shoots me a look that says *did you do something?* I shake my head.

"That reminds me!" Mom's voice has gone up about ten octaves. "Irene says the Millers are thinking of downsizing."

Shannon looks up, eyes kindling at the prospect of the Miller house going up for sale. "Do they have a realtor?"

I slip away while the two of them launch into their favorite subject and head back into the garden, taking my sweet time stacking the folding chairs against the side of the house and then gathering up the table linens under my arm. Dan's definition of *basically done* and mine are very different.

I'm about to head inside when I hear the fence swing open and smack back against its hinges.

"Forgot my wallet," Dan says, coming into view. His smile drops the second he realizes it's me.

"There's still a lot to do here," I say, gesturing around the garden. "Sure you don't want to hang around for a while and head down later?"

"I'm sure," he says.

"So nice to see you're still striving hard for the world's worst boyfriend award. How many years have you won it in a row now, Dan?"

"Got a newsflash for you," he sneers. "It's fiancé. Don't know if you noticed today's theme, but there's a wedding happening soon."

"Maybe." I shrug. "Though no one says you have to be the groom."

"Of the two of us, I don't think it's my invitation we need to worry about."

"Yeah well, we'll see. There's no saying when you might start pulling a few more late nights over at town hall."

"A lot of chairs to put away," he says, like I hadn't just spoken. "Looks like you'll be here a while. And don't forget the cards."

He swipes his wallet off a nearby table and walks out the way he came. I fight the impulse to grab him by the collar and drag him back by force, or even better, to run him out of town with a pitchfork.

I promised to be good, and I was. I did not ruin the party. I have not said a word to Shannon, or to anyone else, about the wedding, or Dan, or how much he sucks, or about how my sister is throwing her life away on this loser.

But now the party is over. And if he thinks I've let it go, he's about to have a very rude awakening.

"I can help with the cards, if you want?" I say, walking back into the kitchen with the box under my arm.

"Oh," Shannon says, clearly torn between what she wants to do (open the cards) and what she thinks she should do (wait for Dan to open the cards).

I go in for the kill. "Makes sense to take a note of all of them now, so we know you haven't missed any?"

"That's true," she says, warming to the idea. "We'll just make a list of everyone who left one. Dan and I can go through them in detail tomorrow."

We set up mission control on the family room floor, the cards strewn out all over the ancient glass coffee table that's been here since before I was born.

Shannon uses a letter opener to neatly slice open each envelope, opening the card and reading out the sender in her most businesslike voice before sliding it back into place and stacking it into a neat pile at her elbow. As the ever-dutiful assistant, I input every detail into my laptop. At this point I'd literally file her taxes for her if it means I'm allowed to be in her presence.

"Uncle Bill and Aunt Irene," she says. "Check. Two hundred dollars." My eyes bulge. The amount of money that changes hands at weddings is obscene.

We content ourselves with small talk while we work. She tells me about which of her friends are pregnant, and I tell her about Sam's attempts at catfishing our neighbor, who she's convinced keeps stealing her packages.

"Any men in your life?" Shannon asks me next. "I remember you saying something about a guy you worked with."

I cringe at this; she can only be referring to Andy, who I used to talk about *a lot*. I'm grateful she doesn't remember his name.

"No one," I tell her, and I can tell she's judging me. But can you blame me? With Shannon and Dan as my model, serious relationships seem like no fun at all.

"By the way," she says, offhand, "I might be coming to New York soon."

"What, seriously?" In all the years I've been living there she's never once visited.

"Yep," she says, sweeping up the stack of cards and tapping them against the coffee table. "There's a realtors' conference. It's a good networking opportunity."

"Are you and Dan going to make a weekend of it?"

"The dates clash with a council thing, so it would just be me, if it happens. But I'm not sure yet. They only send the top salesperson."

Holy shit. This is it. This is my opportunity. How long have I been waiting for a chance to separate my sister from Dan and talk some sense into her?

"You could stay with me," I blurt. "And hang out for the weekend. It would be really fun."

"That might be good, actually," she says. "Everything is so crazy expensive there."

"Totally," I say, adrenaline flooding my system. "I could show you the sights. You've never been to New York before." It sounds like an accusation when I say it, and I see her shoulders tense up. I quickly change tack.

"We could try and check out a few dress shops, for the wedding?" I offer. "That big dress shop from *Dream Dress* is in New York," I add, in reference to a beloved reality show. "You could meet Randy!"

She laughs. "That would be cool."

"I'd die to see what he'd put you in."

"Well, I'll let you know if it comes together."

"Please come," I beg her, my tone desperate. "I really want you to. It feels like we never see each other since . . . It will be fun. I promise."

"It would be good to check out some dress shops. There's one I have my eye on."

"Totally. Send me the dates and I'll check with my roommate? Should be fine."

"Sure," she says, slicing another card open. "Earl and Sheila. Canadian Tire. Sixty dollars."

Nine

I'm up early Monday morning ready to take on my first official duties as a strategist. Though it's true I'm not *actually* qualified to do this job, in some ways it feels like I've been preparing for this for a lifetime.

I begin by strategizing how to get an extra fifteen minutes in bed—skip the shower, dry shampoo, dress the top half of my body but stay in pajama shorts.

Next, I strategize the best way to get breakfast made for me. For this, I settle on the simple yet foolproof method of letting the kitchen cupboard bang shut, which instantly summons my father. This particular kitchen cupboard has been wonky since the dawn of time, and if you don't close it with care, it clatters shut, then swings open again until the metal handle makes contact with the cupboard beside it.

If you ever want to torture my father for information, all you need to do is slam this cupboard once or twice. He'll break instantly.

"Watch, watch, watch," he chides when he sails into the kitchen, shouldering past me to shut it himself. I swear he's attuned to hear the sound of this cupboard from any room in the house.

"Sorry," I say, not even remotely meaning it. "I was looking for the mugs."

"What's for breakfast, kiddo?"

"I was just about to ask you the same thing. I'm *starving*."

He slings an arm around my shoulder. "Then I guess it will have to be pancakes."

I smile back at him. "I guess it will."

He drops a kiss onto the top of my head and releases me to gather his ingredients while I take up position at the breakfast bar to enjoy the live cooking demonstration.

I love watching Dad pottering around the kitchen. It's like seeing him in his natural habitat. While most of our neighbors stripped out their old kitchens and replaced them with sleek, ultra-modern upgrades, my parents have kept it vintage.

They replaced the countertops a few years ago, and upgraded the bar stools, but otherwise, everything right down to the pale-yellow wash on the walls is the same as when they bought it. It's not aesthetically pleasing, and wouldn't work anywhere else but in the suburbs, but I love it.

"Carl," Mom says in exasperation when she comes into the kitchen and sees the maple syrup. "*Again?*"

"Why not?" he reasons. "Annie's not home very often."

She makes a big song and dance about how pancakes are not a nutritious breakfast option, but parks herself at the counter beside me anyway.

A few minutes later, Dad deposits the first pancake on my plate, carrying it directly from the frying pan and flipping it down straight off the spatula. It is, quite simply, perfect. I like to think I played a small part in this—after all, I've had him doing practice runs the last two mornings.

"And where's mine?" Mom asks him when he flips the next pancake onto his own plate.

"You said you didn't want any."

"I said no such thing," she replies haughtily. "Annie, get me a plate, would you? Your father forgot."

Connor has scheduled a strategy induction call for us at 10 A.M. sharp. I'm here first, and then he's late, so I click around and then zone out on *The Cut* while I wait. There's no telltale ding to alert me that someone else has joined the call, so I'm startled when his voice rings out across the room, and hastily close the tab, straightening into business mode as I do. On-screen, he's staring back at me, pitched slightly forward, his face intent.

"Is this your childhood bedroom?" he asks, forgoing any greeting. He's not looking at me at all, but over my shoulder, at all the details he can see in the background behind me.

"It is, yes."

"What's that poster of?" he asks, pointing toward the corner.

I wonder if he'd believe that my computer died if I just shut my laptop down immediately. Somehow, I sense the answer is no.

"That's none of your business," I say primly.

"Justin Timberlake?"

"No."

"Coldplay."

"No."

He pauses, thinking.

". . . Weezer?"

"No."

"Am I close in any way? Will I ever guess this?"

"Probably not," I admit. Am I going to say this out loud? "It's . . . *Ice Age*. I really liked that movie as a kid."

"You're right," he says, laughing as if this is the single greatest thing he's ever heard in his life. "I never would have guessed that."

"Did you actually want to talk about work, or have you just called me to mock my childhood bedroom?"

"Definitely the latter," he says. "Are you still a supporter of the *Ice Age* franchise?"

"No," I say, lying.

"Why's the poster still up then?"

"Time capsule. This place is a living museum," I say, stretching out my hands.

"Your bedroom is absolutely enormous. Hey—where does that door go?"

I look behind me to try and parse what he's pointing at. "The closet?"

"No, that door."

"The bathroom."

"Oh my god, you had a *bathroom* in your bedroom, as a kid? That's bananas."

"It's adjoining. I shared it with my sister, her room's on the other side."

"*Seriously?*" His amazement is writ large.

I rip the plug out from the laptop and tour him around, showing him the bathroom and then my sister's old room, before turning back to my own.

He asks questions about every single thing the camera pans across, wanting to see closeups of every picture, poster, and trophy that adorns the space.

"It's like you live in a palace," he says, when I sit back down at the desk.

"Not really. Honestly, it's just like, a very normal-sized house."

"Not to me. I grew up on the Upper West Side."

"That's infinitely cooler than the Canadian suburbs, trust me."

"I always wanted to live in the suburbs when I was a kid."

"Why?"

"What do you mean, *why*? Riding your bike everywhere, hanging out in the forest with your friends. It sounds awesome."

"It's really boring when you're not in a Spielberg movie," I say.

"What's trick or treating like?"

I boggle. "You never went trick or treating?"

"I did," he says. "But it was nothing like we used to see on TV where the whole neighborhood goes out. Is it true that everybody decorates their houses?"

I scan my memory. "Not *everyone,* but a lot of people on our street did, yeah. When we were all little, anyway."

"Like haunted houses and stuff?"

"Yeah," I say, warming to the topic. "One year my uncle Bill turned his lawn into a graveyard and got a bunch of teenagers to dress up and jump out from behind the graves. It made the paper."

"That's sick as hell."

I assess him through the screen. "I wouldn't have pegged you as a Halloween person."

He reels back, his hand against his chest. "How can anyone not be a Halloween person? It's objectively amazing when you're seven."

An image of a tiny Connor covered in face paint and a cape pops into my head, Halloween enthusiasm radiating off him. Something about his boyishness now instinctively tells me he was a very cute kid. Or maybe he was a little dweeb. Who knows?

I can tell from the background that he's in the office, the gray fabric paneling of the call booth giving him away. He's wearing a cheerful green hoodie today, which contrasts perfectly with the charcoal that surrounds him.

The call booths have the *worst* lighting known to mankind, yet Connor looks fine. It speaks to the strength of his bone structure that he's able to look good on camera. I fight a smile thinking about how shocked I'd have been if I came across him for the first time on a video call like this.

"So, shiny new data analyst," he says. "Are you ready to be inducted?"

"Is inducted a word?"

"It is, and it worries me that you don't know that," he says. A second later, his image collapses into a small square and the mirror image of his screen fills my own. He's got a slide deck locked and loaded. Let the induction begin.

Connor's presentation is as thorough an onboarding as I've ever seen in my life. He runs me through the projects the team is working on, the tools they use and the teams they collaborate with most, followed by a—I have to admit, very charming—slide filled with fun facts about my three other new teammates, Ben, Martin, and John.

I halt him when he flicks forward onto the next slide. "Um, excuse me—"

"Yes, Annabelle?"

I try to correct him. "No one ever calls me by my full name."

"Oh, really?" he says, like I've just relayed a piece of information that has nothing to do with him whatsoever. Something gives me a strong impression there's going to be a lot of *Annabelles* coming my way. Even more so now that I've alerted him to the fact that I hate it.

Anyway. "I didn't see your fun fact up there, Connor."

"That's because I'm not fun."

"I see how it is. One rule for the boss, one rule for the rest of us."

"I'll tell you what," he says gamely. "Pay attention to the last six slides instead of staring off into space and I'll give you my fun fact at the end."

"Fine. The fact better be worth it, though."

"Oh, it will be," he says, flicking onto the next slide.

The final slides pertain to the reporting dashboard, which is finally revealed to me in all its glory. For the last two years, most of the Jotter crew have been dismantling our platform and finding ways to integrate it seamlessly into Taskio. The final piece of the puzzle is a new reporting dashboard, the building of which was a mammoth task that involved trying to wrangle two similar but separate softwares onto a single system so that everyone in the entire company can measure performance in the same way.

That was the idea, anyway. Connor's team has spent the better part of the last year bringing all the data together, creating a single easy-to-use dashboard that every department in the business could access to build their own internal reports. It's complete. But as yet, no one will use it.

"Since you have so handsomely volunteered to take charge of the dashboard rollout, you need to learn your way around it," he tells me. "The more you can do with it the better."

Connor gives me a list of reports he wants me to try and generate. I can't tell if he really needs them or if this is some sort of extended training exercise, but I'm in no position to argue. I'm suddenly feeling very relieved that I'm working from home the next few days where I can do this in private.

"Phone me back if you get stuck," he says, closing out the shared screen of his desktop. His full-size image springs back up to replace it. "I don't have any other meetings or anything this afternoon. When is the next time you'll be in the office again?"

"Thursday," I tell him. "I'll get all this done before then."

"Cool," he says, preparing to wrap us up.

"Hey, can I ask you something? Besides your fun fact."

"I forgot about that," he says. "I better come up with something fast. But yeah, go for it."

"Why did you hire me? Actually?"

"*Did* I hire you?" he muses. "And here I was thinking I was bamboozled into accepting you because you'd tricked your way into being reassigned."

I give him a look like, *very funny*. "We both know you were going to send me packing. Why did you change your mind?"

"I guess . . ." He trails off. "Well, if you want the real reason—"

"I do."

He leans forward, like he's getting ready to reveal a secret.

"I wanted to know . . . all the data I can't find on a spreadsheet."

I laugh, then cringe. "It's all making sense now."

"Where will I find it, by the way?" he wonders. "You never did reveal."

"That's classified, I'm afraid. Any data of this nature will be supplied to you on a need-to-know basis."

"Sounds extremely legit," he nods. "Nothing fishy about that at all."

We both chuckle, then fall into silence. I watch him fidget in his seat, frowning down at the pen in front of him.

"If you want the truth, things have been—difficult. Recently. On the team."

I'm caught off guard by this moment of candor, unsure of how to respond.

"And you were right about the dashboard thing. No one is using it. It's driving me crazy," he says, rubbing at his eyes. "You seemed like you had it in you to bully the right people."

I had an inkling before, but I know it for certain now: Connor is nice.

It's abundantly clear too, after seeing the rundown of the projects Data Strategy works on, that I will not be an integral part of the team, at least not on a technical level. I am the only person among them without a computer science degree, the working definition of a personality hire. I'm just as likely to be a burden as a help to him, and yet he let me stay anyway, and hasn't been a jerk about it either, never asking for any special praise for his good deed. I register a silent vow that I'll make every last person at Taskio use his dashboard, even if I have to stand over their desks and watch them do it.

"OK," I say, switching gears. "Now I want your fun fact."

"You first."

"What? No."

"Boss's orders," he says, pulling rank.

"That's—not how this works."

"I'd just like to remind you that you're in your probationary period and can be let go without notice for the next three months."

"This is an abuse of power," I say, fighting a smile.

"I know," he grins. "Now go."

"Um, OK. Fun fact, fun fact," I stall. What's fun about me? I rack my brains and come up with nothing. "I once bought a purse from a thrift shop and found forty bucks in it?"

"Weak," he says. "I need something stronger for the slide deck."

"All right then," I say. "What's yours? I'm ready to be dazzled."

He pauses like he's about to blow my mind. "When I was a kid I won a chess tournament—at Disney World."

I burst out laughing. "I can't believe it. And yet I absolutely can."

"Wait until you hear about the prize. I got to play chess against Buzz Lightyear!" His tone makes it clear that he still considers this to be a huge honor.

"How old were you?"

"Nine," he says.

"Lifetime dork award," I tell him. "Did you win or lose?"

"Well," he starts, but I don't get an answer. Connor's attention is diverted by something out of my eyeline. "Oh shit. I gotta go."

"Oh, OK," I say, feeling deflated. "No worries."

He says a hasty goodbye and then he's gone. Twenty minutes later, my messenger pings.

> **CONNOR:** I won, obviously. But I'll never truly be sure I beat him fair and square.

Ten

Mom and Dad are driving up north to visit some friends this morning, so it's decided that Shannon will drive me to the airport, even though I tell them over and over I'll just take a taxi. Dad is scandalized at the suggestion. We're not the kind of people who let one of our own spend seventy-five bucks on a cab ride.

Mom insists she wants to lock the house up as they're leaving, refusing reasonable suggestions like leaving me with a spare key or letting me exit through the garage. In her infinite wisdom she decides it makes the most sense for me to sit outside and get some fresh air.

"It's a beautiful day," she reasons, like she is in fact doing me some big favor here, and then they go, leaving me on the front step to wait for Shannon, who won't be here for almost an hour . . . exactly the amount of time it would have taken me to get a taxi to the airport.

The Wi-Fi signal carries to the front lawn, so I can at least get some work done while I wait. In all honesty, though, I just lurk around the company Slack channels aimlessly, which is exactly how I notice the precise moment the little green dot beside Connor's name flickers to life.

ANNIE: Hey good morning
ANNIE: It's your favorite strategist

His reply is immediate.

CONNOR: Oh hey Ben
ANNIE: I meant me, actually
CONNOR: But you said favorite…

I decide not to dignify that with a response.

ANNIE: I just sent over that report you asked for
CONNOR: Wow. Speedy
ANNIE: What can I say, I'm amazing at my job
CONNOR: Where did you pull the data from?
ANNIE: Nowhere. I made it up. Was I not supposed to do that?
CONNOR: No that's fine, that's exactly how I do it

I'll say this for Connor: he never misses a beat. It's refreshing to talk to someone where you don't have to explain you're kidding all the time.

CONNOR: I thought you weren't working today
ANNIE: I'm not, just finishing a couple of things before I head back to nyc
ANNIE: Which brings me to what I really came here to tell you…
CONNOR: Let's hear it
ANNIE: I've got my fun fact
CONNOR: We've been here before
ANNIE: No seriously
CONNOR: This one better be good

So far Connor has rejected the three fun facts I've attempted to give him on the grounds they're not "fun enough," which is rich considering his is essentially a humblebrag about how good he is at chess, the least cool game in the world. But all his talk about competitions got me thinking. This time, I think I've finally got it.

> **ANNIE:** So there's this ice cream shop in our town and when I was a kid they ran a competition where you could invent your own ice cream flavor and if you won they'd make your flavor
> **ANNIE:** You had to do everything—come up with the flavor, the name, design the carton, all of it
> **ANNIE:** I was OBSESSED with this competition
> **ANNIE:** I took it super seriously
> **CONNOR:** That adds up
> **ANNIE:** I entered multiple times with multiple flavors

He beats me to the punch before I can finish typing out the end of the story.

> **CONNOR:** Did you win?
> **ANNIE:** Excuse me, can you WAIT
> **CONNOR:** Sorry
> **CONNOR:** Continue
> **ANNIE:** I won!
> **CONNOR:** haha
> **CONNOR:** What was the flavor?
> **ANNIE:** Sorry, that's not part of the fun fact.
> **CONNOR:** Oh come on

I'm so busy grinning down at my computer screen that I miss the sound of Shannon's silver Mercedes swinging into the driveway, and hastily type *BRB* before slamming the laptop shut and shoving it into my bag. There's a faint mechanical buzzing, and then her head appears.

"I popped the trunk."

The window rolls back up, and I wheel my crappy shell suitcase around and dump it in, closing the trunk with more force than I intended. I brace for her reprimand when I open the passenger side door, but she says nothing.

Apparently we're being nice today.

"Do you have your passport?" she asks when I buckle in.

"Yes."

"Wallet?"

"Yep."

"House keys."

"Got 'em."

"Phone?"

"Jesus, Shannon, yes. I have everything. We're good."

She shifts the car into reverse and looks back over her shoulder. "Well, you better hope so, because I am not turning around."

"History suggests otherwise," I mutter, and when she turns back toward me, we exchange little knowing smiles.

Shannon and I shared a car all through our high school years. We inherited Grandma Ruby's old Honda, which she had no further use for after a particularly grueling drive to ours for Christmas. As the oldest, Shannon was of course the one who held the keys—the only time I was allowed to drive was if she needed me as her designated driver—but the perks of being her passenger were numerous.

Since I was paying for a lot of the gas she was using to drive her and her friends around, she couldn't really refuse to take me with her whenever she went out. Which meant I spent a ton of my life cruising around with the older kids, absorbing their wisdom, and then driving them crazy by doing stupid childish things, like forgetting my schoolbag.

"Whatever happened to that car?" I ask as we whiz along the main road out of town. "I genuinely can't even remember anymore."

"We sold it after Dan took the wing mirror off pulling out of the garage."

"Ah."

The introduction of Dan to the conversation kills it stone dead in an instant. Even when he's not here he's ruining everything.

My phone's Slack app buzzes with a notification. I swipe to open it.

> **CONNOR:** You can't say you won a competition for inventing an ice cream flavor and then not say what the flavor is
> **ANNIE:** Yes I can

I lock my screen, then clear my throat and try again. When in doubt, there is one subject Shannon always wants to talk about. And that is her wedding.

"So how's the planning coming along? Mom said you guys are thinking September?"

"Maybe. Not sure," she says. Her hands tighten on the steering wheel.

"Oh?"

Her eyes flick up to the rearview mirror and back again. "There's just a lot left to figure out. September might be too soon."

Never would be too soon.

"Like what?"

"Well, they're putting a new roof on the church at the moment," she says vaguely. "And that might not be done in time."

It's April, but OK. Maybe church roofs take five months. I can't argue that scaffolding would ruin the vibe.

My phone, now resting in my lap, buzzes again. I discreetly flip over the screen.

CONNOR: Are you seriously not going to tell me?
ANNIE: Ask nicely

"And we haven't even picked a reception venue," Shannon adds, oblivious to the fact that my attention is split.

I refocus.

"I thought it was going to be at The King's Glen?"

The local golf course has been her venue of choice for as long as I can remember.

"A lot of our friends have got married there since I first got engaged. It needs to be different."

I can't tell if that's a dig at me or not, so I say nothing.

It strikes me that Shannon is being incredibly evasive about all of this. Whether it's because she doesn't want to talk about the wedding or just doesn't want to talk about it with *me* is difficult to parse. Like with the engagement party, it might be that she's made the strategic decision to tell me absolutely nothing until forty-eight hours before.

CONNOR: Please

"What about that new hotel on Main Street?" I suggest. "You know the old post office that they did up?"

"Mmm. Too small."

"Really? A girl in my year got married there last summer. I swear she had, like, two hundred people."

"A lot of important people from the town are going to be invited," is all she says. "The guest list is going to be really big."

"Will you go into the city then?"

"No," Shannon says. "Dan is a councilor. We want it to be local."

"Of course. Makes sense."

Again, the conversation stalls. What else does one say to their beloved sister after a long period of estrangement that isn't *why did you forgive Dan but not me?*

> **CONNOR:** I didn't want to have to do this but… if you don't tell me what the winning flavor is I will have no choice but to fire you
> **ANNIE:** That's not very nice
> **CONNOR:** I'm never nice when it comes to ice cream
> **ANNIE:** There's… so much to unpack there

"And I'm really busy with work," Shannon says, as if I've raised another point she needs to counter. "I'm coming into my busy season. So it might have to wait."

Have I heard that right? I have never known Shannon to wait for *anything* where Dan is concerned. This is the girl who dropped out of university in her final year because doing long distance was unthinkable.

I never got the impression that work was particularly important to her, though let's be honest, I don't have a clue what's going on in her life. I've never even been to her house.

Maybe she really is busy. Or maybe . . . she just doesn't want to marry Dan.

My heart leaps at the thought. If Shannon is getting cold feet, I will *happily* make them colder.

"Well, no rush," I say, trying not to sound eager. "The venue is super important, you need to get it right."

She breathes a deep sigh (of relief?) as we slow down at a red light. "Exactly."

A plan is forming rapidly in my mind. If Shannon is having second thoughts about her pending nuptials, maybe all she needs is another option. And I can give her that option. I just need to get her to New York.

"So when will you hear about your conference thing?"

I swear she *growls*. "They're sending him instead."

I am totally baffled by this cryptic statement, and when she points out the window toward a man sitting at the bus stop across from the traffic lights, I'm even more confused.

"They're sending . . . that old guy?"

"No, not him," she says, ever dismissive. "*Him*. On the billboard."

Would we go so far as to call the giant poster on the inside of a bus shelter a *billboard*? I decide not to quibble. I see what she's referring to now: behind the old guy waiting for his bus is a life-size image of a shiny real estate man, extra sexy. Judging by the almost demonic way Shannon said the word *him*, I'm guessing she is not a fan.

"Who is he?"

"The worst person in the world. And unfortunately, the top salesman last year. He gets the trip."

"*Bastard*." I say it with feeling. Now that I look closer, I mistrust his smolder.

"He *is* a bastard," she seethes. "And he wears the *worst* shoes."

"That is truly damning."

"I want to run him over with my car."

"OK, whoa," I say, laughing. She went from calm to venomous in a heartbeat. "Let's just dial it down a little with the murder. You can't run a man down because you don't like his shoes."

The light has changed, and she speeds forward, leaving the bus shelter poster in our rearview and channeling her rage by cutting off another car when she switches lanes.

I watch in fascination as she broods silently, and for the second time in as many minutes I wish I knew what was going on in her life, that I had the context for whatever rivalry she has going on with her co-worker. Instead, I sit quietly while she works through it on her own and wait for the mist to clear.

> **ANNIE:** So my flavor was called…Coco-nutty. On the carton I drew a picture of a coconut with arms and legs holding a barbell. He had a little speech bubble that said "I'm here to get shredded"
> **ANNIE:** Because it had coconut shreds in it
> **ANNIE:** Get it??
> **CONNOR:** I'm speechless

"Anyway," Shannon says, picking up the conversation like the last five minutes of white-knuckling the steering wheel never happened. "The trip's not happening."

"It still can," I say to her, tossing my phone out of reach. "You could just come for a visit. I have a few holidays left I could take."

"I don't."

"A weekend, then. Everyone knows you can do New York in a weekend."

She says nothing.

"Seriously, Shan. It would be so great. We can still go dress shopping. *And,*" I say, like I've come up with the ultimate clincher, "I've already scouted out like half the bars and restaurants where they film *Real Housewives.*"

She cuts me a look. I've got her attention.

"They're all shit," I warn. "But I *do* know where they are."

"I'm not sure. I need to save for the wedding."

"I have air miles coming out of my eyeballs."

"Don't you need them for your own flights?"

"Why? Where am I going? Nowhere, that's where!"

I'm starting to sound like a peppy travel agent, but I don't care. I am not letting this opportunity slip through my fingers.

"We can do it the same dates you were already planning," I tell her. "I'll look up reward flights right now."

"I should talk it over with Dan . . ."

"One weekend," I plead with her. I feel it in the marrow of my bones: if I can just get her to New York, I can turn the tide and convince her to call off this wedding for good. "*Please.* I really want us to spend some time together. It's been ages."

I didn't intend to sound so desperate, and I know she's clocked my tone.

"Fine," she says eventually. "If you can get a reward flight, I'm in."

Eleven

Connor wants me there bright and early on Thursday for a breakfast meeting with my new team. Which I absolutely would have been on time for, if my fucking keycard wasn't deactivated again.

This time, I calmly make my way over to the security desk and wait until I can explain the problem. I'm informed that unfortunately I will need a new keycard, which it is not in their power to give me, since I am unauthorized. I will need to take this up with the reception desk at Taskio on the twenty-first floor. Which I can't access. Because I don't have a working keycard.

I am now ten minutes late for my breakfast meeting.

The security guard, sensing that my mood is turning, suggests I check in as a visitor, so that my manager will receive a notification letting them know I've arrived.

"Could you please let Connor Reid know Annie Winstead is here to see him," I say through gritted teeth.

I then submit to having my photo taken on a small, badly placed webcam. It gets printed out in grainy black and white, then clipped onto a garish yellow lanyard with the word VISITOR stitched across it in lettering so chunky it could be seen from outer space.

I wait for Connor. He doesn't come. After another ten minutes I ask the security desk to email him a second time.

When he finally does appear, I am seething.

"Wow, late on your first day, huh?" he says when he sees me. I am too annoyed to do anything but glower at him.

The security guard buzzes me through the barrier. Connor sweeps me into the elevator and upstairs.

"The guys are up in the Scratch Kitchen," he says.

"Mmm." I nod.

Here's the thing I don't get. Did he not even *notice* I was late? I was supposed to be here twenty minutes ago.

"After that we'll go and sort out your keycard."

I give him a halfhearted thumbs-up.

Where did he think I was, exactly? I'm over twenty minutes late and he didn't so much as *wonder* what had happened to me?

I could have fallen into a sinkhole for all he knew. And that's where I'd still be, with rats *crawling all over me,* probably eating me for breakfast, because my new boss didn't even *realize* I wasn't there. On my first day!

"Can I just say," Connor says, leaning in close. "That. Is a very fetching lanyard."

I look down at the stupid yellow visitor necklace.

He's making fun of me. I KNOW he's making fun of me. His eyes are twinkling at me, willing me not to sulk, but to laugh with him instead. I won't do it! I bite down on the inside of my lip, hard. I refuse to let him charm me.

He seems satisfied with this, chuckling under his breath as he straightens.

"I'll introduce you to the team," he says over his shoulder when the elevator dings open. "They're just over here."

He leads me across the canteen until we come to a halt in

front of three guys, all huddled around a laptop. My first assumption—that they're working on something important—is swiftly corrected when I hear a garbled sound coming through the laptop speakers.

"Isn't that insane?!" the one in the middle says, while the other two marvel at whatever video or meme it is they're watching.

"Good news. I found her," Connor says, calling his teammates to attention.

All three of them push back from their seats and rise, and Connor makes the introductions one by one. Ben, the purveyor of the laptop, a tall, wiry redhead in a striped long-sleeved rugby shirt. John: shorter than Ben by maybe one or two inches, with perfect curly brown hair and glasses that I can only assume were purchased at a Harry Potter gift shop. And finally, Martin: the shortest by several inches, impeccably dressed and sporting a shock of jet-black hair that's actively fighting the earth's gravitational pull (and winning).

We all shake hands, and Connor disappears to order some coffees for us while the guys drag a couple of extra chairs over and then carry on with their merriment like I've been there the whole time.

Unfortunately, I have done that thing where instead of remembering their names, I focused on remembering my *own* name, and already have no idea who is who.

"Sorry," I say, halting the conversation abruptly. "Can you tell me your names again? More slowly this time."

I pay better attention second time around—repeating each of their names several times under my breath and quickly developing nicknames to try and tell them apart. From now on they'll be known as Curly John, Martin Short, and Big Red Ben.

Ben, I realize, is the one Martha told me was hotter than Connor, and honestly, I'm surprised; he isn't. Though I can appreciate he has a certain allure. Of the three, he's the quietest—so far, anyway—and though I couldn't exactly say why, it feels like he's watching me closely. His eyes are the color of what might best be described as *seafoam,* and give the uncanny sensation of being almost transparent.

Though the shortest, Martin is also the loudest, and very clearly the team's court jester. Curly John falls somewhere in between. He strikes me as a little sweetie.

"Nice to have a girl on the team," he says, turning to me with a smile.

Yes, I think. Definitely a sweetie.

"Thank you," I say, "I'm kind of nervous. It feels like the first day of school."

"I get it," Ben says, chiming in from the head of the table. "When I was a kid, my family moved and I had to start fourth grade at a new school. I was so scared I threw up all over my T-shirt when I got there."

"You did not," Martin says, amazed.

"I swear," Ben says. "I had to walk all the way back home with puke all over me."

"What happened then?" I ask him.

"My mom made me change and walk back."

John laughs. "That's savage."

"How have I never heard that story until now?" Martin asks, visibly suspicious that Ben's story is some kind of hoax.

"Ask Connor," he says.

"Ask me what?" Connor materializes at my elbow and drops a coffee in front of me.

"Ben's saying he puked all over himself on his first day of school," Martin tells him.

"Ah, the great Pennsylvania State Move," Connor says. "An important story in the Benjamin Canon."

The guys riff back and forth, Martin interrogating Ben's story and John interjecting now and again to ask for clarification, while I sip my coffee and catalogue as many details about them and the group's dynamic as I can.

It's clear they're all close—I'd be willing to wager they hang outside of work—and judging by Connor's prior knowledge of Ben's first day of school story, those two go back even further.

After five minutes it's official: I love them. I will happily live out the rest of my days with this merry band of dorks.

"You should tell us about yourself, Annie," Martin Short says to me. "Are you in a—"

Connor cuts him off immediately. "No hitting on the new girl on her first day."

"I wasn't," Martin protests, then turns to me: "I swear I wasn't. I was just going to *ask* if you were in a—"

"Band," Ben jumps in.

"Doomsday cult," John adds, hot on his heels.

I laugh. "I am not in a band, a doomsday cult, *or* a relationship, if that's what you were going to ask."

Beside me, Connor groans. "We're going to get reported to HR before 10 A.M."

"You would no matter what," I assure him. "My best friend is in HR."

He looks at me like *ah, this all makes sense now,* but I've interacted with Connor enough to know he won't hold that detail against me. Besides, I'm on the team now. No take backs.

"So are you on any of the apps, then?" Martin asks, like this is all a standard part of the onboarding process.

"Not currently," I say. "But I've been known to dabble."

"I'll add you to my contacts so you don't come up in my matches," Martin tells me. Chivalry isn't dead, folks.

"She wouldn't match you," John ribs him.

Martin shrugs, supremely unconcerned. "Maybe she would. Maybe she wouldn't. I have a very good profile."

As it turns out, Martin is a bit of a legend on Hinge. After years of striking out on the apps, he underwent a rebrand, embracing his status as a short king.

"I just put it right in my bio now. I get so many more matches that way. Really gives me a niche, you know?"

Despite the fact that the guys clearly engage in this kind of rolling back-and-forth all day long, for whatever reason, the subject of Martin's Hinge profile has never specifically come up in conversation before, and gets them all thinking.

"I wonder what my niche would be," Ben muses.

"Antacid king," Connor offers.

"Sun rash king," Ben replies with a grin.

John bounces a pencil against the edge of the desk. "Mine would be like . . . curly king."

"That sounds like a shampoo brand, dude." Martin, it is clear, is the arbiter of king status.

"Yeah, OK," John says, dejected for a moment. He brightens. "Well, see? It just goes to show you. Not everyone has a niche. It's a smart move."

"That's what I'm saying." Martin nods. "You know I even get tall girls matching me sometimes. They like that I own it."

Ben is doubtful. "How do you know they're tall? Does it say *tall queen* in their bio?"

We never get to find out: Connor flips the screen of his phone over and tells us, "Time to go. We have a call in five."

Class is dismissed.

• • •

What was once a bank of four desks is now a bank of five. Martin Short and Curly John take their places at the same desks I saw them at last week. Big Red moves to the head of the table, and Connor takes the seat closest to him, which means . . . I'm sitting beside Connor. Great. Perfect. Loving it already.

His desk, if it's possible, is even more of a catastrophe than the last time I saw it. The mountain of paper has doubled. I assume this is because he emptied the entire contents of his drawers to clear them out for me, and hasn't found a new home for all of it yet.

"So we've got this call," he says, trailing off as he searches under a pile of paper, fishing out his headphones. "Hopefully won't be too long. Then you and I can catch up about the dashboard."

Ah, the dashboard. I spent the rest of my time back home pulling reports to learn my way around it, and I'm pleased to say I mostly got the hang of it after three frustrating days of tearing my hair out and cursing the skies above me.

When Connor said I wouldn't be able to do the job, I was offended on principle, but I have to begrudgingly (and privately—never to him) admit that he had a point. I have no idea how to do any of this and it's really hard.

Which brings me to the other thing I spent most of the last week doing: staying up late into the night hanging out with my good friend Brian the Dinosaur.

I caught him untold butterflies in his little net. He and I also went on a long walk across a field, picked flowers, and built a charming log cabin where—I presume—he'll live out the rest of his days in peaceful solitude.

Since this is more of a secret project, I have no one to brag to about the fact that I graduated the game and have moved on to the next age bracket, where I now gamely assist Stegosaurus Julie on a—frankly insane—quest to find her lost turtle. I didn't set out intending to lose hours on a kids' coding game, but as it turns out, it's pretty fun. Whoever invented Brian the Dinosaur is an absolute genius. And probably a millionaire.

"Important question for you, Annie," Martin says, once Connor and Ben have joined their call.

"Um, OK."

"Would you rather . . ." He raises his brows meaningfully. "Smell like rotten egg for a year, OR have to carry an egg in your hand every day for a year without breaking it?"

"Such a good one," John says. "It took me ages to decide."

"Is this . . . something you discuss often?"

"It's would-you-rather," Martin says. "The best game ever."

Not sure I'd call it a game, exactly, but sure.

"I guess I'd have to say carry the egg for a year?"

"Lies," Martin says. "I don't believe you. Think how annoying that would be. And if you drop it . . . you get fined a million bucks."

"Who is fining me?"

"Are you sure, Annie?" John asks anxiously. "I chose smell like egg, in the end. It just seemed easier."

"You would be *holding an egg*," Martin stresses, pretending an egg is cupped in his hand. "For three hundred and sixty-five days, everywhere you go. Even when you sleep. You seriously think you wouldn't drop that thing?"

I let out a laugh, which alerts Connor's attention, and sends the three of us hastily logging on to our screens.

. . .

It takes me no time at all to identify how I will become indispensable to my new teammates. From now on, my role, as I see it anyway, will be getting everyone in this company to leave them the hell alone.

Formally speaking, the objective of Data Strategy is to improve data quality across the business and introduce a standard set of metrics that (in theory) will make our reporting more consistent.

In practice, however, Data Strategy seems to operate like a little team of internal handymen.

People from every department come to them with a range of different questions at all hours of the day, interrupting whatever they're supposed to be doing and crashing into the DatStrat inbox with subject lines that all riff on some variation of: URGENT *request for [insert request that is definitely, definitely not and has never been urgent here]*.

If someone needs something from Data Strategy they're supposed to raise a support ticket. The DatStrat inbox exists so Data Strategy can follow up on official ticket requests. This is an outbound-only situation. There should be no inbound messages.

And yet.

Every time I open this inbox, it's overflowing. And I'm chagrined to learn that many of the worst offenders are from my old department.

"John," I say, waving my hand above his screen to capture his attention. All I can see from behind the monitor are curls.

He reminds me of a gopher, the way his head pops up over the screen. "What's up?"

"What's the deal with that email Brandon just sent you, to the DatStrat inbox?"

"Oh, sorry," he says. "I'll get to it."

"No, I mean—what's *his* deal?" I amend. "Are you working with him on something specific, or is he just being a freeloader?"

"The second one," Marty confirms, inserting himself into the conversation. "He's always bugging us."

"Not anymore he's not," I tell them. "Let me reply to him, John, OK?"

"Sure," he says.

I roll up my sleeves and start typing. No one bullies John on my watch.

Brandon,

Just jumping in here. While I appreciate this is time sensitive for you, this particular ask falls outside the remit of the Data Strategy team. Given John's existing workload, he's not the best person to handle this efficiently, and in future I'd appreciate it if you used the established ticketing system rather than approaching him directly. The report you're looking for can be pulled from the dashboard, and if you'd like any assistance with this you're welcome to attend a future learning session we'll be hosting soon. I'll be sure to send you a calendar invite.

All best,
Annie

To think I thought of Brandon as a good guy back in Product! My eyes have been well and truly opened. Luckily, there are few things more satisfying in this life than shaming someone in passive-aggressive corporate speak. I feel a surge of satisfaction when Brandon replies minutes later with a surly message of defeat.

"Did you just—" John says, reading the email, his mouth open in shock.

Martin reads over John's shoulder, then punches the air. "Hell yeah!"

"What's happening?" Ben asks from the top of the table, his attention caught.

"Annie just bitch-slapped Brandon over email," Martin says.

"Thanks, Annie," John says, looking bashful.

Truth be known, I have a blast. I underestimated just how much fun it would be to act as their human shield, denying lazy product managers their pointless requests, settling a few of my own scores in the process.

"She strikes again," Martin says, obsessed with reading every reply. "That one was brutal."

I preen. It was, if I do say so myself.

The only person who doesn't seem to get any relief by my taking control of the inbox is Connor, who I quickly learn gets many, many requests that bypass it and go straight to him.

I watch him answer query after query, pulling data, building spreadsheets, writing mysterious pieces of code. He wears it all lightly, but now and then I get the impression that it's intensely stressful. He has a to-do list as long as his arm, which isn't even scratching the surface of all the things he's covering for *his* boss while she's off on mat leave.

As my seatmate, it is impossible not to be aware of him, and I study him with the intensity of a cultural anthropologist.

I notice things about him that I've never paid attention to in anyone before: the set of his shoulders, the way his hair curls around his ears. The freckle on the back of his neck.

His arms, too, are very nice, as are the backs of his hands, which I get to watch typing away on his keyboard all day long.

CONNOR: You'd be a TERRIBLE spy
ANNIE: Excuse me?
CONNOR: You know when you're staring at me you turn your head all the way to the side?
ANNIE: I do not
CONNOR: You do, you're doing it now
ANNIE: I'm not even looking at you
CONNOR: Yeah NOW you're not. But you were
ANNIE: I wasn't
CONNOR: It's like those people wearing dark sunglasses who think no one can tell what they're looking at
CONNOR: Which never works, by the way
CONNOR: You can always tell
ANNIE: How
CONNOR: It's what your nose is pointing at

I try not to laugh when it's clear that I should, in fact, be working, but I can't help the little snort that escapes when I read that. I don't need to look at Connor to know he's smiling too: I can feel it.

ANNIE: Creep
CONNOR: Says the person staring

I refocus on the task in front of me, determined to ignore Connor's presence, which is of course, impossible. I wonder if he's looking at me as much as I'm looking at him. I find the thought strangely thrilling.

. . .

"What was the name of that boy you went to prom with?" Mom says, without preamble, when she telephones me later that week while I'm making dinner. My roommate is out, somewhere. In her absence I made the salmon.

"I didn't have a date to prom."

"Well then, who's that floppy-haired boy in all the pictures? I have an album full of the two of you on our doorstep."

I am at pains to correct her. "He wasn't my date. We went as *friends*."

"What's the difference?"

"And his name was Thomas," I tell her.

"That was it," she says, satisfied to have this mystery solved. "Are you still in touch with him?"

"Other than through social media? No."

"Well, I think it's high time you reached out," she suggests, like this is something important she's been thinking about for a while. "He works at The King's Glen, you know."

"I did not know that. How do *you* know that?"

"I saw him when I stopped by there the other day."

"And you thought, what? There's my daughter's prom date from twelve years ago, I wonder how he is?"

"What I thought was that you could give him a call and see if they can squeeze in one more wedding this year."

Oh, here we go.

"Has Shannon asked you to do this?"

"She doesn't need to ask. I'm her mother," she says. "And it can't hurt to make a few inquiries."

"Maybe hold off for a bit?" I say, annoyed by her eagerness.

Her tone suggests she finds this absurd. "What would be the point in that?"

"Because she might not want you to? Maybe she doesn't

even want to get married at The King's Glen. She said they hadn't settled on a venue."

"Oh, tosh," she says. "She's only saying that because she's worried they won't have any free dates."

I hesitate. "Are you sure? I didn't exactly get the sense she's in any hurry. Maybe—she's having second thoughts?"

Mom sighs deeply, exhausted at the prospect of raking over this subject with me *again*.

"Dan and your sister are in love," she tells me firmly. "They're moving forward. It's water under the bridge."

"That's not the impression I got."

"Sweetheart, I know Dan's not your favorite, but it's time to let this go." The edge in her voice is a warning. "You're not here. You don't see everything. This is what she wants. Your sister is happy."

What I've never been able to figure out: is Mom delusional, or am I? Either way, if this is Shannon's version of happy, it sucks.

"So will you call him?" she prompts.

"I don't know, Mom. Don't you think we should let Shannon plan her own wedding?"

"She is planning her own wedding! This is just groundwork. Something nice you can do for your sister. I think she'd really appreciate the effort."

"OK," I agree, resigned. "I will reach out and see what he says."

"That's my girl," Mom says, pleased. "And ask him if they do gluten-free!"

It's the next day before he replies to my DM, but as it turns out, Thomas is delighted to hear from me.

He remembers Shannon, of course, sees her around sometimes, doesn't mind looking into it for me, as long as I keep it quiet. If people knew he had the power to influence the wedding bookings, he'd be inundated.

He gives me the information, offers to be my wedding date (as a joke), then says his goodbyes.

It's mid-morning. Connor and Ben have both been on a video call with Brad and the rest of the exec team for the last hour. Ben's so bored he's practically asleep, his head leaning on his wrist, his eyes falling in long, slow blinks. Judging from Connor's posture now, he deeply disagrees with whatever is being discussed. He's leaning back with his arms crossed, a deep groove between his eyebrows.

Now that I've had leisure to observe it more closely, I can confirm that (sadly) Connor is occasionally Brad's bitch—though *not* his friend, as was previously suggested to me.

Connor reports to Brad, so he can't easily tell him to fuck off, even when I can tell that he wants to. Which is a shame. Because Brad comes by a lot, always at an inconvenient time, to discuss issues that I'm almost certain are none of his business.

I whisper across to Marty that I'm going to make a call, then decamp to a booth, and dial my sister. It rings so long I don't think she's going to answer. But then the call connects, and the sound of her voice emerges through the garble of her car's speakerphone.

"Hey," I say, trying to pretend like calling her like this is very normal.

"Is something wrong?"

"Nothing," I promise. "Did you know Mom is making wedding inquiries on your behalf?"

"I did not," Shannon says. I can hear the sound of her indicator clicking away in the background.

"Well, she is. She asked me to get in touch with my friend Thomas who works at The King's Glen."

"Who?" Shannon asks.

"My date from prom," I tell her.

"You mean the guy you went with *as a friend* and then made out with on the dance floor?"

"That's the one." I cringe. Never tell Shannon anything. Her mind is a steel trap.

"I'm pulling up to a viewing," she tells me. "Get to the point."

"Right. So, they have like, no availability left for the rest of the year," I tell her. "Unless you wanted to look at the first weekend in December, which is booked, but the couple hasn't paid, so might be canceled."

"I don't want a winter wedding," she says.

"OK. Then your only other option is to go on the waitlist. Otherwise, they're taking bookings for *next* autumn. The summer is fully booked."

"Hmm," she says. I have no idea how to interpret this.

"Anyway, I just wanted to give you a heads-up before I gave this information to Mom."

"Maybe hold off on doing that? Tell her you haven't heard, if she asks."

Are Shannon and I about to have . . . a secret?

"You bet. I will tell Mom *nothing*."

I feel giddy with triumph. It's me and Shannon against the world.

"Great. I have to go now," she says. She cuts out mid-goodbye.

. . .

Since in technical terms I am what's known as "totally useless," Connor leaves me to solve the dashboard problem. Namely, to figure out why no one wants to use it.

This isn't that different from what I spent all day doing on my old team, except instead of collecting feedback from customers as they tested new beta features, I'm collecting feedback internally.

I run a series of small focus groups with squad leaders from Marketing, Sales, and Product, and what becomes clear almost immediately is that poor dashboard uptake isn't a usability issue, but a political one. No one likes that they're being forced to give up their own individual reporting tools of choice and made to use this new one just because the executive team said so. The sessions all have a strong flavor of group therapy, something Connor finds frustrating and which I find totally amusing.

To Connor—the person who has spent the last year building the dashboard—the pointless resistance to a tool that is better, and more useful, than what most teams are using instead makes no sense whatsoever.

But what he's forgetting is how fucking *spoiled* everyone who works here is. Taskio prides itself on hiring the best of the best (vomit), and though this is a nice idea in theory, what it really means is that by the time the golden candidate has been selected and hired, they think they're God's gift to big tech. Every person here truly believes they are the best and smartest person in the room, a position that affords them the license to do whatever they want—and when they can't, complain about it *forever*. Did I say this place was like high school? Maybe I meant nursery school.

. . .

I get to work first the next morning, arriving just a few minutes before Ben, who looks different for some reason. I study him as he empties the contents of his coat pocket onto his desk, depositing his wallet, keys, and phone in front of him.

I tilt my head, taking him in further, trying to pinpoint the source of his allure. "Did you cut your hair?"

"No," he says, dry as ever. "A trained professional named Jim did it for me."

"My compliments to Jim, then. It looks really good."

Connor pulls up just as I say this, and Ben gets really bashful, looking from Connor to me and then down at his feet as he mumbles out thanks.

"Don't you think Ben's hair looks good?"

"Uh, yeah," Connor says. "Nice haircut, Ben."

Ben looks like he would rather *die* than discuss his haircut for even one more second, leading me to wonder if he has ever received a compliment in his life. We all take our places at our desks, the three of us arranged like the points of a triangle. It's awkward, almost, the way we're suspiciously eyeing one another; me watching Ben, Connor watching me watching Ben, Ben watching Connor watching me watching Ben, on a loop. None of us are saying anything.

These guys, I tell you.

Still, Ben's haircut is striking, and later in the morning, when he cracks a very signature Ben joke in Marty's direction, a thought blinds me: *Ben* could go out with Carrie. Ben and Carrie would be *perfect* for each other!

I have no evidence to support this. I can't point to a single tangible reason why I'm sure of it, yet somehow, I am, and when I imagine Ben and Connor tagging along on all our days and nights out—obviously, Ben will bring Connor, that goes without saying—instead of a pit of dread in my stomach I feel a pleasant buzz, like a portal of fun and possibility has opened and all we need do is walk through it.

I love this plan. This is my best plan ever.

A rogue thought shatters the daydream. Is Ben single? Martha thought not; but in the weeks since, I've never heard Ben mention anyone. Didn't we all talk about dating apps that first day? I need to be certain.

For the rest of the morning, I covertly watch Ben, who avoids making eye contact with me, very pointedly. I know Connor notices me doing this—he gives me a look like *stop it you're being weird now*. But I can't. I'm a woman possessed. I have to know.

When Ben eventually gets up from his desk, I wait three seconds and then follow him, trailing behind him at a distance until he's at the elevators. I dart in just as the doors are closing.

"Hey, Ben," I chirp.

"Whoa, where did you come from?" Ben says, jumping at the sound of my voice.

"Just a quick question for you," I continue, crowding him back into the lift. "I was wondering: are you single?"

He presses himself against the back wall, like he's trying to physically distance himself from the question. The look on his face is one of muted terror.

"Wh-what makes you ask that?"

"Just wondering," I say, trying not to spook him further. He's really squirming here. "I haven't heard you mention anyone."

"Hah, right," he says, his shoulders lowering.

"So are you?" I press.

He tenses again. "Er. Yeah."

I beam at him. "That's *great* news."

"Is it? I mean, we all are. Me, Marty, John. Connor," he adds meaningfully.

"Right, yeah. I knew that. You were the question mark."

Ben forces out a strangled laugh. "Well, now you know. The whole team is. Look at that. All of us. Equally single."

I was not expecting Ben to be this nervous just having to *admit* that he's single. It doesn't bode well for his first date with Carrie, who is a very confident woman. Maybe I will have to chaperone.

"So, was there any reason you were wondering . . . ?" Ben asks again, still wary.

"It's just good to know these things," I tell him, not wanting to reveal my true purpose. Subtlety is key when it comes to matchmaking. "You never know who might be interested in hearing that information."

"Hmm, right, yeah. Of course. But you know . . ." He trails off for a second, then light dawns. "Office relationships are forbidden."

"They . . . are?"

"Yeah. Super frowned upon," he says, nodding with vigor. "You could get fired. *I* could get fired. My boss is really against it."

"Your boss . . . Connor?"

"And your boss," he agrees. "Connor. Very against workplace relationships. He wouldn't even like that we're talking about this sort of thing right now."

"Seriously?"

"Seriously. Oh look at that, we're here," he says as the elevator dings.

I step out into the cafeteria and wait for him to follow.

"Do you know what, I just realized I forgot something," he says, jabbing at a button in front of him. "I'll go back down and get it. No need to wait for me. I'll see ya!"

The door slides shut.

I'm baffled by what just happened there. Workplace relationships are forbidden? If that were true, this place would have no need for annual layoffs; we'd lose ten percent of the workforce after every Christmas party.

I can't imagine Connor taking a firm stance on it, either. Though you never know; he is a stickler for the rules at times. I don't think it's a deal-breaker. I hope not, anyway. I'll figure it out.

It takes me a week to get a working list of the most common objections to the dashboard and then come up with a plan. I summon the entire team to a meeting room early one Thursday morning to reveal it, sending around a calendar invite titled *Operation Use the Dashboard*.

Ben is first to arrive, followed immediately by Connor, who comes in carrying a coffee for himself, and one for me too. John is next, and then finally Martin, who whistles as soon as he sees me.

"Damn, Annie, all dressed up today. You got a big date tonight or something?"

I blush, immediately conscious of the fact I'm in a miniskirt, which makes everyone except Connor heckle at me, certain that they've called it and I have some mystery hot rendezvous that starts immediately after work. My denial sounds weak, which only sets them off further, and though I insist I *don't* have a date, and am not that dressed up, the damage is done. I am on track to receive a light ribbing about going on a date after work for several days.

Finally, finally, we turn to work conversation, and I'm allowed to begin my presentation.

"Gentlemen," I say, clicking my remote to pull up the first slide. "Welcome to Operation Use the Dashboard."

I start by walking them through all the feedback sessions, pulling out a few choice quotes here and there and dividing the feedback into the three most common objections I heard, then walk them through how we can address each of these.

Most of the stuff is minor. There are a few usability issues that I need the guys to agree to address, but most of the other work I can do on my own. I show them the folder of training videos I've filmed on my computer already. John promises to watch every single one.

"This is awesome, Annie," Connor says, with such genuine warmth that it makes my insides glow.

"I'm glad you think so," I tell him, "because that brings me to the final phase of our rollout plan."

I click the remote and the final slide springs up on the projector in front of us. It reads LUNCH AND LEARN in animated font.

His eyebrows go up. "You're going to host a Lunch and Learn?"

"Actually, you're going to host it. Next Wednesday."

"No," he says flatly.

"Yes," I insist. "I already signed you up."

Ben crows at this, slapping his hand down on the desk. "I love it."

"Great, because you're going to be up there too," I tell him. "Connor will need some help with the demos."

"I do not want to do a Lunch and Learn," Connor says, looking mulish.

"It carries more weight coming from the department head," I tell him. "And will be a really good chance for us to get a bunch of people onside with the dashboard in one go."

"Nobody attends the Lunch and Learns," he says.

"I have a plan for that too," I promise him. It's already in motion. "I just need you to get up there and talk about it."

Connor, as it turns out, is not that keen on being in the spotlight, and spends the next few minutes arguing with me, before realizing resistance is futile and finally giving in, or appearing to. The public part of this conversation is over, but I have a feeling it's about to continue privately over messenger.

"Legendary behavior," Ben congratulates me as we leave the meeting room.

"Legendary bullying, you mean."

"Whatever works," he says cheerfully, patting me on the back.

As expected, seconds after we return to our desks, my messenger pings.

> **CONNOR:** TRAITOR
> **ANNIE:** Consider this your skills test revenge my friend
> **CONNOR:** Revenge??
> **CONNOR:** I gave you a job. Aren't we even?
> **ANNIE:** Not even a little bit
> **CONNOR:** Are you going to throw tomatoes when I get up there too or will watching my public humiliation be enough for you on its own
> **ANNIE:** I *think* it will be enough, but I reserve the right to change my mind about that
> **CONNOR:** Unbelievable
> **ANNIE:** It will be great. If we want more people using the dashboard, first we need more people to know about it. Just go up there and don't be yourself
> **CONNOR:** Very inspiring words
> **ANNIE:** If you're thinking about how much extra work it's going to be you don't need to worry

ANNIE: I'll make the slide deck
CONNOR: Will you do my homework for me too?
CONNOR: I can make my own slide deck. I don't trust you not to mess with me.
ANNIE: Fine. But take it seriously
ANNIE: I think it's important we come across as professional for this
CONNOR: And how does one come across as professional, exactly?

He turns his head toward me and raises an eyebrow, his silent signal that the rest of this conversation will take place out loud. I wheel my chair back and turn toward him, crossing one leg over the other. His eyes track the movement. I'm suddenly very aware of the fact my legs are on show. Is he looking? Is it warm in here? Why am I flustered?

I refocus on the conversation at hand.

"Well," I hedge. "I was thinking maybe you could . . ."

I trail off, gesturing vaguely at his sweater.

"Maybe I could . . ."

"You know," I say.

"Oh, I think I'm going to need to hear you say it."

"Get dressed up a bit," I blurt, my cheeks burning. "Like, put on a blazer or something."

"A blazer."

"Maybe not." I try to picture Connor in a blazer and simply cannot do it. "Never mind."

"You think I dress like a slob?"

"*No,*" I say emphatically. "I just mean like, maybe don't wear a hat that day. Whatever. It doesn't matter. You know what, forget I said anything."

I turn back toward my desk and delve into my unopened emails with vigor.

He lets the conversation drop, but later that afternoon I

catch him looking pensively down at his sweater, a hand running up and down his chest.

Did I hurt his feelings? All I wanted to tell him was that if he dressed more like the extremely competent adult he is rather than cosplaying the goofy frat boy he pretends to be, people might take him more seriously. Should I turn back to him and add an amendment like, *Actually Connor, that's one of my favorite sweaters on you. It looks nice with your eyes. You always look great no matter what you're wearing. If you really want the truth, I'm finding you so hot that it's becoming a problem for me. Please don't change.*

I say none of that, of course. I don't dare broach the subject a second time, but instead make a silent vow to inconspicuously compliment him for being a nonslob at the next available opportunity and hope he forgets all about it.

Twelve

In the end, Connor doesn't so much agree to the Lunch and Learn as he just stops resisting it. Once Ben threw his might in with mine, it was game over.

We've been busy all week tweaking the dashboard ahead of the big unveiling, trying to incorporate as much of the feedback from the product managers as we can, and while the guys are busy geeking out over a bunch of things I don't understand at all, I keep busy convincing my friends one by one to attend the Lunch and Learn.

Slowly but surely, I extract attendance promises from most of Product, then Marketing, then Sales. Come to Data Strategy's Lunch and Learn, or face my wrath.

On Wednesday, I'm deeply absorbed watching back a dashboard training video when Connor arrives. I sense him beside me but don't look up straightaway, and when I do—fuck me.

He's wearing a blazer.

It's so incredibly Connor: it's corduroy, and a deep, dark olive, just the right mix of casual and dressy, and looks perfect with whatever dark knit he's wearing underneath. He's turned away, saying something to Ben at the head of the table, giving me precious seconds to regain control of my jaw, which is currently hanging open. I'm still staring when he turns back toward me, a lurking twinkle in his eye.

I give him an exaggerated once-over.

"Did you have to go out and buy that specially?"

"Dickhead," he laughs.

Connor and Ben spend most of the morning making final tweaks to their presentation, though I don't know how much you could truly call it preparation. Most of their energy is directed at putting together a deck where a little animated turtle appears on every single slide in a slightly different way. It reminds me of the turtle I've been hunting on *DinoCode*. I should alert Stegosaurus Julie.

While the guys discuss the pros and cons of Connor opening with one of their signature would-you-rather questions—for the record, they're leaning toward no, in case the debate gets too heated and cuts into the presentation—our building manager Priya appears on the edge of the floor.

Priya and I bonded through shared experience. We were the only two people working late one day when one of the taps flooded the women's washroom. After a lengthy mission that soaked us both to the bone, she promised that if I ever needed anything all I had to do was ask. This week, I called in the favor.

"We're good to go," she says, stopping beside my desk. "Everything gets delivered at twelve."

I dance in my seat. "Amazing. You're amazing. Thank you so much, Priya."

"I'm excited," she says. "I can't believe you pulled it off."

"Neither can I," I say frankly. "Will you send a reminder out?"

"You bet," she says. "Slack is about to go off. I'll see you over there in a little bit." She waves as she goes.

I smile, pleased with my own cunning. This is going to be

the best-attended Lunch and Learn this company has ever seen.

"What was that about?" Connor asks from beside me. I realize belatedly he watched the entire interaction.

"The catering for the Lunch and Learn. We're getting Subu."

Across from me, Martin Short bolts out of his chair. "Did you just say the word *Subu*?"

I don't even bother trying to hide my grin. "Yes, Martin, I did."

"Subu. As in, *the* Subu," he confirms.

"The one and only."

Subu is an extremely New York–famous food truck, achieving viral status online for seamlessly combining three things millennials absolutely love: sushi, burritos, and hipster branding. They regularly have lines around the block. And that's if you can find them.

"I had no idea they catered," John says.

"They don't," I tell them. "But I asked very nicely."

What I really did was stalk their socials relentlessly, then show up at the food truck and beg: aka the mysterious date the guys were ribbing me for last week. Carrie suggested we might have better success on this mission if we both looked, and I quote, "as hot as fucking possible." She wasn't wrong.

Martin and John's excitement goes from zero to one hundred in the blink of an eye. They're acting as if I've just told them Sabrina Carpenter will be coming to perform a song about the dashboard rather than a local food truck providing a bunch of giant hand rolls.

Still, if this is the reaction from these two, it bodes well for when Priya sends out her reminder. If this is my one contribution to the success of the dashboard, I am happy.

Connor hasn't said anything, and when I turn to gauge his approval, the look he gives me holds so much affection it sets my heart racing. I've kept my promise, and he knows it. We are going to launch this dashboard to the moon.

The turnout is amazing. We get there fifteen minutes before the session starts to set up and even then, the room is already buzzing. Subu is as tempting as I hoped it would be. Connor will have a full house.

Lunch and Learns always take place in "The Pit," a purpose-built space laid out amphitheater-style in a semicircle around the stage. Priya introduces us to an IT guy who mics up Connor and Ben and tests all the slides to make sure they're appearing on the screen as expected.

By the time Priya returns, ushering in several trolleys of food, the place is packed. John and I swoop in and fill up a plate for the guys, knowing everything will be long gone by the time we're done. Up front, Connor and Ben are both serene. It's only me that's vibrating with nervous energy.

I scan the room and am pleased to see most of the product team have actually showed—even Andy, who was very iffy about the whole thing the three times I stopped by his desk to beg him to come and bring the rest of his squad with him. I leave the guys to guard the food and go over to say hello.

Andy usually skips the Lunch and Learn, as this is exactly the kind of forced bonding that is typically beneath him. But having Andy in the room matters. If he takes up the dashboard, the rest of his team will too, and so will the rest of Product.

"You came," I say, sliding onto the bench beside him.

"Don't tell me you're surprised. You've been reminding me all week," he teases.

I shrug. You never know with Andy.

"Plus," he adds, the corner of his mouth curling up, "I figured I owed you one, for forgetting you're Canadian. I still don't know how I did that."

I laugh, nudging into his shoulder. "You're forgiven."

Connor and Ben are hanging around beside the stage, waiting to get started. I can see him watching me talking to Andy, and I give him a wave from where I'm sitting, mouthing *good luck*. I catch Carrie sliding in at the end of the back row over my shoulder just as the lights start to dim, and then we're off.

Any anxiety I felt on his behalf is wasted. As soon as he opens his mouth, goofy Connor is gone. In his place is this other person: one who takes control of the room, cracks little self-deprecating jokes that people laugh at, who fields questions from the audience with ease.

I'm a strange mixture of proud and possessive watching him up there. Pleased he's doing well, but also territorial, too, like Connor's laughs and smiles were my own personal discovery, and thus meant to be exclusive to me.

He and Ben make the perfect double act, so natural with each other that you'd think they'd done this a hundred times before, each sticking to their own side of the stage and seamlessly passing their jokes back and forth, Connor in his blazer and Ben in his smart shirt. They're refreshingly unpretentious, never once using words like "paradigm-shifting" or "cross-platform alignment" like the rest of the execs usually do when they make minor announcements about anything. When I scan around the room, people seem genuinely engaged with what they're saying.

We'd agreed in advance that if no one asked any questions I would raise my hand so that Connor and Ben could demo a report, but as it turns out, we needn't have worried. The crowd is genuinely enthusiastic about the dashboard. There are so many people asking him to troubleshoot their reporting issues that his presentation runs over by twenty minutes. Even Andy raises his hand.

None of us can get near Connor and Ben when the lights come up—people are literally lined up to speak to them. But by the time I make my way over to John and Martin, Ben has managed to slip away from the crowd. He gratefully accepts the plate of food we saved for him and the four of us settle into the debrief.

"How good was that?"

"Way better than we were hoping," Martin answers. "Connor is going to be so jazzed."

Ben takes a huge bite, groaning as he does. "You're in the hall of fame for this one, Annie, for real."

We all watch as Connor chats away, and John points out a few of the people buzzing around him, including the head of paid search, who has just pulled him aside for a one-on-one. We all agree: it's a good sign.

With that under control, it's now time for the second part of my secret plan: introducing Carrie to Ben. I wave her over, watching as she weaves her way through the crowd.

"Hey, Ben," I say, wrapping a hand around his arm and pulling him away from the conversation he'd been having. "Have I introduced you to my friend Carrie?"

"No?" he says, face quizzical.

"Well," I say to him as Carrie comes to a halt in front of us. "Carrie, this is my teammate Ben," I say.

I've already lightly primed her for this; I've been talking up Ben, and the rest of the team, all week, telling her how great they all are and how they make a refreshing change from the losers we're used to.

Ben and Carrie chat away, and soon we're joined by Martin and John. I'm not exactly sure how we got there, conversationally, but by the time Connor makes his way over to us we're all deeply engrossed in a debate about whether it's better to have arms for legs or legs for arms.

"Glad that's over," he says when I hand him a plate of food.

"You were so great," I tell him. "I think the blazer really made it."

He tugs at the jacket, a smile lurking. "You like this, do you?"

Yes. I like it.

"So here he is, the famous Connor," Carrie says, stepping forward, turning the attention of the whole group in the process. "We finally meet in real life."

He accepts this compliment with a smile, and I watch in detached horror as his eyes quickly scan down her body and right back up again. "And you are?"

"Carrie," she says, holding her hand out to Connor. "It's me you talked to about Annie's role transfer."

"Of course," he says, extending his own in return. "I thought I recognized your voice. Nice to meet you in person. You look just like your emails."

Carrie is simply *delighted* that Connor's aware of who she is, shyly tucking her hair behind her ear as she thanks him for smuggling me onto their team.

"It's definitely you who did me the favor," he says. "Thanks again for helping sort all that out."

"That's what I'm here for," she says. Highly suggestively, I might add. Her voice drops about four octaves.

There's a martial light in her eye that fills me with misgiving, a feeling that only intensifies the longer she hangs around. Carrie is extremely good-looking, attractive in a way that defies classification. She appeals to everyone. Rarely, however, does anyone appeal to her.

My roommate Sam often jokes that she's in Manhattan's top 2 percent of singles, not just because she's hot but also because she's fun and smart and—most importantly—just a little bit rude. If she sets her sights on Connor he won't stand a chance. My stomach lurches at the thought. She's supposed to go out with Ben!

Alex from my old team summons me from across the room, and I move off reluctantly, leaving Carrie with the guys.

"*Hey-o*," Alex says, giving me a high five. He's so tall I practically have to jump to reach it.

"What's the verdict from Product?" I ask him. "The dashboard's pretty good, right?"

Andy joins the circle just as I say this. "Annie has truly crossed over to the dark side. You're really drinking the data team Kool-Aid."

"Are they the dark side? I wasn't aware of it."

"She's lost to us," Alex laughs, a hand on his heart. "Taskio claims another good woman."

"*Never*," I promise. "Jotter forever."

But I look over at my new team when I say it, not ready to admit that secretly, I like it so much better in DatStrat than I ever did in Product, or at Jotter. It feels disloyal to even think it.

Connor is still in conversation with Carrie. Considering how hard I had to convince her just to attend this thing, she's acting awfully interested in it now. While I watch them, Connor turns his head toward me. I point a thumb toward the door. He nods.

"I have to go," I say. With a promise to Alex that I'll crash the next Product stand-up, I start heading toward the elevators.

Carrie hangs back.

"You failed to mention how hot Connor is," she says, sliding up beside me. "I thought you said he was a dork."

I bristle. "He is a dork."

"Your definition of dork and mine must be very different."

There's no time for anything else, since we catch up with the boys then, all piling into the elevator, riding together until we get to Carrie's floor.

Connor tells Carrie it was nice to meet her. I tell her to hurry, that the elevator doors are closing. He raises an eyebrow at me as the five of us continue onward, which I do my best to ignore.

"Here's one," John says with a snap of his fingers. "Would you rather spend an hour alone at the bottom of the ocean, or an hour alone in deep space?"

I spend the rest of the day in a state of flustered agitation, confused about why the thought of Carrie prowling around Connor makes me want to scratch my best friend's eyes out. But having slept on it, I've mellowed considerably. It was childish to assume they'd be interested in each other romantically. *Of course* they'd be curious about one another: they've each heard stories of the other from me. And wasn't she flirting with Ben just as much yesterday, when I introduced them? I decide that she was.

See. Everything's fine!

I'm feeling extra gracious by the time I arrive at work, going so far as to get a coffee for Connor to make up for my unexplained grouchiness yesterday. I slide the cup across from my desk to his as he slings his jacket over the back of his chair.

He eyes it with suspicion. "This feels like a trick."

"I get you a coffee and you automatically assume I'm up to something?"

"Yes," he says frankly.

"Fine, I'll give it to Ben then," I say, reaching for the mug.

He swats my hand away and quickly takes a huge gulp. "No way. No take backs."

A minute later he admits he burned the roof of his mouth, and I laugh.

I slowly become aware that Connor is amused by something; the telltale call and response of typing quickly, pause, typing quickly, pause is what gives it away. I watch out of the corner of my eye as his face splits into a big grin, his fingers flying across the keyboard in reply to what he's seen. It goes back and forth like this for another ten minutes. It's not one of the guys: their keyboards are mostly silent.

The mystery is solved when, a little later on, I look up and see Carrie walking toward us. She smiles at me, but before I can say anything, turns her attention to Connor. "Ready to go?"

Excuse me. What?

He locks his screen, pushes out from his desk, and grabs his jacket from the back of the chair without so much as a look in my direction.

I watch in openmouthed horror as the two of them walk toward the elevators. The last thing I see before they disappear from view is Carrie playfully squeezing Connor's arm.

"Interesting," Ben drawls. I'm not the only one whose attention has been captured by this unusual series of events, it seems.

"What'd I miss?" Martin asks, his head poking up from behind his monitors. Ben just shakes his head like *don't worry about it,* but then seconds later I hear the clack of his keyboard. Then Martin's. Then Ben's. WHAT ARE YOU ALL TALKING ABOUT WITHOUT ME, I want to scream, but don't. I pretend I don't notice at all.

It takes Connor seventy-two minutes to reappear. I feel both hungry and left out and have spent the last hour letting my rage grow steadily, ready to unleash it on him. I glower at him as he sits back down.

"Nice lunch?"

His whole body stills at my tone. He swivels his head toward me in slow motion.

"It was," he says.

"Where did you two lovebirds go?"

His eyebrows disappear into his hairline. "Lovebirds?"

I have nothing to add, so say nothing, opting instead to be very absorbed in the spreadsheet in front of me.

"We went to Lola's," he says eventually.

"You're only supposed to take an hour for lunch," I reply, as if it matters, or anyone cares. They don't.

"Oh my god." He laughs under his breath.

"What?"

"Are you jealous I went for lunch with your friend?"

My face is on fire. "No."

"You are," he says, his tone one of obvious delight. "You're jealous."

"That's not it at all."

"What is it then? Are you mad I didn't bring you back a sandwich?"

This has backfired badly. I stare resolutely at my screen. "I have work to do."

"So do I," he says, preparing to put his headphones on. "I just had a long lunch."

The more I try and focus on my work, the less I succeed in doing any. Every time I see Connor's hands move over the keyboard out of the corner of my eye, I imagine he's busy flirting with his new girlfriend Carrie. Anger and embarrassment war within me for top billing. When I can take it no longer, I go upstairs to steal some snacks and sulk in private.

As it turns out, two packs of Oreos can do a lot to restore your inner calm. I swallow the last of my feelings back down with a full-fat Coke and return to my desk determined to ignore Connor for the rest of the day.

It takes him less than sixty seconds to message.

CONNOR: Would you forgive me if I promise never to have lunch with anyone else ever again
ANNIE: Fuck off please I'm very busy

His laugh filters through my headphones. He types again.

CONNOR: This is so surprising
CONNOR: I never pegged you as the jealous type
ANNIE: I'm not!

The exclamation might have been a little much there. Too late now. I click out of the chat box and return to my spreadsheet. He messages again.

CONNOR: It wasn't a date

And then:

CONNOR: If that's what you're assuming.
ANNIE: Ok Connor

The clack of his keyboard becomes more pronounced.

CONNOR: Carrie had some questions about a report she wants to set up

I guffaw so loudly that Martin pokes his head above my screen. "Nothing, sorry," I say to him, and he pops back down. To Connor I type:

ANNIE: SURE she did
ANNIE: Boys are so fucking dumb
CONNOR: ...?
ANNIE: Carrie has never thought of reporting in her LIFE
ANNIE: That was obviously just her excuse to talk to you
CONNOR: She said this to you?
ANNIE: She doesn't need to! This is how girls work
CONNOR: Really??
ANNIE: Yes

A minute passes. Then two.

CONNOR: What do you use as your excuse to talk to me

I want to die.

ANNIE: I am exiting this conversation now
CONNOR: Are all these dashboard questions made up just to spend time with me?

ANNIE: No
CONNOR: But you just said…
ANNIE: That's different! I actually have to work with you
CONNOR: So does Carrie
ANNIE: I give up

The events of the workday continue to unfold around us. We don't talk in person or online for the rest of the day, but every time we make eye contact he gives me the most satisfied, shit-eating grin of his life.

At four o'clock he opens his drawer and pulls out a pack of candy. The rustling of the plastic bag is especially loud, and just when I'm about to snap at him to take it somewhere else I realize he's only doing it to get a rise out of me. I give him a stern look—his face is a portrait of innocence. He tips the open pack toward me in offering. I decline.

Connor is adamant he wasn't on a lunch date, but so what? He wasn't the one who initiated it, so technically he has no idea. Nor did he deny being interested in Carrie. What I need to find out now is if *she's* interested in *him*. Dancing around the subject will get me nowhere. I decide to go bold.

"Knock, knock," I say, inviting myself into Carrie's office.

She's not alone. Andy is here, perched on the edge of the desk.

Perfect, would you look at that. Another man who likes my best friend more than me.

"Two seconds," Carrie says without looking up. "If I don't send this email before six my boss will freak."

She hammers out the rest of her email, sends it off with a little *woosh,* then spins her chair toward Andy and me.

"What's up?" It's unclear whether she's addressing this to me, or Andy, or both of us. He and I exchange wary glances. I motion to him like, *after you.*

Andy straightens up off the desk, clearing his throat.

"I thought we might go for a drink after work," he says. He looks pointedly away from me as he says this, lest I get the impression he is including me in this invitation.

"Oh," Carrie says. I can practically hear the cogs of her mind turning. Her eyes dart toward me and then away again—a silent plea to supply her with an excuse. Fortunately, I have one.

"Sorry, Andy. Carrie's spoken for. My roommate invited her to a gallery opening tonight."

"Yeah, cool," he says. "I love art stuff."

I scoff at this. "No you don't, you've told me a million times you hate—"

Carrie cuts me off. "Did she actually?"

"Hmm? Did who actually," I ask, our last topic of conversation already forgotten.

"Sam. Did she actually invite me."

"Oh," I say. "Yeah. She told me to bring you."

What she actually said was: *bring that rude blonde you're friends with.*

Carrie retrieves her bag from under her desk. "Give me a minute to freshen up. Then we'll go."

Carrie locks us out of her office, so Andy and I loiter around by the elevators, trading gossip while we wait. He tells me about the conspiracy theory that has riveted the product department this week: people are convinced Brad doesn't own a computer.

"It was a joke at first but seriously, Annie, no one has ever seen him use one."

"Do you know what," I say, picturing all the times I've seen Brad hovering around the space between Ben and Connor's desks, thumbing notes into his iPhone, "now that you mention it, I've never seen him with a computer either."

"We've got a Slack channel going. Every time someone sees him in the wild without a computer you send NC in the chat." At my puzzled look he adds, "No computer."

I crack up. "That's funny."

"We've clocked up over forty sightings of Brad NC."

"Wow," I say. "Does he really hang around that much?"

"Oh god yeah. He's like the phantom of the product department."

"What's he doing?"

Andy shrugs. "Poking around, crashing meetings. Being a general pain in the ass."

Sounds very similar to his dealings with Data Strategy, frankly.

"You know what has to happen, don't you?" I tell him. "Someone's going to have to break into his office and check once and for all. That's the only way to end this."

"If we did, I'm convinced the only thing we'd find is a phone charger and a box of protein bars. You know he has no tech background at all? He's from McKinsey or something."

"Really?" This surprises me. Though maybe it doesn't. He's exactly like another consultant I dated briefly. "How did he end up here?"

"Classic Taskio whimsy. They're always putting people in roles they're not qualified for." The corners of his mouth tip up. "You, for example."

I gasp. "Why, you little—"

"Ready?" Carrie materializes looking noticeably hotter than she did ten minutes ago.

Andy, it's clear, takes this transformation as an invitation to put the moves on her. Within seconds I'm relegated to third wheel status, his attention now wholly focused elsewhere.

Sam's gallery, Le Nal, is on the Lower East Side, its name an anagram of its address on Allen Street—Anell felt too on the nose.

It's a small, run-down space with shitty lighting and white stippled walls that Sam and her collective of fellow artists use to stage immersive art experiences. The last one caused a bit of a stir, actually; a performance artist who goes by the moniker Chewy invited all his exes, then stood at the front of the room, held out his arms, and invited them to scream.

We find Sam passing out glasses at a makeshift wine bar, set up directly beside the door. Her black hair has been teased high, bombshell-style, and she's decked out in a scoop neck and pinstripe cigarette pants, a mix between Beetlejuice and a goth Brigitte Bardot.

Her lip curls when she sees Carrie and Andy locked in conversation behind me. He is not on the approved guest list.

"Oh, look. You brought a man."

"Er—Sam, this is Andy. And you know Carrie already."

"Do I?" she says cryptically, turning away without handing either of them a glass.

I do the honors instead, shrugging at them like, *that's Sam for you*.

"That's your roommate?" Andy asks, mystified.

"She's unexpected, I know."

"Don't mess with her," Carrie warns him. "She bites."

For tonight's exhibition, dozens of iPhones have been installed in various corners of the room like security cameras, live-streaming footage of the gallery onto other phone screens also mounted around the space. She's called it WATCHED/WATCHING.

At any given time, the gallery can accommodate about a dozen people—our living room is honestly bigger—so Sam is keeping a strict watch on who gets to go in when.

Optics are key. I've learned over the years that there must always be more people milling around the sidewalk than there are inside the gallery. How else will you attract passersby to stop and ask what the fuck we're doing in there?

To that end, she taps Andy on the shoulder and tells him bluntly to go inside, and when he hesitates, drags him by the arm.

It's a warm evening—sunny, pleasant, humidity still bearable. Traffic is the backing track to everything you do in New York City, and tonight is no different. Everyone chats against the sound of bikes whizzing past and the occasional blaring horn.

"Sooo," I say to Carrie, once Sam has shoved Andy through the gallery door, "how was your lunch with Connor?"

"HA," she says, pointing a finger at me. "I knew it. I fucking knew it!"

"Knew what?"

"That you're hot for your boss."

"I'm not—"

"Save it," Carrie says. "I could just tell when you got all weird at the Lunch and Learn. Why didn't you say anything, you dumb freak?"

I stutter, trying in vain to deny the allegations against me: that I like Connor, and that I withheld this information from Carrie.

"So, you—it wasn't a date?"

"It was a trap," she tells me. "I wanted to see if you'd react."

"By asking him out?"

Carrie ignores this. "I say this as your friend, and also as an officer of the HR department. It's absolutely against company policy to go out with your boss."

"I'm *not*—"

"That said," she continues, cutting me off, "I got the impression there's more than a professional interest there. He asked a lot of questions about you."

"He did?" My voice goes so squeaky that she laughs. I cough, then say again, in a tone that I hope conveys my nonchalance, "I mean—he did?"

"Yes, you loser. But of course, none of that matters, right? Because you're not interested."

"Absolutely," I say, taking a sip of warm white wine. "Not interested."

"Mmm," she says. "Convincing."

Sam returns, inserting herself neatly into the space between Carrie and me. Andy, I notice, is now being entertained—or held against his will—by one of the other gallery staff.

"Your turn," she says to Carrie.

"You could start with hello," she replies.

Sam smirks. "Oh, were you waiting for me to acknowledge you?"

I jump in quickly before the two of them can come to blows. "So—inside?"

Sam casts me a dismissive glance. "Not you. Go and say your hellos to Ari."

"Oh, is she here?" I ask, scanning behind me for signs of Sam's . . . Actually, I don't know how to describe Ari. It feels rude to call her a fuck buddy.

"Come," Sam orders, leading Carrie away. "You'll need it explained to you."

Carrie looks at me and rolls her eyes.

While Sam tours her through the gallery—with absolutely no regard for her personal space, I might add—I catch up with Ari, then say hello to the few other people I recognize milling around. I'm refilling my wine glass a few minutes later when Andy stumbles back out into the fading sunlight.

"Your roommate is crazily intense."

"Yeah, sorry about her. She's mostly harmless."

"I tried to say something to Carrie and she said if I didn't leave, she'd hex me." He has the look of a man trying to decipher the most confusing interaction of his life. "What is that?"

"Um, I think it's a curse," I say. "She's kidding, obviously."

Probably.

"I'm not sure I want to take any chances," he mutters, pausing to pull out his phone. Even from here I can see he's texting someone on an app—now that Carrie is a nonstarter, he's assessing his other options.

"You heading off?" I ask him eventually.

"Yeah, going to meet a friend," he says, still staring down at his screen. "Tell Carrie I said bye?"

Totally unnecessary, as it turns out, because Carrie doesn't ask. She returns to my side looking flustered, her cheeks flushed.

"Sorry," I say. "Was Sam on one in there?"

"Just her usual," Carrie says, taking a deep swig of wine. Sam is back outside too, now holding court in the middle of a group of friends, telling an animated story we're too far out of earshot to properly hear.

Carrie and I look on for a minute, then lose interest.

"Hungry?" I ask her.

"Starving. Let's get out of here."

"I'll just tell Sam we're leaving."

"Don't," Carrie says over her shoulder, already walking in the opposite direction. "Let her wonder."

I'm so mollified by Carrie's extended report of her lunch with Connor that evening that I decide to say no more about it at work the next day, and for the second morning in a row greet Connor as if nothing untoward has happened.

He makes no mention of it either, and when he doesn't reference anything of that nature for the rest of the morning, I consider our disagreement—if you can even call it that—totally over.

Today I'm working with John on some data inputting and spend most of the morning with my chair rolled over to his side of the table so we can work off the same screen. The other guys are deeply immersed in some task that needs to be presented to management later this afternoon, so there's no time for the usual pointless joking around.

Around lunchtime, Ben pops up from his chair and says to Connor: "Should we get food before we run out of time?"

"Sorry, I can't," Connor says mournfully. "Annie doesn't like it when I eat lunch with other people."

I try and punch him on the arm, but he jumps out of the way. "OK, OK," he says, laughing. "You can come with us."

Thirteen

On Thursday morning a product manager sends a waspish message to the dashboard Slack channel, saying that they're trying to pull a report but only getting a blank page that reads:

```
IndexError—please provide a valid index
```

All the guys are either busy or absent, so I decide to take a look for myself. If I can't figure out how to fix it, my logic is that if I can at least try and find *where* the problem is, I can quietly nudge my curly-haired champion John to fix it when he's off his call.

I log in and start to comb for the reports, looking for the function I need. The odds of me fixing the broken report are low. The odds of me crashing the entire dashboard with an errant keystroke are a lot higher, but luckily I have enormous experience in this field—I have been haunting my sister's socials for years, careful to leave no trace.

After several minutes of scrolling, I *think* I might be in the right place but am no wiser as to what the problem is, and am just about to give up, when a line of code catches my eye.

Brian the Dinosaur is with me in this moment, whispering, *is the index out of range?* It is. It is out of range!

I can actually fix this. Holy shit!

I tweak the code, switching it from (my_list[5]) to (my_list[4]), hit save, then refresh the dashboard. The error is gone.

I am—no exaggeration—a fucking genius. My chest swells. I flap my hands like a baby duck hitting the water for the first time. I am high on life, with absolutely no one to share it with.

John is the first one to reappear, and I pounce immediately. "GUESS what."

He deposits his computer back on his desk. "What? No wait, I want to guess. OK," he muses. "You . . . just found out you're the lost princess of a small European country."

"Be serious."

"You saw a ghost and it tried to speak to you."

"Where do you even come up with these? No."

"OK, tell me."

I can't contain my excitement. "I fixed *a line of code!*"

He blinks. "I'm going to need more information."

"One of the product managers was grousing they kept getting an index error when they tried to pull a report. So I went in to look, and I fixed it!"

John leans forward and gives me a high five across the desks. "That is awesome. What was the fix?"

"It was out of range!"

The enthusiasm I'm feeling about this is not normal. Next I'll be learning chess.

John is pleased. "Four weeks in DatStrat and you're already one of us. Now all you need is a cool pair of glasses."

. . .

Connor returns from whatever long, drawn-out meeting he's been in, looking particularly harassed. I watch as he logs back into his desktop, checks his inbox, sighs deeply, closes it, then checks the Slack channel and starts scrolling.

I see the moment he reads the message about the report error, and then my reply. He turns toward me, eyebrow raised.

"What's this?" he asks, pointing at the screen.

I don't even bother to pretend I haven't been watching his every move. "All taken care of. I figured it out."

"Did John fix it for you?" He's almost petulant when he says this, like the only person I should be asking to fix things is him.

"*No.* I did it myself. It was easy."

"It was easy," he repeats, unconvinced.

"It was no big deal, just a small fix. The index was out of range."

"How do you know what that is?"

I shrug, showing him how breezy and nonchalant I am. "I've been working through a few levels on *DinoCode*. I knew what to do."

The *hours* I've spent secretly playing a children's coding game have all been leading up to this. And I can tell you it was one hundred percent worth it. Connor is completely, utterly speechless. I feel like I could take over the world.

When he finally speaks again, his voice is kind of squeaky, like he's straining every muscle he has not to react. "You've been doing *DinoCode*?"

"Yes."

He does laugh now.

"That is . . . " He trails off, scratching at the back of his neck. "Wow."

"What?"

"Nothing. That's great, Annie. Well done." His voice is like a warm hug.

He's still chuckling minutes later, when Ben reappears. "What's funny?" Ben asks.

"Annie's been doing *DinoCode*."

Ben freezes, then says, "Annie's . . . been doing . . . *DinoCode*?"

"Yes," Connor says, his smile huge.

I look from one to the other, suspicion flaring. "What's so weird about that?"

"Nothing," Ben says hastily. "Absolutely nothing. That's cool. *DinoCode* is sweet."

I get the feeling I'm missing something, but none of the guys say anything, and they're all suddenly very focused on their work, and my calendar pings with a call reminder, so the moment is gone.

I don't see the guys for the rest of the afternoon, until we're all due to sit in on a weekly stand-up meeting with Software Engineering. Stand-ups are one of the stupider customs of the tech industry, designed to be an informal team meeting where people share what they're working on, and they do it—you guessed it—standing up.

Except, no one *ever* bothers standing, making a stand-up meeting just . . . a meeting. While I'm at it, no one in Software Engineering is an *actual* engineer, either. Rather, it's just a team full of developers who use—get ready to die—an "engineering approach."

You can see why I love it here.

Sven, the department head, is a highly respected yet temperamental Swede with hair so blond that when I first met him I genuinely thought it came from a bottle. Shannon would die if she realized the color she spends hundreds of dollars a month to maintain is simply growing out of this man's head naturally.

He is exactly what you'd expect from the head of software engineering: technical, smart, efficient—and scary, with no people skills. That last part is something I've only ever dared say out loud to Connor, who laughed and said, "He's a really good guy." I never did figure out if this was because of his lack of people skills, or in spite of them. I may never know.

I catch up with the rest of DatStrat (Martin's shorthand has infected my brain) as they're hanging around by the elevators, deep in animated discussion.

"No way," Ben says, throwing his whole body into it, like a human slingshot. "*Nothing* tops the pistachio."

"That's insane," Martin parries back. "White chocolate is the original. The classic!"

"It's too much," Ben insists. "That's way too much for a cookie."

"Only you would like a *savory* cookie."

"We have to stop this," John groans, clutching his stomach. "I'm getting too hungry. I want them so bad I'd go and line up for them."

"Insanity," Connor says. "No cookie is worth the hassle."

"What's insane is *you* saying *that*," Ben says, as if Connor's words go completely beyond the pale.

"What are you guys talking about?" I interrupt as I come to a halt beside them.

Connor grins. "Krumes."

"Who now?"

Martin boggles. "The *bakehouse*."

I shake my head. "No idea."

This sets them all off immediately. Martin mimes the sound of a bomb exploding, while the other three pile into the elevator with exclamations of *what do you mean* and *best cookies in the world* and *have you been living under a rock?!*

Apparently, yes I have.

Anyway, the stand-up is uneventful: it turns out Sven likes Connor a lot, and the two of them get into a sort of heated brainstorm about whether he can help Engineering do something that's frankly way above my pay grade and therefore too boring to listen to. Blah blah data pipeline blah blah machine learning blah blah API. You get the idea.

"Anything to add, Annie?" Connor asks just before the meeting wraps up.

I glance up quickly; I'm a rabbit caught in a snare. Connor is watching me with what I can only describe as an extremely reprehensible twinkle. The man has an instinct for the second I tune out of the conversation. He always, always knows.

I've spent the last five minutes doodling a picture of a small castle into the corner of my notebook. Obviously, I have absolutely nothing to add here.

"I'm going to take some time," I say, adopting the air of a great thinker. "Really process what we've been discussing here. Before I give my opinion."

Sven seems satisfied with that. The meeting adjourns.

"Dickhead," I murmur, as we file out of the room.

Connor only grins. "It seemed like you were working on something pretty full-on over there."

"I was taking notes," I say loftily.

"Were you? That's great," he says. "You can send the meeting recap across to everyone."

I smack him on the arm with my notebook and continue walking.

• • •

"What did you think of that ask from the customer services team?" I ask Connor when we're back at our desks.

He's already tucked into a pack of Skittles. He keeps them on him at all times. "I think it won't work."

"Even if we just imported the data? They say they can get it."

"Even then," he says.

"I think you're wrong."

"Why does that not surprise me, Annabelle?"

"Would it really be that hard?"

"I get it," he says, smiling. "You fix one line of code and now you're ready to build a whole dashboard."

"You'd be surprised how much they teach you in *Dino-Code*."

"I promise you I wouldn't."

"I bet I could do it."

"I bet you could not," he says, adding, "and before you go all fire-breather on me, not because *you* can't do it. Because it can't be done."

"A wager then," I tell him.

"What are we wagering?" John asks.

"Annie thinks she can import the third-party reviews data to make the report CS is asking for."

John says nothing but when he looks at me his face clearly states: *why would you think that?*

"And I think it's not possible," Connor says. "Which has instantly made her certain that it *is* possible, and now she wants to bet on it."

I stick to my guns. "Martin will agree with me. Martin, don't you think if we did the same thing as with that other app from last week it could work? It's not *that* different, surely."

"Umm," Martin says, leaning back in his chair. "Um um um um. Maybe. Maybe."

"See," I say to Connor, spreading my hands. "Martin agrees with me."

"Would we call that Martin agreeing with you?"

"Are you scared, Connor? Afraid a *girl* is going to show you up in front of all your little friends?"

"Your trash talk is truly something to behold," he tells me. "Are these guys my little friends?"

"Take the bet," Ben says. "What's the prize? Better yet, what's the forfeit?"

"Good question," I reply, thinking quickly. "If I win, Connor has to be my assistant for a week."

He laughs. "It's disturbing how quickly you had that ready to go."

"And if I'm wrong," I say, "which I won't be . . ."

"If she's wrong, Annie has to go and get us all Krumes for the stand-up on Monday morning," Ben says.

John leaps up from his chair, punching the air. "Yes!"

"Fine. If I can't do it, I will go line up at your little cookie emporium on the weekend."

Connor looks me over, thoughtful. "Are you sure you want to do this?"

"I've never been surer of anything in my life. I figure this out, and you have to do everything I tell you."

"In twenty-four hours," Connor verifies.

"In twenty-four hours," I agree. "But I'm allowed to ask the guys for help."

"Sorry, Annie," Martin interjects. "I'm rooting against you now. I really love Krumes."

"Fine." Connor nods, then holds his hand out for me to shake. "You can ask for help. In twenty-four hours, if you haven't figured out how to integrate the data, you're waiting in the insane bakery line. I hope you don't have plans this weekend."

"It won't matter," I say, taking his hand. It's warm. "I am going to win."

Fourteen

I'm disoriented when my alarm goes off on Sunday morning, instinctively reacting like it's Monday, before the world comes into focus and the memory of my defeat comes flooding back. I roll over and groan.

With twenty-four more hours I could've gotten it. I had some very good leads.

The thing is: just collating the data took a lot longer than I expected. By the time I was finished gathering everything I needed, the day was over. I had to convince John to stay late and look at it with me, but though he said he could import my data for me *in theory*, he didn't have a clue how we'd go about actually integrating it into a report.

I refused to accept this, sending John home and scrolling coder forums on Reddit instead. I posted what I was trying to accomplish, eventually making contact with a hobby hacker in Germany called Vunderkid, who said he could do it for a price, until I told him I needed it by the next day, at which point he disappeared.

Instead, I wrote a very long, very intricate email, telling Connor how my custom report *could* work, to which he simply replied: *time's up you lose*.

The memory of Connor's satisfied grin when I read his stupid email is enough to get me moving. I'm going to wipe that smug smile off his face by stuffing it with an enormous, overpriced cookie. If I can't be a winner, I'm determined to be the next best thing: a really good sport.

My bedroom is in a state of disarray. It looks like a small child broke in and pulled every single item from my wardrobe and then just tossed it up in the air to see where it would land. Really, it was Carrie, who decided she had to change ten minutes before going out last night.

I dress in a version of my doing-nothing-on-the-weekend uniform, throwing on a pair of leggings and a huge, baggy sweatshirt, which I attempt to elevate with a jean jacket. I'm trying for "off-duty model," but in reality am looking more "quarantine, day seven." What does it matter? The only other person who's going to see me this morning will also look like the living dead.

I make my way out to the living room and around to the front of the sofa, taking in Carrie's lifeless form. She's lying facedown, her backcombed hair now a wildly knotted bird's nest of platinum blond highlights. A threadbare bedsheet is draped across her—Sam's, I think—and her arm dangles off the edge of the sofa. Even in sleep she reaches toward her phone, which lies on the floor beneath her, its cracked screen face up.

"Wake up, sleepyhead," I say, poking her with my toe.

A garbled moan is my only reply.

"It's time to go to Krumes," I say. "Remember how you promised you'd be fine this morning and would definitely be joining me?"

"No," Carrie whimpers, rolling over and croaking out a plea for water.

The current state of affairs is not exactly a surprise to me. When I finally gave up and went to bed around three thirty last night, I left Carrie and Sam in the middle of a deep and meaningful about the nature of creativity, endlessly arguing the particulars of what did, and didn't, qualify as the creative act.

Both Carrie and Sam can be big personalities at the best of times, but last night felt like a death match. All night, any conversation we fell into, on any subject, one always had to disagree with the other. Sam said red wine was better. Carrie disagreed. It must be white. Carrie argued Pinterest was basic; Sam insisted it was refreshing and ironic instead. On and on it went, until the two of them wound up on the dance floor, staring one another down, angrily swaying to the music. Like a dance-off in *Zoolander*.

The wild thing is, we weren't even planning to go to that rave. Carrie and I were going to have a movie night on the couch. Sam was going to a gallery thing. But the three of us convened in the living room and it's like the fuse was lit. Before I knew it Carrie was going braless in a tank top she fished out of the back of my wardrobe and Sam was in a leather miniskirt and we were at a blacklight party at an old warehouse in Brooklyn's armpit.

I fill the cup of water and hand it to her. She's sitting up now, sheet tucked under her arms. She has the air of a Victorian monarch, ruling from her bedside.

"So, Krumes?" I ask again. "We need to get there before they all sell out."

"If you think I'm going uptown right now, you are insane," she says, taking a huge, two-handed gulp of water.

"You'll feel better once you get moving," I reason. "And we can get brunch!"

"I will not be eating today," she says. "Please let me die in peace."

I sigh. I've dealt with Carrie's hangovers enough times to

know she's not going anywhere fast. "Fine. But if you think I'm saving you a cookie, you're in for a shock."

"Have fun," she mumbles, rolling over.

I head back to my bedroom and swipe my tote bag off the door handle, then grab the book on my bedside table and stuff it inside.

I pull on my running shoes, fill my water bottle, and with one forlorn look at Carrie's inanimate form, slip out of the apartment.

When I emerge from the subway at 72nd Street I have the errant thought that I'm deep in Connor territory now; I've heard him describe the wacky hot dog stand on the corner many times.

I don't often have occasion to come up to this side of town. It's early, and mostly deserted. The shopfronts along Amsterdam Avenue are still closed, and there's hardly any traffic at this time of the morning. The city feels extra spacious today—there must be a million people within a square mile of where I'm standing, yet it feels like I've got the place to myself.

I walk a couple of blocks with the sun on my face and then turn down 74th Street, the map on my phone guiding me to my final destination. I don't find Krumes so much as I find the *line* for Krumes. I'm getting a feel for why this place sells out so early—it appears to be the size of a basement cupboard.

There're already at least a dozen people hanging around, but not so many that I'm worried, so I join the line, then fish my book out from my bag. The bakery opens in thirty-five minutes. If I'm quick about it, I can be back home and napping within an hour.

• • •

A shadow falls across my page. I glance up quickly, then jerk my head up again, certain I can't truly be seeing what I'm seeing, which *appears* to be the shape of a human man that looks exactly like Connor. Grinning at me.

"Good book?" he says by way of greeting.

Any ability to form words has deserted me in this moment, and all I can do is stand there mutely while my body attempts to process the shock of this encounter.

The Connor of the weekend is very much the Connor of the weekday, though with a few slight tweaks: today he's in faded black jeans, with a white shirt and a plaid shirt-jacket (shacket?) over the top. There's a brown thread running through it that matches perfectly with his eyes. Not that I'm noticing!

The longer I stand there gawking the bigger his smile grows.

"I'm surprised to see you, actually," he says casually. "I didn't think you'd show."

"Not that surprised," I argue. "You brought two coffees."

You know what it is, it's the hat: he's wearing it backward.

"Oh, this isn't for you," he says glibly. "They didn't have any large cups left so they put mine into two small ones."

"I—Are you serious?"

He laughs. "No, you lemon. Here."

I take a sniff. "Does it have—"

"Cream? Yes, Your Majesty. Regular cream, not the weird flavored stuff you ingest at the office."

"Thanks," I whisper into the lid.

He considers me a moment. "Would you honestly notice if it was milk?"

"Oh yeah, one hundred percent. It just tastes like . . . coffee without it."

"I thought that was the point."

"Spoken like a man who does not appreciate the value of a good creamer."

"You've got me there."

"Why are you here?" I ask, suspicious. "Were you just walking by and came here to gloat? Wasn't the point of the bet that you didn't have to do this?"

"That's true. But I was feeling guilty."

"Why? Because you won?"

"Because I cheated."

Excuse me? "You what?"

"I cheated," he repeats, showing exactly zero signs of remorse. "I knew what the outcome would be when the bet was made."

"You—how?"

"Because we already tried that a while ago and couldn't do it."

"And yet you took the wager!"

"I did *try* and tell you, at the time. You wouldn't hear reason."

"Oh my god, you are so—"

"Smart?" he offers. "Cunning."

"Annoying!"

"*I'm* the annoying one?" he says, laughter in his voice. "You're the junior developer with five levels of *DinoCode* under your belt who thought they could build a new reporting function in twenty-four hours."

I want to hit back at these claims, prove him wrong in some elaborate way, but I don't know how. The glint in his eye says he knows exactly where my thoughts are going.

"*FINE*," I say, admitting defeat. "But I'm *not* buying you a cookie."

"That seems fair."

"Since this wager is now forfeit, you have to buy your own."

"I will even buy you one," he offers.

"It would serve you right if I made you go to the back of the line."

"But then who would you talk to?"

"Anyone but you."

"I did get up early and bring you a coffee. That has to count for something."

"Well, it doesn't."

"Liar."

I am lying. It does count for something. That Connor came all the way to meet me here is doing things to my insides.

Lucky for me, I don't have to admit it. There's movement at the front of the line. The bakery has opened.

Fifteen

It's like we've crossed the threshold of another dimension when we step out of the bakery and into the bright morning sun. The city is waking up around us now, the area a chorus of balls bouncing and children laughing, the hum of people out enjoying the weekend. The whole morning has taken on a surreal quality, like I was living my life when I walked into the bakery and living someone else's by the time I walked out of it.

The rules at Krumes were absolute: strictly one box per customer.

As per the conditions of our wager, I buy a box of cookies that will be saved for our team meeting tomorrow. Connor's box is for eating today.

He points me toward a stoop across the street, and we dodge traffic as we wander toward it, settling down with our two cookie boxes keeping a respectable distance between us.

"Well, Annie," Connor asks me, "are you ready to be changed forever?"

"I'm not sure," I say, peering inside the box as soon as he tips open the lid. "They do look good. But they also just look like cookies."

"We'll check back on that opinion in five," he says.

Not sure if I mentioned, but these cookies are *enormous*. Famously almost half a pound of dough goes into each one. They look more like mini hamburgers than your garden-variety cookie. Every inch of space is covered in something, like chocolate chips, or cookie crumbs. I'm certain if you tried to eat a whole cookie in one sitting you'd die.

We agree that for the purposes of taste testing, we'll break each cookie into quarters and sample them all one piece at a time.

"What do you want to start with?" Connor asks me.

"Which flavors were the guys fighting over?"

Connor points into the box. "That one is white chocolate, Martin's favorite. And the one with the pistachio bits is Ben's favorite."

"Let's go with white chocolate," I decide.

Connor breaks a piece off for each of us, then holds his up and gives me a jaunty *cheers* before popping it in his mouth. I do the same.

It only takes a single bite to understand what the fuss is about. "I think I get it now," I say between bites.

"Worth giving up your Sunday morning for?"

"One hundred percent," I say. "Though whether it will be worth ever giving up a *second* Sunday for is another question."

I decide we need to try more flavors before we can make a full assessment. We agree to keep eating until one, or both, of us feels sick.

Connor hands me a napkin. "OK, what's next?"

"Pistachio, one hundred percent," I tell him. "It's time to try the flavor that got me into this mess."

He laughs, breaking off a piece of pistachio and handing it to me.

It only takes a single mouthful to convince me. That might be the best cookie I've ever had in my life.

"Oh my god," I say with a whimper. "I am one hundred percent team Ben. White chocolate has been completely forgotten."

"I always forget how good these are," he agrees. "They look so intense but they're really not that sweet."

He pulls his phone out of his pocket, snapping a picture of the box between us. Texting it to the group chat, he informs me.

"You guys have a group chat?"

"Of course," he says, like this is the most obvious thing in the world.

"Wow, thanks for the invite," I say.

"No girls allowed."

"What do you guys talk about?"

"You, mostly."

I level him a look. "Very funny."

He doesn't say anything. Just ducks his head and smiles to himself.

"Did you know all the guys before working here, or just Ben?"

"Just Ben. Naomi poached John from Google. Marty was originally in Engineering but moved across to our team a few years ago."

"Is Ben your bestie?"

"Kinda," Connor says.

"Just at work, or out of work too?"

"Is there a difference?"

I shrug. "Sometimes."

"Both, then, I guess. We were roommates in college. We've always worked together."

"Sometimes I don't think Ben likes me that much," I admit.

"It feels like he's always got his eye on me." Sometimes I get the niggling sense—usually, honestly, when I'm flirting with Connor—that he doesn't approve. But I'm never quite sure if his objections, if you can even call them that, are personal or professional.

"He does, for the record," Connor says.

"How do you know? Has he told you?"

"Yes," Connor says. "Multiple times."

"That's a lie."

"I promise you it isn't," Connor says, then sighs. "You know Ben resigned the morning of the layoffs?"

"For real?"

"Yeah," Connor says. He seems weary, somehow. Like even talking about this is exhausting for him. "He'd been threatening to do it for a while, but he still kind of blindsided me with it. Our team has been understaffed for a long time. And as you know yourself, our remit is kind of all over the place, even more so since Naomi's been gone. When the layoffs happened, and it was clear we weren't going to get anyone to help us, Ben decided he was done with all of it. He wants to do other things."

"Whoa."

"But then you turned up," he continues. "And I at least had a temporary solution. It was clear you'd be an enormous pain in the ass but also a really effective project manager. I begged Ben not to quit, to just stick it out a little longer. If things didn't get better after you joined the team, then he could leave. And as you will notice, he is still here."

"Oh," I say, trying to reorganize my memories in light of this new information.

"If you're getting a vibe off Ben, I promise it's not because of you. It's because of me. He's just waiting to see what happens. Next cookie?"

We decide on a classic: chocolate chip.

"Can I ask you something else?" I say around a mouthful of cookie.

"I have a feeling you will either way," he comments.

"How did you end up as acting department head? It just feels like . . . you hate it."

"Well, Annabelle, when two people love each other very much—"

"Yes, thank you," I say dryly. "I understand the concept of maternity leave. I mean why didn't they hire someone to do it?"

"Naomi's idea of a sick joke, I guess. She wanted me to push myself and go for a management role. She thought I'd like it," he adds.

"Do you?"

"No," he says, sighing deeply. "What's there to like? I spend all day in calls and meetings and taking flak from my direct reports. That's you, by the way."

"No idea what you're talking about," I say. "You were one of the early people in at Taskio, weren't you?"

"Employee number five."

"Wow. So like, early early."

"Yes."

"Like 'Taskio is my religion' early."

"We like to think of it as more like a family."

"The best cults always do."

I mull over how to ask him my next question. "I guess I'm just curious about what you like so much," I say eventually. "Or is it just that you have equity and can't leave?"

Connor shifts forward, resting his elbows on his knees and rubbing at his eyes with the heels of his hands, like he's trying to scrub away whatever thoughts are behind them.

"I know you probably won't believe this," he says, "since

everyone from Jotter hates Taskio. But it used to be different here. It was genuinely exciting, back in the early days, what we were doing."

"I get that."

"Maybe five years ago now, the leadership team decided to pivot and start aggressively going after enterprise clients."

"And you disagreed?"

"No," he says, surprised at my question. "It made way more sense for us to get off the hamster wheel of funding rounds and try and turn a profit. As soon as we won a couple of those big enterprise contracts, everything got easier. But it also changed the vibe a lot. We had big clients and we had to service them. We weren't some scrappy little startup anymore."

"You weren't Jotter, essentially."

"Before you start your sermon, just a reminder that Jotter sold out too. Literally. To Taskio."

I look him over. "Hey, Connor? Want to know a big secret?"

"Yes," he says.

"I like Taskio's interface better than Jotter's."

He gasps. "*Annabelle.*"

"It's true. I always thought it was better. So do a lot of people at Jotter. We just can't admit it now because you're our overlords."

"Unbelievable. And after all the shit you've given me."

"Someone around here needs to keep you on your toes."

"You're right, I'm doing such a great job of staying on top of everything otherwise."

He says it like it's clear he's doing the exact opposite.

"You are," I tell him. "Honestly."

"Thanks," he says. "Though I don't believe you."

We sit in companionable silence, watching life unfold on the street around us.

"Do you ever think about leaving?" I ask after a few minutes.

"Sometimes. Not really. And not now," he adds.

"Why not now?"

He stands. "Shall we walk?"

Sixteen

Connor takes me on a guided tour of the neighborhood, which is, I learn, not only where he grew up, but where his mom still lives. It's like the whole city springs to life before my eyes. He points out all the little landmarks of his childhood: the homes of his school friends, the playground where a friend accidentally split his lip open, the dessert restaurant that was the site of his first date. He doesn't recommend it. The relationship only survived as long as the ice cream sundaes, he tells me, so in a way, this was also the site of his first dumping.

We've been zigzagging up a couple of blocks and then back down again, roaming nowhere in particular, until he turns us down 77th Street toward the gates of an enormous basketball court, taken over by a bustling weekend flea market known as the Grand Bazaar, which, he informs me with the authority of a local historian, is the oldest flea market in the city.

I need no further urging to look around. I have always loved yard sales, and this one is huge. There's all the usual junk sellers you'd expect at a flea market, but also lots of vintage clothing too. I hand my coffee over to Connor and get to work.

He trails behind me from stall to stall without complaint, one coffee cup in each hand, amusement writ large.

"You really love this, don't you?" he asks me, a smile hovering around his mouth.

"I'm addicted," I admit.

When I first moved to New York I was single and didn't know anyone, and never had anything to do on weekends. I'd literally spend hours just going to little vintage sales and hunting around the racks. Practically everything I own is secondhand. It's a very jazzy wardrobe.

Connor, as it turns out, is well-trained in the art of vintage shopping; his mom is also a connoisseur. He spent a lot of his childhood trailing around after her at this very flea market.

"You two would get along great," he assures me as I sling two denim jackets across his waiting arms.

"I'd like to meet your mom. I bet she has a lot of embarrassing stories about you."

"Millions," he agrees.

This flea market is even bigger than I realized. When we finish outside, he points toward the doors and says it extends all the way into the cafeteria too.

Before we get inside, though, someone hails him, and Connor turns.

"Young Mr. Reid. We haven't seen you in a while," the man says, standing from behind his stall and reaching out to shake Connor's hand. He is in his sixties, maybe, with a huge salt-and-pepper mustache.

"I haven't been here in a while," Connor admits. "How are you, Mr. Shaw?"

"I've got something for you," the man says, hunting through the stack of records in front of him, eventually brandishing an album with *Talking Heads* emblazoned across the front. Really, it's for his mom; she sold off all her old records years ago, regretted it instantly, and has been painstakingly rebuilding her collection ever since.

Connor agrees this is a find, and the two merrily haggle back and forth until the man cracks a huge smile and says: "Only for my best student."

"This was one of your teachers?" I ask, as Connor counts the cash out of his wallet.

"One of his *favorite* teachers," Mr. Shaw amends. "I taught him science in that room right there," he says, pointing up to a window in the building behind us.

"Oh my god," I say, looking around me with renewed interest. "This is your school?"

"It is," Connor confirms.

The flea market is forgotten. Mr. Shaw is now the most interesting man in the world. I beg him to tell me stories about Connor, peppering him with questions until the tips of Connor's ears burn bright red.

Mr. Shaw reveals he was not just a science teacher; he was also the supervisor of the chess club. A club that Connor *founded*. He was also, Mr. Shaw tells me grandly, a very active member of the computer club for several years.

Connor looks ready for the ground to swallow him whole. I have never been happier.

"OK, and that's enough," Connor says, turning me away from the stall by the shoulders. I protest immediately—Mr. Shaw was just remembering something about a seventh-grade winter formal.

"Mr. Shaw, it was great to see you, I'll see you soon," he says, waving off his former teacher. "Annie, the exit is that way, you're fired, you know too much."

I cackle, and move toward the school's back entrance instead. Two enormous doors have been propped open to let people in and out and I'm determined to keep exploring. Connor follows with a resigned sigh. Secretly, I think he's also loving it.

"I've never played chess," I muse, as we pass through the doors. "You're going to have to teach me."

"Not sure you'd be able to sit still long enough to learn it."

I am riveted as we make our way down the hallway. It's lined with vendors, and most of the school is closed off to visitors, but I can see down a long corridor covered in red lockers. He walks me right up to the metal shutters, pointing at a bank of red lockers beyond it, and the one that used to be his. I would kill to slip under the gate and check it out for myself.

The cafeteria is basically like any other, the pillars covered in huge murals proclaiming what I assume must be the school's stated values: determination, honesty, inspiration, bravery.

"Kind of intense," I say, pointing at one of the pillars, which simply says *dream*.

He looks at it, then looks back at me, his mouth quirking.

"Am I going to tell you this?" he muses, as if he's handing me a classified state secret. "It's a school for gifted kids."

I burst out laughing at the revelation. Of course. Of *course*. This day just gets better and better.

"I'm so surprised," I tell him. "But also not surprised at all."

Connor being gifted makes perfect sense to me—he has a certain intensity that reeks strongly of getting his homework done before he'd even consider going out to play with the neighborhood kids. All things considered, he's turned out to be quite normal.

We do a loop of the room, then head back outside, our time at the flea market at an end. I quiz him on his school days the entire time. A gifted kid and a childhood chess champion. Truly a gold-plated geek. I love it.

We turn and wander up Columbus Avenue, and the area is bustling now. It's a perfect spring day, and the sidewalk is lined by a farmer's market. We stop at each stall.

Gradually, it dawns on me that Connor and I are on a date. There's no other way to describe the events of this morning. We have spent the last two hours flirting our way up and down the Upper West Side.

We stop by a few more of the stalls, then Connor turns to me with a smile and says: "Well, there's only one thing for it."

We are now strolling through Central Park, as ~~lovers~~ colleagues do.

"Am I keeping you from anything?" he asks.

"Not really. My plan today was just to get ready for my sister."

"Oh?"

"She's coming to visit on Friday for the first time. I want it to be perfect."

"Define perfect."

"Just the usual," I say. "A weekend so fun she leaves convinced to dump her fiancé and move here instead."

"I think there's a '36 Hours' guide for that." He nods. "What are your ideas so far?"

"Not that many, to be honest."

"Well, what do you usually do on the weekends? What did you do last night?"

"Went to a rave in an abandoned warehouse."

He pauses. "I was not expecting that."

I start to tell him I'm not much of a raver, but then I have a flashback of the three of us losing our minds to a remix of Avicii's "Levels," me screaming over and over that it's my favorite song, and think better of it. "Carrie loves house music," is what I admit to him instead.

"Carrie as in, Carrie human resources manager who you accused me of taking on a lunch date?"

I cut him a look. "Yes."

"I wouldn't have taken her for a raver."

"It comes and goes."

"OK, so no raves. What else have you got?"

"Um," I stall, knowing he's going to make fun of me. "Visit Times Square."

"I thought you said you wanted to have a fun weekend."

"Ha ha," I say, shoving at his arm. "I feel like she'll want a picture of it for her Instagram."

"I think we can probably source you some better options. Luckily for you, I was born and bred right here in Manhattan. They rarely let me leave."

"You said you live in Brooklyn," I point out.

"They let me leave to sleep," he concedes.

"Didn't you tell me you went to college in California?"

"Yes, but if you read my Wikipedia page, you'll notice I came right back."

"Why did you?"

"Mostly because I didn't want to be so far away from my mom. Is this the same sister whose engagement party you were at?"

I take a deep breath. "Yes."

"What's her fiancé called again?"

It pains me to even speak his name. "Dan."

"I can tell he's a good friend of yours," he says, dryly. "But good news. It's time for your next cookie."

Somewhere around cookie number four, Connor implemented a thirty-minute rest period between flavors, so we don't get too hopped up on sugar. But deep down I wonder if he did it to give us a concrete reason to spend more time together. We still have three flavors to go.

"What sorts of things does your sister like to do?"

"I don't—I don't really know. We're not that close."

I turn to look at him. He says nothing.

"I'm nervous, I guess. Before I went home last month, we hadn't spoken in more than two years. Not since their last engagement party, in fact."

"Seriously?"

"Yes."

"That's—why?"

"Uhh . . ." I've always stood by my actions at the party. I know it was shitty, but I did what I had to do. But something about saying it out loud to Connor makes me feel uneasy. Like the memory doesn't sit so well with me anymore. "So, remember how I said my sister's fiancé was a shithead?"

"Yeah."

"Well. So." I rub my temples. I don't even know where to start. "So, at their first engagement party, I made a toast and called Dan out, in front of everyone, for having sex with someone who was *not* my sister at town hall."

Connor chokes on the piece of cookie he'd just popped into his mouth. "Come again?"

I shrug. "He was never going to tell Shannon, and I was pissed off that he was going to get away with it."

"What did people do?"

"The place went, like, deathly silent. And then Shannon turned to Dan and said, 'Dan, what is she talking about?' and everyone just exploded. Shannon stormed off, Dan went after her. My mom *flipped* out at me. And the party just kind of . . . dispersed."

"Fucking hell."

"Long story short, Shannon was obviously *super* pissed off at me."

"Not sure I blame her," Connor says.

"No, I know. I don't either, honestly. I didn't mind being the bad guy because the ends justified the means, you know? But then she and Dan got back together. And she still wouldn't talk to me."

Somewhere over the course of my confessional, Connor has slung his arm over the back of the bench.

It's almost, *almost* like he's put his arm around me.

"Anyway," I say. "So now they're engaged again and she's coming to visit, and this is my chance to make her see reason and get my sister back. I have to get it right."

"Hmm," Connor says. "And if she marries this guy anyway?"

"I won't let that happen."

"You might not get any say."

"If I honestly thought she was happy I'd butt out."

I definitely would. Maybe I would.

"But Dan is the same as he always was. And I don't even think she wants to marry him. I just need to show her she can have a different kind of life."

"That's a tall order for one weekend," he says eventually.

I give him a weak smile.

His arm does come around me now, and he pulls me into a reassuring squeeze.

"Well," he says decisively. "I guess we've got work to do."

I look up at him. "We?"

"What, you think I'm going to leave you to make this itinerary on your own? Your best idea was Times Square."

"That wasn't my best idea. That was *one* idea. I have many more."

"Really." I can tell he thinks I'm full of shit. He's doing his *Annie you are full of shit* face as he rises from the bench.

"I *do*," I insist. "I have a list."

"Let's see it, then."

I should have foreseen this would be his response. "It's more of a . . . bucket list, from when I first moved here. Of all the things I wanted to do in the city."

We're up and walking again, meandering down the path past dog walkers and people out on their afternoon stroll.

"Now I *really* need to see it," he says, swerving to let a toddler zip past on her tiny pink scooter.

"Absolutely not. It's private."

"OK, how about this, I'll guess what's on it and if I'm right, you have to tell me."

"Fine."

"Perfect. Now, what would be on Annie's bucket list?" he muses.

He stops walking and turns toward me, looking me over carefully while he pretends to think. My tote bag full of cookies hangs from his shoulder.

Not for the first time this morning I wish I'd taken the time to look more presentable, especially since Connor looks, and I am reluctant to admit this even to myself, irresistible. But how could I have imagined this is how my Sunday would pan out?

"Is it written down?"

"Yes. On my phone."

"Get it out. How many items are on the list?"

I roll my eyes but comply, pulling up my Notes app and scrolling until I find it. "There's ten."

"Ten. Wow, OK. Ten." Again he makes a big show of thinking about it, then starts firing off guesses. "Cycle across the Brooklyn Bridge."

"Incorrect."

"Smart. It's steeper than it seems, you know."

I start walking again. He falls back into step beside me.

"Sit in the audience of *The Tonight Show*."

"No." My list seems lamer and lamer with every good suggestion he makes.

"I'm going to die of curiosity. Please tell me what's on it."

I consider denying him but instead meekly pass my phone over, feeling more and more self-conscious as he scrolls down the list.

"*Go up the Empire State Building . . . ?*" His tone is completely incredulous. "Annie, haven't you lived here for like, six years?"

"Yeah, so?"

"Your bucket list reads like an alien's who's beamed down to earth with a travel guide from the mid-'90s."

It's an oddly accurate observation. I do feel like an alien here, sometimes. Wandering around wondering how to make myself a proper New Yorker.

"OK, *finally*, here we go. Something normal."

I pinch his elbow. Hard.

"Ow," he says, holding his arm.

"Which one?"

"*Find the best pizza slice in the city,*" he says. "A worthy yet impossible goal. Many brave people have tried before you."

"Connor, I'm surprised at you. Of *course* it's possible. It just needs a dashboard."

He laughs at this, and my stomach does a little flip of satisfaction. Making Connor laugh is one of the best things.

"You're right, what was I thinking. All we need to do is input the datapoints."

"Exactly. Ergo, it stays on the list."

"It stays on the list," he agrees, smiling at me as he passes my phone back. "But we're going to need some better options for your sister."

Seventeen

After Central Park we wander through the neighborhood until before I know it, we're turning the corner and my subway stop is in view. Whether Connor knows I take this train or it's just a coincidence that he's depositing me here is unclear, but something tells me it's the former. Him seeing and remembering little details like that is just so incredibly *him*. I know the walk to the subway is for my benefit. He's already told me he's staying uptown so he can drop in on his mom.

Now that our time together is almost over I'm desperate to extend it, to eke out just a few more minutes of Connor's company rather than go home and spend the rest of the day without him. I stall for ages outside the subway entrance, scanning my brain for a conversational gambit that will keep us talking for the rest of the day. If he's wise to my ruse, he doesn't show it. Maybe he doesn't want to go, either.

Desperation leads to inspiration. "I meant to ask you," I say, snapping my fingers. "What did you think about the whole free tier thing? What will they do?"

"That question has been haunting me since I was cc'd on the email."

Brad, our brilliantly stupid VP of corporate development,

has recently come up with a new initiative he's extremely enthusiastic about: a free tier of Taskio.

We run on a subscription-based model, and Brad believes we could capture a bigger share of the market if we rolled out a free tier, where we'd generate revenue by showing users targeted ads. Connor and Ben have been banging their heads against the wall at the stupidity of this—yet Brad won't let it go. He genuinely believes spamming our users with in-app ads will usher in the golden age of Taskio.

"Please bring me to that meeting. I would pay good money to see Brad and Sven duke it out on that one."

"I would if I trusted that you would sit quietly and not put your hand up to volunteer your own even more insane solution," he says, referencing another meeting where I did exactly that.

"Hey! You said yourself that was a good idea."

"I said it was an *idea*," he corrects. "The word 'good' was never mentioned."

"You're just upset you didn't think of it."

"I think it would be more accurate to say I'm upset that you did."

I realize, then, why we're still here: neither of us has a clue how to wrap this up.

Even if I did want to leave—which I don't—what do I even say to Connor in this moment? *Thanks for the best date I've ever been on, see you Monday? By the way, did you think it was a date too?*

He, at least, looks just as awkward about this as I do, like now that we're about to part ways it behooves us to acknowledge what exactly it is we've been doing all day.

"Do you know how to get home from here?"

I scoff at what he's implying. "I do have a basic working knowledge of the New York City Metro, you know."

"Seeing as you have *go up the Empire State Building* on your bucket list, I didn't want to make any assumptions."

I've already been fighting for composure all day, but the evil little smile he gives me tips me over the edge. Connor is never more irresistible to me than when he's teasing me like this. His tiny, gentle little insults are subtle reminders of just how much I'm on his mind.

I'm leaning forward before I consciously realize what I'm doing, rising on my toes and dropping a kiss onto his cheek. It's warm and smooth and the second I make contact it's nowhere near enough for me, so I regroup, grab his shoulder and kiss him full on the mouth. It's startling in its novelty, but also familiar—like some secret part of me has known about kissing Connor all along.

I can *feel* his surprise in the way his shoulder tenses under my hand, and though it can be said that I am kissing Connor, in this moment it could not be said that he is kissing me. But then a split second later he catches up with me, tilting his head just a fraction and sending the pressure right back. Our lips move together softly, tentatively. I slide my hand up to the back of his neck, closing my fingers around his hair, launching myself into kissing him with everything I've got.

Too much, maybe: he jolts back to earth and releases me, taking a hasty step back. The look on his face is one of extreme shock. I'm sure mine mirrors it.

It feels like a giant speech bubble is floating above the two of us reading *what the hell was that, exactly?*

"Did I—" I say reflexively, just as he says, "I don't think we should—"

We both halt.

He tries again. "This isn't a good idea."

I scramble to take it back. "I—sorry. I didn't mean to—"

I'm stammering, trying to string together a sentence that will erase the last thirty seconds and vanish me off the face of the earth. It feels like a bucket of cold water has been tossed over my head. The mortification is bracing.

"Annie—"

"No, my bad," I say, shaking my head, holding my hands out in front of me, as if I can physically stave off the humiliation. "Forget it—I don't know what I was—"

"It's just—"

"I'll see you tomorrow," I say, cutting him off before either of us makes this worse than it already is.

I give him a small wave—though am no longer looking at him to verify if he actually saw it—and then I turn and hotfoot it down the subway steps.

I could win a marathon at the speed I'm moving. Nice to know, I guess, that my fight-or-flight response is in good working order.

Miracle of miracles, a train is pulling into the station, the doors gliding open just as I push through the turnstiles. I rush onto the train, power walking to the farthest possible corner of the carriage, wishing I could keep going and continue walking straight off the edge of the map.

A short eternity later, the doors close, and we move: Connor hasn't followed me. I sink into the closest available seat, hugging my tote bag to my chest. I squeeze my eyes shut, but it does nothing. The image of Connor's grave face saying *this isn't a good idea* is seared into my brain. It burns me the entire way home.

Eighteen

An hour later, I burst through the apartment door, hoping against hope that Carrie is still on my sofa, too hungover to make her way home.

Turns out I needn't have worried—she and Sam are side by side smoking a bowl.

Carrie is infinitely more presentable than when I left her. She's freshly showered and back in her jeans, wearing an oversized sweater she's stolen, I notice, off the back of my desk chair. The table has been tidied away, the sheet is gone, her water has been replaced by a huge iced coffee. It's like she lives here.

Sam looks as she always does—head to toe in black, her sleek, straight black hair falling to her shoulders. As far as I know, she sleeps in her eyeliner. People sometimes ask me what my roommate is like, and over the years I've learned I can sum up her entire personality in a single fact: she has microbangs. She trims them to deadly precision using a laser tape measure.

"Were you making those fucking cookies yourself?" Sam says, cackling at her own brilliance. Even without the smell of weed gently perfuming our apartment, her slow blink would be a dead giveaway. Sam is very high.

"That took a *lot* longer than I expected," Carrie says, emitting a perfect smoke ring with the tilt of her jaw. "So glad I didn't go with you. No offense."

"What kind of loser gets up at dawn after a rave and goes uptown to a bakery," Sam muses.

"The kind of loser who made a pointless bet and lost it," I say, throwing myself down on Carrie's other side. She holds her ridiculously pearlescent glass pipe toward me in question, but I decline.

"So do we get to try them?" Sam asks.

"I told Carrie she wouldn't get any if she didn't come. I feel like I should stand my ground on principle," I reply.

"That doesn't apply to me," Sam says, reaching for the box. "Hand them over."

When I told Connor that I knew the girls would want to try some, he wrapped one up for his mom and then sweetly sent me home with the rest of the leftovers, something I'm extremely grateful for now that I know my two best friends have the munchies.

Sam and Carrie rifle through the box of half-eaten cookies, busying themselves for several minutes by breaking off little pieces and sampling each flavor with impressive speed.

"Good, I guess," Sam says, chewing, then immediately deciding, "No, amazing. These cookies have changed me."

"Same," Carrie agrees. "It was absolutely worth Annie lining up all day."

"I wasn't lining up all day," I tell them, segueing nicely into what I really want to talk about. "I was lining up for an hour. Then . . ."

Sam side-eyes me. "Then . . . ?"

"OK, so you know that guy I work with?"

"No."

"You do. The one I sit beside."

"From the gallery?"

I feel the heat spread up my neck. "No, that's Andy. I'm talking about Connor."

"Try saying his name without looking like you've committed a crime," Carrie says, grinning.

I clear my throat and continue. "So when I went to wait for the cookies . . . he was there."

Carrie reanimates at this tidbit, her hand closing around my knee in a vise grip.

"Oh my god. Are you banging a guy from work?" Sam exclaims, her tone one of awe, or maybe revulsion.

"*No,*" I say, but my voice cracks, ruining everything. I try again. "Nobody is banging anyone. We're just . . . " We're just nothing. Why am I so embarrassed? "I don't even know if we qualify as friends. We're colleagues."

"'Kay," Sam says.

Carrie guffaws. "Colleagues don't hang out on Sundays."

"That's the thing," I tell them. "It *honestly* wasn't planned. Or," I pause, thinking. "I didn't plan it. He just showed up."

"Do you know what that sounds like to me? A date."

"It felt like one," I admit. "Later on, I mean. We went on a big walk through the neighborhood. He took me to a flea market!"

This detail feels particularly damning. You can't just take a woman to a flea market and expect her not to get ideas.

Sam is quickly losing interest in this conversation. "Straight people are so corny."

"Shut up, fake goth," Carrie says, rolling her eyes. "You'd fucking love that and we all know it."

Interestingly, Sam does not argue the point, but simply crosses her arms with a little *humph*.

"Keep going," Carrie orders me, and I do.

I tell her about Connor showing up unannounced, how he brought me a coffee, how we got another coffee, how we wandered around the Upper West Side for *hours*. All the flirting.

"He likes you," is Carrie's official assessment when my story comes to a close. Sam has no opinion—she has left the room.

I shake my head. "He doesn't."

"He does," she insists.

"He *doesn't*, Carrie. He's not interested."

"How do you know?"

"Because I kissed him, and he told me not to do that."

"*YOU WHAT?*" I have never heard Carrie's voice reach those decibels. She says it with so much force that she launches herself off the sofa.

Sam comes galloping back through from her bedroom. "What happened?"

Carrie points at me. "She kissed her boss and he told her to stop."

"You little slut," Sam says, a grin on her face. "Lead with that next time, that's way more interesting."

"I need the particulars. What happened, how did it happen, what did he say *exactly*," Carrie says.

I throw my head back and groan, covering my face with my hands. "I'm really embarrassed."

"You should be," Sam says, at the same time Carrie says, "Don't be."

"Gah," I say, wishing I could scrub the humiliation right off me. How am I ever going to look him in the eye again? "He walked me to the subway and I was just getting a *vibe*, you know? And I thought fuck it, and I kissed him."

"With tongue?" Sam clarifies.

My cheeks flame. "Umm."

"Oh my god, she kissed her boss with tongue!" Carrie squeals.

It's physically painful to have to say this part out loud. "That's what stopped it. I kissed him and then tried to stick my tongue in his mouth and then he stepped back from me and said it wasn't a good idea."

Even Sam is struggling with the level of cringe. She's biting on her knuckle, her hand balled into a fist.

"I just—" My gut twists at the realization that I called it so wrong. "I don't know. He's really *nice,* you know? He referred to us as a *we* at one point! He put his arm around me! I got confused."

"Fucking hell," Carrie says. She looks completely shell-shocked.

"How am I ever going to come back from this?"

"You aren't," Sam says simply. "You will have to move back to Canada."

"*Sam.*"

"I'm kidding, don't be so dramatic," she says. "It's *fine.* Just pretend it never happened. Pretend you don't even know who he is the next time you see him. Kiss one of those other guys you work with, so he just thinks you're a big slut."

I look to Carrie, who has been quietly pacing. "Maybe he does like you," she says eventually. "Maybe he takes the whole no-dating company policy thing seriously."

"No one takes that seriously," I argue. "We all know that."

"I know, but, you have to admit it is a tiny bit messier when the person in question is your direct report. Really not a good look."

"I guess," I say. Maybe that's it. Could that be it? Ben's warning that Connor is against workplace relationships resurfaces. But I'm not convinced.

I was hoping to discuss this for the rest of the night, so I'm chagrined when Sam changes the subject and suggests some arthouse screening starting in an hour. A return to an earlier conversation, I think; Carrie seems to know exactly what she's referring to.

"No," Carrie says decisively. "I'm going home."

Sam is not impressed with this response. She sniffs and retreats back to her bedroom—since we won't do her bidding, she has no further use for either of us.

"Bye then," Carrie calls after her, an edge to her voice. She turns to me and shrugs. "See you tomorrow?"

"If I make it through the night." I shudder.

She gives me a squeeze, tells me not to worry, and then she's gone.

I look around the empty living room. Something about the last few minutes felt off, though I can't exactly put my finger on what. Sam left the room in something close to a flounce. Carrie, too, seemed displeased. What was that about?

It might just be that they have both reached the maximum amount of time they can tolerate in each other's company—they've been together nonstop for twenty-four hours now. After a rocky start to the weekend, it *seemed* like they were getting along, though what do I know? I'm just someone who kisses their boss!

The thought sends a fresh wave of shame through my entire body. I'm too jittery to sit still, so I start tidying, beginning with the clothes on my floor and moving through the apartment room by room until I've scrubbed the shower clean and organized the junk drawer.

At one point my phone pings, and I practically vault the sofa to get to it, in case it's Connor texting to say *sorry, you're fired* or maybe *sorry, I'm gay,* but I don't know why I'd think that, because as far as I know he doesn't even have my phone number. Turns out it's just Shannon, replying with a thumbs-up to a text I sent her two days ago.

"What's the deal with your friend," Sam says later, standing in my bedroom doorway.

"Jesus Christ," I say, jumping back from my pile of laundry. The woman is as stealthy as a cat. "You scared the shit out of me."

"I knocked."

She didn't. I resume my sorting. She folds her arms impatiently.

"So?" Sam repeats.

I pause, then turn to face her, my senses on high alert. It's such an un-Sam question.

"Why do you ask?"

"She's . . . interesting," is all Sam offers.

I scan her face. "She's—very straight."

Sam smirks. "You sure about that?"

"Pretty sure," I tell her frankly.

"Her loss," Sam shrugs. "Anyway, I need her number."

I stare at her, searching for some hidden motive.

Sam rolls her eyes. "Calm down. She just asked me to give her the details of Mel's piercing studio."

That, at least, makes sense. Carrie already has about eighteen holes in each of her ears. It wouldn't surprise me to learn she's planning more. I read out Carrie's number. Sam types it into her phone, then salutes me.

"Please don't terrorize my best friend over text message," I say to her retreating form.

"No promises," Sam says, her voice floating down the hall.

Nineteen

Every Monday morning we have a weekly team meeting. It starts at 10 A.M. I have done the mature thing and waited until 9:57 to arrive.

Dread is too mild a word for what I'm going through when I round the corner toward DatStrat, clinging to my Krumes box like a life raft. The top of Ben's head is the first thing that comes into view, his bright red hair leading me to my doom like a beacon. He's standing beside his desk—hanging around, really—while Martin drums a pencil against the arm of his chair. John hovers beside him.

Connor is not there.

Is this feeling relief, or despair? I'm glad not to have to face him, but the realization that he's avoiding me too is a wrench.

"Good morning, Annie," Ben says when I reach the desks, prompting an instant chorus of *Hi Annies* from both Martin and John. All three stare at me expectantly. What do they know?

"Everything OK?" I ask, looking from Martin, to John, to Ben.

They all hesitate just a beat too long.

John recovers first with an extra cheerful, "Definitely!"

It is clear to me: they know everything. I will never live down my shame.

"Is that box what I think it is?" John asks.

"No," I deadpan.

"Too late, already saw it," John says.

"*Please* tell me there's white chocolate in there," Martin pleads.

I feign confusion. "Oh shit, you *wanted* white chocolate? I thought you said *no* white chocolate."

"I know you're joking and it's still not funny," he says.

"Time to go," Ben says, marshaling us into order.

I look around. No sign of Connor. Where is he?

As if he's heard my thoughts, Ben falls into step beside me and says quietly, "Connor had to talk to Brad. He'll see us there."

Whatever. Don't care!

Connor arrives to the stand-up fourteen minutes later. He's already looking at me when he walks into the room. I can tell he wants my attention, but he can't get near me. I'm stationed between Martin and John, and there's actual work to be getting on with; Martin is in the middle of discussing the proposed roadmap for some new dashboard features. The box of cookies sits untouched in the middle of the table.

"How did it go?" Ben asks when Connor takes his seat.

"Later," is all he says.

I can withstand a split second of eye contact before my stomach flips violently and I'm back to inspecting my nails.

Martin finishes presenting his findings, the guys bat a few questions back and forth, and then the conversation goes dead.

"Annie, I think we should probably address the elephant in the room?" John says a moment later.

I look up. They are all watching me. Oh god, please no. Are

we *all* going to discuss me kissing Connor? Speech is totally beyond me. The only confirmation I can give John that I've heard them is a strangled *hmm?*

He looks at me quizzically. "The cookies?"

I blow out a breath. "Of course. The cookies. Go for it," I tell them.

He's on it like a predator to its prey.

Tearing through a box of gourmet cookies does a lot to release the tension in the room, though not all of it, since not a single person has ribbed me for losing the wager or made me present the box to Connor on one knee as part of my punishment.

Connor has stayed mostly quiet. When Ben slides the box toward him he simply says, *Annie first.* I retrieve my cookie of choice (chocolate chip—the one I know Connor will want) without making eye contact.

If he thinks he's going to give me the *let's pretend this never happened* speech he can save his breath. I am already pretending. I have gone fully method in my new role of *woman who never kissed the boss.* I am about to win an Oscar for it.

While the boys chatter around me, I chance another look at him. His eyes jump to mine immediately, as if by looking in his direction I set off some sort of trip wire that alerted him to my presence. This time he gives me a real *look*. One that I am at a complete loss as to how to interpret.

I'm seized with a new, even *more* embarrassing dread than the one I've been feeling since yesterday afternoon. Does Connor feel *sorry* for me, like he knows I like him, and knows *I* feel stupid about it? Does he want to make me feel less bad?

No. Absolutely not. Nope, no way. I would sooner lie down and let a pigeon pluck my eyes out before I allow Connor to let me down gently. So glad we never had this talk!

With the cookies mostly demolished, conversation turns to the product department's uptake of the dashboard. Or lack thereof.

Mostly, I pay no attention whatsoever, and instead torture myself with a moment-by-moment replay of the day out with Connor yesterday, growing steadily more desperate and indignant with each remembered moment.

If he didn't want me getting the wrong idea, then pray tell, *why* did he put his arm around me? Why did he say *we* would come up with ideas for Shannon's visit—which he probably won't even help me with now, that jerk. Why did he even show up there in the first place? Why did he kiss me back? I didn't imagine that; I know I didn't. If he wants to pretend he was only kissing me back because he was surprised, then I will tell him he is a liar! He can only write off the first 1–2 seconds to surprise. The rest was intent.

". . . something we could potentially look into further, but I'm not really sure. Do you have any opinions on that, Annie?"

Shit. I only came back into my body partway through John's question and have no idea what he's talking about.

"A few," I say, acting as if I've been paying attention this whole time. "But I suppose it depends."

"That's true," John agrees.

"We could ask," Ben says, his tone suggesting he has very much thrown a cat among the pigeons here. "After all, at least one person at this table has a pretty good line into that squad."

I take it he means me.

"I don't want to open that can of worms," Connor says.

I'll bet you don't, Connor. I'll bet you don't. Well, too bad. "I'll do it. Who do you want me to speak to?"

"Andy, ideally," Ben says. "If we could get a better handle

on why they think the dashboard isn't matching the metrics on the other reporting tool, we might be able to fix it."

Ah. This again.

"OK. I will try. Actually, I'll go now," I say, taking this golden opportunity to slip out of the meeting before I get stuck talking to Connor.

He tries to stop me. "You don't need to—"

"No, it's fine," I say, resolutely avoiding his eye and addressing the whole room. "Andy and I are really good friends. He'll tell me what's up."

Andy, as it turns out, is more than happy to unburden himself on the subject of the new dashboard and its *bullshit metrics* when I swing by his desk.

The way that Jotter tracked user engagement was a lot different from how Taskio does it with the dashboard—the end result being that a lot of features, like the template library, now show really poor performance.

Andy is convinced this is a conspiracy, and after a morning spent back in my old stomping grounds, the product department, I'm chagrined to learn he is far from the only one. The product leads—especially the Jotter product leads—still do not like this dashboard. They think it's being used to squeeze them out.

Since my only real objective today is *avoid Connor at all costs,* I stay downstairs and talk to every product lead I can find. Considering it's mostly a time-wasting exercise on my part, it's also surprisingly fruitful. By the time I'm done, I've taken pages of notes on what the average product manager likes about the dashboard (nothing) and doesn't like (the entire dashboard) and have a few ideas of my own about how we can implement some changes to get them onside and keep Andy happy.

"I'll talk to the guys," I promise Andy. "There's got to be a way to get some better metrics."

"You're our only hope," he says, pressing his hands together in prayer.

I instinctively know if I don't go back soon it will *look* like I'm hiding, so with huge trepidation, I make my way back to DatStrat to face the music.

Connor and Martin are both on a call when I get there, giving me the perfect excuse not to talk to him. Or so I think.

CONNOR: have you had lunch
ANNIE: Yes

I actually haven't.

CONNOR: Coffee then
CONNOR: I'll be off this call in five
ANNIE: Can't. I'm sitting in on the marketing update

Another lie, but needs must. If he thinks I am going to have a coffee with him while he tells me that it's best we never kiss again in a kind, managerial way, he can forget it. I log off before he can suggest anything else.

Twenty

I make it another two hours before my luck runs out and I come face-to-face with Connor in the corridor.

He is marching toward me, his determination evident in the length of his stride.

"I need to talk to you." He's at my side in the blink of an eye, wrapping his hand around my elbow and turning me around to follow him.

"Now's really not a great time," I try to tell him as he frog-marches me back in the direction I just came.

"Too bad."

He pulls us into the closest available meeting room, which unfortunately, turns out to be the music room.

Why do we even *have* a stupid music room? Despite what its existence suggests, it would absolutely be frowned upon if you got caught in here playing an instrument in the middle of the workday.

It's a comically inappropriate setting for this conversation. There's literally a drum set in the middle of the room. My eyes dart frantically around the space for something I can plausibly distract us with, but unless my plan is to start an impromptu jam sesh (which it is not) I have nothing.

Connor is on to me. He has strategically placed himself between me and the door.

"What's your plan here, Annie, just avoid me for the rest of your life?"

I cross my arms. "I'm not avoiding you."

"Really? Could have fooled me."

"It's been a busy day."

"Yes, all those fake calls and meetings must have kept you really tied up."

"I was *not* on fake calls!"

"I have access to your calendar."

I hesitate. "I forgot to put them in."

"Fine," he says, his tone making it clear he has no further energy to waste on my pointless lies.

"Look, if this is about yesterday, we don't need to—"

"Yes, we do need to," he insists.

"It's *really* not necessary—"

"Annie, will you just shut up for one minute and listen to me, please? Jesus."

His exasperated use of *Jesus* has rendered me mute. Well, almost mute. I mutter a begrudging *fine*.

"Yesterday afternoon, when you kissed me—"

NOPE, sorry, unbearable. Can't do this.

"It's OK, Connor, honestly. I get it. Please stop. We don't have to make this awkward. It didn't happen."

"What? That's not what I'm saying at all."

A dreadful suspicion crosses my mind. "Are—are you about to fire me for kissing you?"

"*Annie.*"

He draws a deep breath. I can see his chest rising through the gray marl of his T-shirt.

"You caught me off guard," he says. "When you kissed me yesterday. I wasn't expecting you to do that. I handled it badly."

My stomach sinks.

"You didn't, Connor, really. It's me who should be apologizing."

"Sorry?"

"I get it," I insist, like this is all no big deal. "You don't like me like that."

He looks absolutely dumbstruck by this statement. He makes a strangled noise like he's about to say something, but nothing comes out.

Instead he steps forward, grabs either side of my face, and kisses me, full on the mouth. Like this is his last desperate act to silence me once and for all.

I am so stunned by this turn of events that I can do nothing. A marble statue has more movement than I do in this moment. I realize vaguely that I now understand what he meant when he said I caught him off guard. It *is* surprising when someone kisses you out of nowhere.

He leans back to look at me, his hands still holding me in place. "I think you might be the most annoying person I've ever met."

Then he tilts my chin up, ducks his head, and kisses me for real.

His first kiss was to shut me up. The end of the conversation. This kiss is the start of a new one. And I would like to talk all night.

Connor releases my face, wrapping his arms around me and pulling me into his body. I am all too happy to comply. My hands slip under his T-shirt, his muscles rippling as I slide them up his back. Somewhere in the back of my mind there's a megaphone blaring *Not an appropriate thing to do!* But it's distant—I can barely hear it through the sound of the pulse pounding in my ears.

His teeth graze my bottom lip, eliciting an instant hum from somewhere deep in my throat. When my lips part, he slides his tongue into my mouth, and I lock my arms around him to make it clear I expect him to continue moving in this direction. His mouth quirks into a smile—strange how I can *feel* him do that—which falls away just as quickly when I press into him even more.

By the time he pulls away he's supporting my entire body weight. One arm is wrapped around me, the other is planted on the back of my head. Our noses hover an inch apart. His chest bobs against mine with the shallow rise and fall of his breath.

"OK, fine," I say, my voice husky. "You handled it badly."

"Dickhead," he says warmly, his mouth catching mine again.

I'm hoping this means we're about to go back to kissing, but it was just a ruse. His arms drop away from me and he steps back. I feel the loss of warmth immediately.

"Is—that what you wanted to talk about?"

Connor chuckles, scrubbing a hand down his face. "No."

I have never been more thrilled than in this moment, watching Connor try and wrangle himself back into seriousness. Every time he gets his smile tamped down it slips free again. Flustered Connor is my new favorite Connor, I will accept no other.

I step forward, but he stops me, catching my shoulders and holding me at arm's length.

"I realize you'd rather saw your arm off than have this conversation with me," he says. "But we need to have it."

"I'm listening," I say, but really I'm just looking at his lips.

"About yesterday," he says gently. "It's not that I don't like you, Annie. It's that I do."

My gaze travels upward. His eyes are like gooey molten chocolate.

My brow furrows. "Sorry?"

His arms drop away. "I like you a lot," he says, looking me dead in the eye.

My smile blooms. "Well, that's nice," I tell him. "I thought you didn't."

"I panicked," he tells me. "When I came to meet you yesterday, I wasn't thinking about what could happen. I just wanted to spend time with you. And then when you kissed me, I realized with stunning clarity how easy it would be for you to blow my life up."

"Bit dramatic."

"Is it?" he asks, searching my face. "I don't know, Annie. Sometimes I get the impression that none of this is serious to you."

I frown at this. "What do you mean?"

"Work, me, all of it. It's all just a lark," he says, lifting his arm and running it down the back of his head. "There are moments when I think you like me too, and then others where it feels like you're just passing the time. But—"

I can feel him hesitating, weighing up whether or not to keep going.

"It's not that for me. I know you think this place is stupid but I care about it a lot. And I'm technically your boss and we'd be working together, and I just had no idea how to deal with any of it. It felt like everything was on the line all of a sudden. And I let all that get in the way."

Is that what it seems like, that I don't care? I almost laugh; if he only knew.

"So to recap," I say, trying to parse everything he's told me. "You wanted to kiss me so badly that you . . . refused to kiss me?"

"I felt like such an idiot afterward." He laughs. "I wanted to slingshot myself into outer space."

"You are such a loser."

"I know," he says, bashful again. "I guess we've settled the question about whether or not I have any game."

"Well," I say, stepping toward him. This time he doesn't stop me. "You might have some game."

I skate my fingertips lightly over his chest, and he reaches up to clasp my hand.

"Can I have a do-over, please? Maybe ask you on a date, properly?"

"Is this you asking me now, or asking to ask me?"

He shakes his head. "I'm doing it again, aren't I? I'm asking you now."

I squint at him. "Have you ever talked to a girl before?"

"It's been a while," he admits. "Will you please go on a date with me this weekend, Annabelle?"

"I will go on a date with you, yes," I say. "But not this weekend. My sister is visiting, remember? Consider that your punishment."

"I accept that."

"Your punishment is also to help me plan it."

"Fair enough."

"And you have to kiss me again," I tell him.

"Don't push your luck."

Twenty-One

By the time Friday rolls around, I'm nervous, but I'm ready. True to his word, Connor helped me plan the whole weekend down to the last detail, never once teasing me about the intensity with which I selected every bar and restaurant, or why I believe my sister's entire future hinges on how much fun is had this weekend.

Tonight I will begin Operation Liberate Shannon. But first, I have to get through the workday.

Things get off to a shaky start. Connor is summoned to Brad's side first thing, Ben joins him not long after and they're gone for hours, only increasing my unease. It feels like there's something going on that they're not telling me, a feeling that grows when I ask Connor how it went and all he manages to say is *yeah, good*.

While Ben and Connor are busy with their mysterious backroom dealings, Martin, John, and I wade through the backlog of dashboard support requests, which come at us thick and fast now that we've succeeded in getting more people to use it.

It's amid these stirring activities that an email comes in letting me know I have a visitor waiting downstairs. This is unexpected; I *never* have visitors.

I consider the possibilities as the elevator glides downstairs and decide that my mystery visitor is most likely to be my old teammate Leon, who emailed last week letting me know he'd found a new job and wondering if his desk cactus had survived. His new office was also based somewhere in FiDi, and I promised we'd meet for lunch one day soon to return the precious cargo back to him.

I've taken less than six steps before I realize how far off the mark I was—I'm just rounding the security gates when I catch a glimpse of my sister sitting on a leather bench by the window, scrolling on her phone, when she wasn't supposed to arrive in New York for another four hours.

I rush toward her, and she glances up when I approach, popping up and sliding her phone into her pocket. She looks as pristine as always, though not dolled up today like Real Estate Barbie. She's in jeans (surprising) and a camel-colored trench coat, rolled up to the elbows so she can showcase her many bracelets. Though hers are about four times the price of the bangles Mom wears, the effect is the same. I wonder if I could point this out to her or if it would be considered an act of war.

We embrace, and I search her face when I pull back, looking for signs of distress.

"Is everything OK?"

"Why wouldn't it be?"

"I just—what are you doing here?"

"Visiting you for the weekend, remember? You didn't hit your head or anything, did you?"

Her exaggerated concern draws a small smile from me, but I won't be deterred. "No, I mean, what are you doing *here*, at my office? Your plane hasn't even taken off yet."

She opens her mouth to reply, when I see an arm snake around her shoulder. Daniel.

"What is *he* doing here?" My voice drips with venom.

"Hello to you too, Annie."

If I don't look directly at him, maybe he'll disappear. I keep my focus firmly on Shannon, hoping she'll have some reasonable explanation for all this.

"Well," Shannon begins.

Dan interjects. "We thought we'd make a weekend of it."

"*We* already were making a weekend of it," I reply. "Shannon and me."

"Dan wanted to come and see the city too," Shannon says. "He'll make himself scarce tomorrow when we're dress shopping. It's no big deal."

No big deal to you! I want to scream. I can't believe she's falling for this crap.

"You should have told me," I say, ready for mutiny. "Sam won't want more people in the apartment."

"I know," she says, contrite. "Don't worry. We got a hotel."

The mention of a hotel room irritates me further. It suggests a level of premeditation I don't care for.

"Where are your bags?"

"In our room. We got here yesterday."

Yesterday. I cast a wounded look at my sister who drops her gaze the second our eyes lock, guiltily looking at her feet.

"Wow. Thanks for telling me."

"I wanted to surprise you," Shannon says. I can't tell whether she truly means this or it's a flimsy justification she's using to make this all seem OK. "We got in really late last night."

"But—what about the reward flight?"

"I'll pay you back, OK!" she says, an edge in her voice, like I'm giving her shit here for absolutely no reason.

I shake my head to clear the thought.

"Where are you staying?"

"Dumbo."

"But I live in Manhattan."

Dan just shrugs. "I'm sure this place has Ubers."

My nostrils flare. If I shoved him hard enough, I wonder if I could send him flying back through the revolving door.

"Looks like you've got it all figured out," I say flatly. "But I still don't understand. What are you doing *here*?"

"I was hoping you could give us a tour of the office," Shannon says. "I really want to see where you work."

I did offer this to her when we were first planning the weekend. I childishly thought it would be nice to show my big sister what I do all day. But I will take Dan upstairs over my dead body.

"We're not really supposed to bring people up during working hours."

"I thought you were kind of a big deal around here, Annie," Dan almost sneers. "You can't make a special exception for family?"

"Oh, I can make an exception for *family*. But *you'll* have to wait downstairs."

Dan is winding up for some blistering comeback, but Shannon halts him with a squeeze of his arm.

"Never mind," she says. "We don't want to hassle you. I thought it would be a fun surprise. We'll go, and meet you after work instead."

It's been two minutes and the weekend with my sister has already gone pear-shaped. I could howl at the injustice of this. But sending them away will make things even worse. I need a new plan. And fast.

"It's fine," I say through gritted teeth. "You're here now. Let me show you around."

We ride the elevator up to the twenty-fourth floor in near silence. Shannon's only comment is that we're so high she felt her ears pop.

I give her a forced smile but say nothing. Beside her, Dan is radiating smugness. He's ruined my weekend, and he knows it. That's exactly why he's here.

I realize, belatedly, that I should have taken them straight up to the canteen and left them there, rather than walk them through the office, but it's too late now. My only instinct is to get to Connor. He'll fix it. Somehow.

"Just be quiet," I tell them, gesturing at them to follow. "People are working."

Dan rolls his eyes. "They do have offices back in Canada, you know."

My fingers curl into a fist.

I lead them toward my desk. Connor's head pops up as soon as I'm in his eyeline.

I telegraph a silent plea for help. If there was ever a moment for him to read my mind, now would be it.

"What's up?" he says, his focus darting between me and the two mysterious strangers behind me. "I was wondering where you'd snuck off to."

"I had a visitor," I tell him, my eyes bugging out to try and make him understand the enemy is among us. He stands, pushing back from his chair.

"Connor, this is my sister, Shannon. Shannon, this is Connor," I hesitate, and then add, "my boss."

A shadow crosses his face, there and then gone again. He turns, devoting himself to Shannon. I watch as the two of them briefly exchange pleasantries, and I'm reminded once again of his good manners—he gave me just the same smile the first time I met him.

He casts a glance at Dan, then looks back at me, waiting.

"That's Dan."

His eyes widen ever so slightly, but he recovers immediately, shaking Dan's hand with a *nice to meet you, man,* which I sincerely hope he does not mean.

"They came early to surprise me," I say to Connor. "Isn't that fun?"

"So fun," he rallies back, his eyes full of mirth. "You must be over the moon."

"That's one way of putting it."

"We wanted to see where Annie worked," Shannon says. I get the impression she's trying to save face.

"Annie's always bragging about how cool her job is," Dan adds, with the obvious intention of embarrassing me. "So far this place just seems like an office, though."

"Well then," Connor says, swiping his keycard off his desk. "We better give you the grand tour."

When Connor said grand tour, he meant it. He leads Dan and Shannon around every floor, introducing them to department heads, showing them inside all our cool conference rooms, and even emptying out a merch closet that before this afternoon I didn't know existed. Shannon and Dan are now the happy owners of a Taskio-branded pen, notebook, T-shirt, beanie, umbrella, and USB stick.

There were also Taskio tote bags in the supply closet—which would have been useful to help them lug around all this crap—but Connor, surprisingly, didn't offer those. It is, in fact, the only branded item in the whole room that he didn't gift to them.

Prior to this, I thought the overzealous tour was a reflection of his commitment to Taskio, but I gradually realize that Connor is demonstrating commitment to *me*. Shannon and Dan have long since lost interest, if they were ever even interested in the first place, and it dawns on me that Connor knows it. This tour isn't a perk. It's a punishment. He's making Daniel eat his words. The gleam in his eye when our gazes connect confirms it.

"Well, that's pretty much everything," Connor says after a lap of the engineering department. "Unless you want to see the server room?"

"That's OK," Shannon cuts in hastily. "We've taken up so much of your time already."

"In that case, follow me. We've saved the best for last."

One short elevator ride later, Shannon and Dan are staring out over the enormous cafeteria and the panoramic views beyond.

"Wow," she breathes, for once not faking her enthusiasm. Even Dan looks impressed.

"And all this is just for Taskio?"

"Yep," I confirm. "Cool, eh? And everything is free. You can have whatever you want."

"Seriously?"

"Seriously. They'll even make you that weird skinny foam thing you like."

Shannon and Dan need no further prompting; I let them loose in the cafeteria to plunder its spoils.

• • •

I don't know if I decide it or Connor does, but we silently collude to give Dan and Shannon the impression that we must get back to work, and they agree to head back to their hotel, where I promise to meet them at the end of the workday.

We wave goodbye at the elevators. My smile drops the second the doors slide shut.

"You have to come to dinner," I say as the two of us make our way back to DatStrat.

Connor gives a humorless laugh. "Absolutely not."

"*Please.*"

"No."

"Connor."

"Annie."

"You're the one who wants me to be the bigger person," I reason as we get back to our desks. "How am I supposed to do that without you?"

John and Martin are working from home today, so it's only Ben there to greet us. He pulls his headphones off.

"Brad was looking for you," he says to Connor. "I told him you were gone."

"Thank god for that," Connor mutters, and then turning back to me, "I'm busy."

"I'm *begging* you."

He shrugs.

"Please," I wheedle. "I'll do anything you want. I'll even go talk to Brad."

Ben perks up at this briefly, tilting his head toward Connor like *maybe not a bad idea?*

Connor is unmoved. "No. It would be a little weird to bring your boss to dinner, don't you think?"

He logs back into his computer.

I open my mouth to reply, then shut it again. Is he . . . mad?

Across from us, Ben is not even *pretending* not to eavesdrop. I look back at him. All he does is raise his eyebrows like *well?*

I sheepishly avoid his gaze and take the conversation to messenger.

> **ANNIE:** Are you............mad that I called you my boss
> **CONNOR:** No.

He is. He *so* is. How the tables have turned!

> **ANNIE:** I'm sensing a bit of a tone there.
> **ANNIE:** How would you like me to introduce you, just for future reference?

He does not dignify this with a response, but I can see the messenger open on his screen. He's listening.

> **ANNIE:** I'm sorry Connor
> **ANNIE:** You're so much more than my boss. You're my....
> **ANNIE:** Line manager.

I can't believe it. Calling him my boss hurt his feelings. I find this absolutely delicious.

> **ANNIE:** My...mentor
> **CONNOR:** Can you stop
> **ANNIE:** My fearless leader
> **CONNOR:** Trying to focus here

I sneak a glance at him. I sense his defenses weakening. I can't say for certain, but it feels like he's trying not to smile.

ANNIE: My.... overseer?

CONNOR: Friend would have been fine, for the record

ANNIE: Are you sure you wouldn't prefer... my inspiration?

CONNOR: Get back to work

ANNIE: Really getting some mixed messages here

ANNIE: Should I be following your orders or not?

CONNOR: OK that's enough

CONNOR: Settle down

ANNIE: Yes BOSS;)

In the end, Connor never agrees to come with me, only asks me the name of the hotel they're staying at, and then ten minutes after that, gives me an address and instructs me to tell Shannon and Dan to meet us there after work. I feel a huge wave of relief, both at the fact Connor is coming, and that he has once again swooped in to make the plans. Maybe this night won't be a disaster after all.

In general, Fridays can only ever go one of two ways. It's either extremely quiet because most people have already checked out for the weekend, or it's manically busy while people overcompensate for all they didn't accomplish earlier in the week. Today, it's the second one. I'm shocked when I look up from my spreadsheet to see Ben shucking on his backpack. It feels like I blinked and lost four hours.

"Have a good one," Ben says to me, pushing in his chair.

"You too. Up to anything good this evening?"

"Nah," he says with a crooked smile. "My friend bailed out on me last minute so I'm just going to head home."

"Oh, that sucks—" I stop when I realize he's referring to Connor. "Sorry."

Ben laughs, patting me on the shoulder as he passes. "It's all good. You two crazy kids have fun."

"Where is Connor, anyway? I haven't seen him in a while."

"Hiding from Brad in the sound booths, I think."

"Ah."

He salutes me and then is gone, his bright head of hair bobbing down the corridor.

My phone buzzes, Shannon's name flashing across the screen. I texted her earlier with the details of where to meet for dinner. She's only just replied.

> **SHANNON:** We're just in Times Square. Dan says the Hard Rock Cafe here is supposed to be really good?

Ah yes, Dan who has been in New York for one day. Thank *god* he's here to be our tour guide. Where would we be without his amazing suggestions?

> **ANNIE:** Trust me when I tell you it won't be worth it. This place is a lot less touristy and also close to your hotel

I watch as she types, then stops, then starts again.

> **SHANNON:** Dan wants to have a drink here first so we'll need to meet a bit later. 7:30 instead?

Everything about this message is annoying. How have I become the third wheel on my own girls' weekend? Last time I checked, she was here to visit *me*. There's absolutely no point arguing with her, so I don't. It would be easier, geographically, for both her and me to meet at Times Square, but I decide to stay petty and let them experience the joys of trying to get from midtown to Brooklyn at this hour. Seems only fair to Dan—he is, after all, very passionate about Ubers. I'd hate to deprive him of the surcharge.

I text her back with a thumbs-up and then quickly check my sister's Instagram. Just as I predicted: she's already posted a picture of her standing in Times Square. I stand and go looking for Connor. I want to tell him I was right.

Of all the styles of meeting rooms we have in this building, these ones are extra insane—a corridor filled with compact, windowless rooms designed for recording audio and video. Each has a little screen beside the door to say who's booked it, plus a lightbulb that flashes red or green, depending on whether or not they're in use.

It doesn't take me long to find Connor's name on the door, and I listen before knocking to make sure he is in fact hiding, as Ben suggested, and not on a video call that I'm about to rudely interrupt. When I'm confident, I rap a knuckle lightly on the door and then poke my head around it.

He looks up at me, and I hold my hand up to my ear in the universal sign for *are you on the phone?* When he smiles and shakes his head, I let myself in. The room is extremely simple, just a table with two chairs, pushed up against a wall with a TV mounted above it. There's padding on the walls for soundproofing.

"Just came to tell you I'm not such a bad tour guide after all. Look at this," I say, handing my phone to him. He squints down at the screen then laughs.

"Looks like you know your sister better than you think," he says, smiling at me.

How I wish that were true.

"Not wearing any of their Taskio merch, I notice," he says, passing the phone back to me.

"I bet they binned it instantly."

"Oh, no doubt," he agrees. "Probably before they'd even left the building."

He smiles and I smile, the glow of our shared joke passing between us.

I look around us. "So you're hiding from Brad in here?"

"Hiding from you," he says, then adds: "You're very distracting."

I raise an eyebrow at him. "You seem to get plenty of work done."

"It's a constant battle."

It doesn't feel like he's kidding. I clear my throat.

"They're having a drink at the Hard Rock."

He nods. "Are we meeting them there?"

I shake my head. "I told them to stick with the plan. They'll meet us in Brooklyn."

"Evil," he says. I only shrug.

"So you've got some extra time on your hands," I tell him. "To . . . work."

He closes his laptop. The look he's giving me is heated.

"I'm done."

"Oh?"

He stands. Steps toward me.

"So, um—how should we pass the time?"

Another step closer. Then another. It's like there's a circuit looping between us, from him to me and back to him again. I can feel the charge.

At the edge of my vision I see his arm move. A second later the sound of the lock clicking into place.

"I don't know," he says, voice low. "Any ideas?"

So many. Judging by the way he's staring at me, I'd say his are much the same as mine.

I'm cross-eyed from watching him at close range. He's near enough that I could count his freckles, but I'm too busy having an almost-out-of-body experience to try. He hovers there a moment, his mouth a millimeter away. When he grazes his nose against mine, I'm not sure, but I might actually whimper.

Then he kisses me, and I definitely do.

Kissing Connor is every bit as amazing as I remember. He is methodical, mapping the contours of my mouth, then sliding along my jaw, down my neck. I have never been kissed like this, ever. It's slow and firm and certain, like he's pouring a world of feeling into every movement, and I'm overwhelmed. By all of it.

When he returns to my mouth and bites down gently on my bottom lip, I'm done for. It goes from chaste to raunchy in a heartbeat. I can feel his hard-on press against me. I'm scrabbling for purchase; my hands on his face, in his hair, clinging to his shoulders. I'm seconds away from climbing him when he peels me off the wall.

I'm vaguely aware that we're moving, but it's not until my ass meets the edge of the desk that I realize we've changed direction. I lift myself onto it—he offers a helping hand, gripping the back of my thighs to give me the boost I need, those extra few inches lining us up in a way that feels almost indecent. He releases my mouth while his hands find my waist and slide me farther up the table. I have no patience for this interruption. I pull him back to me with force, my legs locking around him. He laughs into my mouth.

"No teasing," I say breathlessly.

"No teasing," he agrees, his lips sliding back against mine.

It feels like we're magnets, pulled together by force. I wrap my arms around his neck, and kiss him, hard, drawing us backward, until his palm hits the table. The strength of his arm is the only thing holding us even remotely upright.

Another minute of this, then I drop my hands behind me on the table and lift my chest toward him. His hands start roaming, up my sides, then everywhere, cupping, squeezing, his thumbs brushing across my nipples through the fabric of my dress. His pupils are blown all the way out as his eyes track the movement. Seeing him like this only increases my desperation.

Had I known we'd be doing this today I'd have worn something more accommodating. The neckline on my dress leaves no room for maneuver, unless he's going to unzip it and take it right off me. I'd be open to the idea, but am in no state to make suggestions. I'm practically nonverbal.

Eventually, his hands move downward, sliding across my bare thighs and then up beneath the hem of my skirt until he's gripping my ass, holding me firmly in place and pressing me tighter to him. We're aligned so perfectly now that every movement from one sets off a chain reaction in the other, until we're both panting for air, our mouths coming together before moving away again. My hips move of their own volition.

I can feel myself getting close to something, but it's not enough. It's nowhere near enough. "Connor," I plead, unable to find words for what I want from him.

He understands. His hands start to roam again, gliding up the inside of my thigh. I gasp when he finds the edge of my underwear, stroking the lace, and then sliding beneath it. He rubs his fingers up and down the very core of me, humming into my neck.

"Is this what you wanted?" he says, slipping inside me, slowly at first, then firmer, deeper. One finger. Then two.

"Here?" He breathes into my ear. "Or here?"

"There," I gasp, canting my hips against him. He presses

his palm up exactly where I need him most, and then I'm nothing but pure need.

"Yes," I gasp.

"Yeah?" he says, a smile in his voice.

His hand works me while I desperately move against him, the pressure building so quickly all I can do is cling to his shoulders as he murmurs words of encouragement in my ear. It goes on like this for seconds, or maybe hours.

"Connor," I gasp. "I'm—"

I don't even get the words out, but he knows. One moment I'm there, and in the next the world tilts sideways, then stars explode across my vision, obliterating every thought I've ever had.

I slump forward, breathing heavily into his neck. Ten seconds ago I wouldn't have been able to tell you where we were for all the money in the world, but it dawns on me now that we're still in the office. Instead of banking my desire, the last few minutes have only set it further alight. I don't care where we are, or what time it is, or how long it takes. My mind is on a single feedback loop: *more more more*.

I kiss him again, arms around his waist. He cradles the back of my head, gentle as ever, but he can't hide. I can feel his erection pressed between my thighs.

I reach for his belt, but his hands close over mine, halting my progress.

"Wait," he whispers, our mouths separating, then joining again. "Annie."

I try to release my hands from his grip, but he holds them tighter.

"You don't want to?"

"I want to so badly," he says, thrusting against me.

"OK," I say breathlessly, rubbing the front of his jeans.

Every sentence is broken up by more kissing, a delightful contradiction to his words. My body is humming—with adrenaline, with pleasure, with desire. I want to see him undone in the same way.

He groans when I press with more firmness, dropping his head to my shoulder.

I dip my hand beneath his waistband, my fingers grazing him ever so lightly. That does it.

"Screw it," he mutters, kissing me again, his hands reaching for his belt himself. A thrill shoots through me when I realize that he's as desperate for me as I am for him; that Connor, *my* Connor, dorky, diligent, chess champion Connor has been driven to madness at his place of work. By me.

I am triumphant, eager to help him with this task, desperate to keep going. Our hands are clumsy, knocking against one another, slowing the removal of his jeans down rather than speeding it up, but I don't care.

"Stop." He laughs, swatting my hand out of the way as he opens his belt. I giggle into his mouth. Kissing resumes at a frantic pace. This might be the best moment of my entire life.

He finally succeeds in undoing the button. I'm clawing at his zipper when a door slams somewhere along the corridor, shutting with such force the entire wall vibrates.

I gasp, and Connor straightens, on high alert. He looks like he has no idea where he is, and I watch in real time as he takes the room back into focus, his chest heaving.

He steps back, giving me a rueful smile, then turns his attention down to his pants. Reality takes over. He buttons his jeans and I slide off the table, smoothing down my disheveled hair.

I hold my breath, waiting for the moment he tells me this was all a big mistake, but he doesn't. Instead, he draws me into him, holding me lightly against his chest. He drops a kiss on the side of my cheek.

"Later," he promises me.

"Later," I agree.

Twenty-Two

"You need to be ready for *anything*," I tell Connor, on the train to Dumbo. We're standing. His hand is wrapped around the bar above my head, mine on the bar closest to the door, both of us jostling lightly as we speak. "Dan loves to start arguments about the most pointless things."

Connor smiles. "I think I can handle it."

"Ask them about the wedding. See if you can find out what they're thinking," I instruct him. "Whatever you do, don't mention Dan's job, he'll never shut up about it. If he brings it up, change the subject. You can ask Shannon about her job."

"Noted." He nods.

"Avoid giving an opinion about anything, if you can. Don't ask for Dan's opinion on any subject."

"Roger that."

"*Unless* it's about their wedding," I amend.

"Annie," Connor says, nudging my chin up to look at him. "You know this is going to be fine, right? We're going to have a nice time."

He's wrong, but I don't argue. He'll find out soon enough.

. . .

The bar Connor has picked out for us is perfect. Just the right side of dingy, softly lit by candlelight, with lots of wood accents. There are basically no windows in here, taking us from day to night when we cross the threshold. I clock Shannon and Dan as soon as we arrive, sitting side by side at a four-person table. They stop talking the second they notice our approach, both jumping up from their seats and greeting us with exaggerated cheerfulness.

I didn't tell Shannon I'd be bringing Connor—payback for this afternoon—and though she looks a little surprised to see him, she recovers quickly, and seems genuinely happy he's here, like she's as desperate for a buffer as I am.

Both of them have changed, looking like glamorous nighttime versions of the people they were this afternoon. She's in a silky black camisole and black blazer, accessorized with gold everything: gold earrings, gold rings, gold bracelets, gold chains. Her hair is up, her lips are glossed, her eyeliner is immaculate.

As teenagers, Shannon once matter-of-factly told me on the drive to school that she was the hot one, and I was the cute one, as if this was an official designation in every family, and there was a maximum of one in each category. I never once doubted her, then or now. Shannon has always been, and continues to be, the hot one. As in: she looks like she could burn you.

Beside her, Dan is Shannon's bargain-basement counterpart. Though he's dressed well in a dark knit polo with indigo and white stripes—Shannon's doing, no question—he still makes it look cheap. His hair has been gelled to within an inch of its life, slicked back from his face, his beard groomed so sharply it looks like he drew it on. I can smell his aftershave from here, and I don't care for it. It just goes to show the old saying is true: you can't polish a turd.

A waitress mercifully appears the second we sit down, saving all of us from any further small talk while we grapple with the logistics of our drink order. Connor recommends the margaritas, a suggestion approved by everyone except Dan, who always has to be different. He, of course, orders a Paloma.

"So how are you enjoying New York so far?" Connor asks them.

"A little overwhelming," Shannon admits at the same moment Dan says: "Really overrated."

Connor pauses, taking in these dueling bits of information, deciding which conversational off-ramp he wants to take. He goes with Dan.

"Oh yeah? How so?"

"Well, it's insanely expensive, for starters. New York is always painted like it's the city that never sleeps, but really there's just traffic everywhere. It's noisy. The streets reek of garbage. I don't really get it."

"Maybe you're just not a city guy," I say.

"That's true. Cities are huge resource drains. Smaller towns offer a lower cost of living, higher quality of life, and less competition than sprawling urban areas."

"Dan's a town councilor," I say to Connor. "He's a *very* big deal."

Under the table, he pinches my thigh. To Dan he says, "That's cool."

Shannon pivots. "So where are you from originally, Connor?"

"New York," he admits, the corners of his mouth twitching. "I grew up on the Upper West Side."

"Oh wow, cool," she says lamely.

"You're not wrong about all those things, by the way," Connor says to Dan. "It is expensive, and there's a lot of people. My mom calls it friction. But there's a lot of good things about this place too. Hopefully you'll discover a few of them before the weekend's out."

Dan mumbles something like *for sure* into the rim of his glass.

It's not long before Connor's easy manners put Shannon and Dan under his spell, and for a few blissful minutes I imagine what life would be like if Shannon lived here and Dan were a person I liked.

Connor continues to steer the conversation, asking Shannon what she does, if she also works in government? No, she tells him, but she's very involved in local affairs. HA. *Ironic*.

She goes on to tell him she's a realtor, a profession she fell into by chance but now really enjoys. It's a refreshing change to hear Shannon talk passionately about something that has nothing to do with Dan, that there's at least one piece of her life he's never managed to infiltrate.

I can see why she loves it. Shannon was always popular, amazing at persuading the people around her to do whatever she wanted. Competitive, too. What people don't realize is that though he behaves like he's the successful one in this relationship, Dan owes most of his lifestyle to Shannon. Town councilors are not particularly well paid. Shannon, on the other hand, is making a mint selling houses for all the guys who had a crush on her in high school.

When the waitress comes to take our orders for another round, Connor suggests we order a pitcher of Palomas, a move that visibly flatters Dan and enables him to give us his expert opinion that they're the better, more underrated cocktail (and *way* more popular in Mexico, something he experienced first-hand when he visited Cancun for a whopping four days).

"So Annie tells me you're planning your wedding at the moment?" Connor asks when the drinks arrive.

"That's right," Dan says, his arm going around Shannon. "It's time to lock this one down for good."

Oh, *gag*.

"What about you, man?" Dan asks, taking a swig of his drink. "Are you married?"

"Uh," Connor says, looking at me, then back at Dan. "No."

"I recommend it," Dan continues, oblivious to the daggers I'm shooting him. "It's the best thing you'll ever do."

Beside him, Shannon titters. "Not married yet, babe," she says, patting his chest.

Not married ever, if I can help it.

"Well, you know what I mean," Dan says, smiling down at my sister, then looking back across the table to Connor and me. "We split up for a while, a couple of years back. I had to see what living without Shannon would look like. It was a dark time. After a few months of that, we knew we had to make it work."

"Aww," Shannon says. "I feel exactly the same."

Gross. Across from me, my sister is looking flushed, but happy—a telltale sign she's tipsy. The alcohol has helped loosen her up in every sense of the word, her hair gradually falling out of the sharp bun she'd slicked it into and framing her face, and to me at least, she looks gorgeous, a closer semblance of the sister I remember rather than the high-definition glamazon who replaced her.

Dan, on the other hand, is starting to look a little shiny. I thought he was just being a dick a minute ago, but now that I observe him closer it's only fair to acknowledge that he's probably drunk, rather than spiteful. He's never handled his alcohol well in my opinion, and Drunk Dan is Everyday Dan dialed up to eleven. He's loud, he's opinionated, and he thinks he's a lot more profound than he is.

Dan has taken a real shine to Connor, offering up his unsolicited advice on everything from fantasy football to cryptocurrency, and he and Shannon both take the opportunity to share with Connor as many stories as they can think of from my teenage years, which are embarrassing, but not quite as embarrassing as starting a chess club, so I let it pass.

Connor is doing the thing I sometimes watch him do in meetings, where he pretends to consider something that I know he's not considering at all. I want to run a wire between his brain and mine so I can hear all his thoughts in real time. Is Dan's conversation annoying him? Was he being honest when he said the breadsticks were good? Does *he* think Shannon is hot and I'm cute?

When another pitcher comes down, I judge it to be time to wrap things up before they manage to drink it. Connor switched to beer a while ago, and I've been nursing my drinks, knowing instinctively that getting drunk tonight would be a terrible idea. Shannon and Dan, on the other hand, are two walking tequila bottles.

In the original version of this weekend, I made dinner reservations at an Italian restaurant in the Village and got tickets for Shannon and me to go and watch some stand-up at the Comedy Cellar. And honestly, I was just going to let them go to waste. But unless I want to subject Connor to four more hours of these two—which I don't—it makes much more sense to give them the tickets instead.

"So, guys," I say, when Connor gets up to use the bathroom. "I have a bit of a surprise for you."

"No. I'm good," Shannon says, dismissing me immediately.

"Don't you want to know what it is?"

"Considering the last time you gave me a surprise it almost ruined my life, probably not."

I lock eyes with my sister. I can't believe she just said that, and judging by the look on her face, neither can she.

Dan's glass hovers midair, frozen somewhere between his face and the table beneath him. His eyes dart back and forth between us, like a swimmer who's realizing he's out in shark-infested waters. This has all the makings of a bloodbath.

I'm on the verge of testily asking Shannon to repeat herself when Connor slides back into his seat and finds us all sitting in tense silence.

"Everything OK?" he says uneasily, tugging on the underside of my chair until it's flush with his.

"Absolutely," I say through gritted teeth. Shannon is glaring at me. I glare right back. "I was just telling the guys about the *surprise* I have in store for them. Tickets to go and see some stand-up."

"Oh," Shannon says, her eyes dropping to the table.

"Stand-up, wow," Dan says with exaggerated (or maybe just drunken) excitement. "I love stand-up. Stand-up is so good. How great is that, Shan?"

"Great," she agrees, inspecting the rim of her glass.

I feel Connor slide his arm around my waist and pull me into his side. I chance a peek up at him. He raises an eyebrow. *Bigger person.* Right.

I heave a huge breath, releasing Shannon's shitty comment on the exhale and charging on. "It's back in the city, but I think it will be really fun. So here," I say, handing the tickets across the table. "My gift to you. Welcome to New York."

Twenty-Three

We stand side by side, the red brake lights of Shannon's Uber disappearing around a corner and out of sight.

"That went well, I think," Connor deadpans.

I look up at him standing there beside me with his hands in his pockets and feel a surge of affection for him, my partner in crime. Connor, who toured my sister and her fiancé around to teach them a lesson and then gave up his Friday night just because I wanted him to.

And now it's just the two of us.

He's watching me watch him, a little smile playing at the corners of his mouth.

I push up onto my toes, wind my arms around his neck until my wrists hook around my elbows, securing him into place.

I've been waiting all night to do this again, and from the way his arm curls around me, I think he has too.

His right arm glides up my back until his hand closes around the back of my neck, and then we're kissing.

He kisses me like we have all the time in the world, and like we're the only two people in the world here to do it. Everything about him feels so nice and so easy and so good, like kissing is the most obvious thing we could be doing and every part of him just effortlessly clicks together with every part of me. This is the later he promised me earlier. It's finally here.

"You know," he says, pulling just far enough away to speak. "I live really close to here."

"You do?"

"Yeah."

"Where?"

His dimple peeps. "Over there."

I feel, rather than see, where he points to, somewhere behind me.

"What, like, across the street?"

He nods. I burst out laughing.

"You're not serious."

"Do you honestly think that I would joke at a time like this?"

"Is that why you picked this restaurant?"

"You said you wanted a spot in Brooklyn."

"Are you inviting me to your apartment?"

He stares at me steadily. Nods. He knows what I'm asking. I nod my agreement.

I lean forward and peck his lips. "Then let's go."

Connor wasn't exaggerating when he said he lived *just over there*. We can see the front door of his building from the street corner.

It's one of those nights that hints that summer's coming. Though it's past ten, the neighborhood is filled with the pleasant buzz of happy people starting their weekends, and we amble up to his apartment complex, an old industrial building of gray stone that's been redeveloped into a condominium.

His hand catches mine just as we reach the awning over the glass front doors, and he leads me inside, through the paneled lobby past the doorman, Joe, who he stops to introduce me to, then into the elevators and up to the eighth floor. We walk down to the end of a gray corridor, each door painted the same shade of navy blue, matching the skirting that runs along the perimeter.

When we get to his apartment, he fishes his keys out from his jacket pocket, unlocking the door and holding it open for me to pass through. I step inside but am greeted with nothing but darkness. I wait patiently while he closes the door and reaches around me to flick on the light.

I stand there for a moment, taking in my surroundings, then peek over my shoulder.

"Go ahead," Connor says, one side of his mouth kicking up.

I need no further invitation to snoop.

We're in a small corridor, with doors on the left and right. The end of the hall opens out into the main living space, a modernish-looking loft conversion with a vaulted ceiling and warm wooden floors.

I do not know what I was expecting, but it was not this. It's cool, but not flashy. The whole space is one big, easy rectangle, with enormous windows running along the back walls offering waterfront views. To my left is the kitchen area, divided from the living space by a counter-cum-breakfast-bar and an enormous concrete pillar that looks sturdy enough to support the weight of the entire building. I vow to return to that later, but for now step past it, to get a closer look at the living room.

There's a rectangular dining table to my left, and on the wall to the far right of the room is an enormous cream couch, wide and deep and smattered with cushions. Behind it, on the wall, is a huge framed poster, and in front of the sofa, a plexiglass coffee table. On the wall opposite the sofa is his TV, with a unit underneath it that's home to books and records, and a couple of framed photos sitting on top. Maybe most surprisingly of all, there's plants: a tree-looking thing beside the couch, and a few smaller ferns and vines dotted around on the other surfaces. The whole place feels comfortable, and supremely inviting. It's tidy, but lived-in. Grown up.

"Do you have a roommate?" I ask him tentatively.

"Just me." He smiles.

I wander around, poking at all the little things I can find, running my fingers along the spines of his book collection—mostly a mix of biographies and Stephen King novels.

I feel like an archaeologist on a dig site, each new finding an undiscovered piece of Connor I never knew about before.

I rifle around the kitchen for ages, poking around the cupboards and snooping through his fridge, and then once most of the living space has been explored, I turn back toward the corridor.

"Now where am I heading?" I ask him.

He leads me down the hall, stopping at the first door, which turns out to be a closet.

"This is famously where I keep my coats. Also shoes."

"That's genius."

"Here is a bathroom," he says of the next door, opening it for me and flicking on the light. It's small, and clean—just a vanity, a toilet, and a small shower cubicle.

"Another closet?" I ask, pointing at a folded door beside the bathroom entrance.

"Laundry," he says, sliding it open to reveal a stacked washer and dryer. Jeez. Talk about living in the lap of luxury.

I can only assume the last unexplored room in the corridor is his bedroom. My stomach flips over in anticipation as he flicks on the light.

Only when we get there, it's not a bedroom at all, but a home office space. There's a double-doored closet at one end of the room and a desk against the wall on the other side, the two enormous monitors a perfect match to the set he has at work.

I stare at the room blankly.

"I don't understand," I say slowly. "Where do you sleep?"

A smile dawns. "In my bedroom, if you can believe it."

"There's *another* bedroom?"

He nods.

"The rent on this place must be insane."

There's another bookcase in here, revealing a whole new treasure trove of artifacts for my discovery. Connor watches me the entire time, waiting patiently for my reaction.

My eye alights on a familiar figure.

"Oh my god, is that Brian?" I say, picking up the toy dinosaur resting on his shelf. Sure enough, it *is* Brian: the *DinoCode* logo is stamped on the bottom of its foot.

I look back at the shelf and gasp. "You have Julie too?"

"I forgot they were friends of yours," he murmurs.

"And yours, clearly," I counter, waving the toys at him. He only laughs. "I can't believe this. All this time you've been teasing me about liking *DinoCode* when *you're* the super fan."

"Busted."

"I don't get it," I say, clutching Brian and Julie to my chest. "Did you used to work there or something?"

He pauses for way too long. "In a way."

I glance up from my inspection. "Why are you being so shifty?"

Connor does the thing he does whenever he's uncomfortable. He scratches the back of his neck.

"Well, the thing about *DinoCode* is . . . " He takes a huge breath and on the exhale he says, "I invented it."

I laugh, that's funny. When I see the look on his face, I stop. "It doesn't feel like you're joking."

"That's because I'm not."

"You . . . invented . . . *DinoCode*."

"Yes."

"You invented—" I break off, holding the dinosaur right up in front of his face. "Brian."

"Yes."

"And Julie."

"Ben invented Julie."

"*BEN INVENTED JULIE???*"

"Yes."

I stare off into the middle distance, trying to make sense of what he's saying to me. I'm getting nothing.

"Connor Reid, you explain yourself *right* now," I demand. "Is this one of your weird nerd jokes I don't understand?"

"One of my—what?"

"Did you invent this the same way I invented Coco-nutty ice cream? Because that doesn't count!"

I'm still clutching the dinosaur figurines. They're now being used to punctuate my surprise. Like little prehistoric pom-poms.

"This is going about as well as I thought it would," he mutters, gently prying the toys out of my grasp and putting them back on the shelf.

"Back in college," he explains, "I made up Brian as part of an assignment for a game development class I was in. Ben was also in this class. We had the idea for this little kids' game where they learned to code through a series of tasks. Our professor at the time really liked it and told us to apply for this grant through the school so we could develop it."

"OK."

"We won the grant and used it to make *DinoCode* in senior year."

"But," I say, not remotely getting it. "You work at Taskio."

"After graduation, Ben and I kept working on it. We worked with an elementary school near campus to get kids to interact with it and give us feedback and stuff. A lot of them really liked it, I guess, and one of the dads of a student there worked at an education software company and got in touch. Eventually, they offered to buy it."

I have nothing to say to this, so I don't. My mouth is hanging open, like I'm a fish caught on a line.

"Ben and I were still in California, working out of the kitchen of our house share. We had no big plan for it. Mostly we just hoped it would help us get jobs after graduation. And building up a company is hard. We were running out of money and needed a lot more than just the two of us if we were going to turn it into anything. And then we got an offer."

I take this information in, picturing Ben and Connor working and living in close quarters fresh out of college. It is not hard to imagine; they still work in close quarters and look like they're fresh out of college. Which explains a lot.

"Did you ever consider running it yourselves instead?"

He shrugs. "Ben wanted us to try. I wanted to sell. I had a girlfriend back in New York and was dying to get home. I overruled him."

"How did Ben feel about that?"

His smile twists. "Pissed, but eventually he agreed with

me. We were in way over our heads, and there was a company offering us a ton of fucking money to buy a game we made up in college. It made sense to sell. We figured we could eventually use the money to do other things."

"And then you joined Taskio instead."

"After the acquisition, we both stayed on to consult for *DinoCode*. And then a guy at the new company had a sister in New York who was looking for an engineer to help build out the software for a startup she was working on. That was Naomi, by the way."

"So you took the job?"

He nods. "I came back to New York, then Ben followed me out here six months later."

"And the rest is history."

"That it is," he says, abstracted now. He picks the Brian toy up again and turns it over in his hand.

"Do you regret it?"

"Not really," he says, setting Brian back on the shelf. "Sometimes I do wonder if we gave up too soon. Or if I gave up, I guess. But I still think it was the right call."

"I don't get it. If you made all this money from *DinoCode*, why work at Taskio?"

"Well, we were like twenty-three when we sold it. I had to do *something*. I liked the energy of a startup but not the stress, so Taskio was a good fit for me."

"Makes sense."

What he doesn't say is that he's also practically a founder of Taskio, something he hinted at last week but hasn't explicitly said. I wonder how big his stake is. Someday it will also make him millions.

I look at Connor like I've never seen him before. He's like, an actual grown-up. Who invents things. That's hot.

"You've gone very quiet on me there, Annabelle," he says, gently drawing his index finger down the bridge of my nose.

"Just—processing. How come you never told me? You know I've been playing *DinoCode*."

"I figured if I told you, you'd stop."

I smile. "That is probably true."

"And honestly," he continues. "I liked that you were playing it. It felt like my worlds colliding."

"Man," I say. "I feel like such a slacker now. No one told me we were out here inventing things. I feel like I need to come up with something."

"Oh yeah?" he says, pulling in close. He slides his arms around my waist, kisses the side of my neck.

"Definitely. Something's coming to me, actually."

He turns me toward the wall, hands guiding my hips.

"Just go with me on this. It's an educational game for grown women who need to learn to code."

I feel a warm hand at my neck, then the slide of a zipper. Cool air on my back.

"I'm thinking it's an animated coconut who loves . . . body-building?"

My dress slides over one shoulder, then the other. Down my arms.

"You're right. Too obvious. An animated coconut with an ice cream shop."

His thumb brushes across the lace of my bra.

"I'll keep working on it," I say breathlessly, and spin toward him.

Twenty-Four

His mouth is on mine, hungry and urgent, and we stumble backward until my shoulder blades press up against the wall. It's like it's been the other times we've kissed, but better: this time, we don't have to stop.

My hands tangle in his hair as his palms settle against my chest, an action that has me moaning my approval. His hands move against me heavily, breaking off only for a second so he can tug at my bra. As an idea, it's inspired. I reach behind me to unclasp it and then toss it away. His shirt joins my bra in a crumpled heap on the floor.

Connor feels like an electric blanket just switched on; every inch of his skin is warm. I run my hands over the lean, hard lines of his arms and stomach, raking my nails down his back, goose bumps following in my wake. His hands smooth up and down my sides, then slide around my rib cage. Until finally they're right where I want them—he cups me fully, his thumbs gliding back and forth across my nipples. I arch off the wall and lean into his touch, and he hums in approval, repeating the motion again and again while my lips try and find purchase on his neck.

He presses a gentle kiss just beneath my earlobe, then

traces a path lower, across my collarbone and then down, until his mouth drops to my chest. I gasp when I feel his lips close around me, my fingers knotting into his hair and holding him in place, every move of his mouth eliciting a whimper. I stare at the ceiling, unfocused, and when his thigh slides between mine and his hips hitch forward I think my eyes might actually roll back so far they do a complete revolution.

My dress is still pooled around my waist. Connor didn't finish unzipping it—must speak to him about this—so I have to tug at it, then shimmy it over my hips. The dress slips down my legs and then I step out of it, kicking it away.

I watch him take in the sight of me, his eyes roaming over my nearly naked body, snagging on the only stitch of clothing left on me.

"Are you trying to kill me," he breathes.

"Yes," I say, fighting back a smile. "I really want that dinosaur toy."

"No jokes, remember," he orders, hauling me against him and kissing me fiercely.

It has never been like this before, for me. I feel as giddy as I do horny. I could laugh out loud at how surprised I am to be here, doing this, with Connor. *I can't believe it, it's you,* I want to tell him. I want to ask him if he can't believe it either, that we were once just two people working in the same building, who didn't even know each other, and now we're this. I can't believe we're this. I can't believe we weren't this all along.

We're pressed together completely now, and I slip my hand inside his waistband. His breath judders when my hand closes around his cock, and I can feel Connor, hard and urgent against me, desperate for what I'm offering. My grip tightens, and he rocks into me, shifting so I can feel more of him.

"I think we need to lie down on something," he says, panting into the crook of my neck.

"You mean you don't usually have sex in your office?" I ask, my mouth closing around his earlobe.

"Annie," he pleads, dragging his mouth back to mine. He pulls me away from the wall, his hands sliding over my ass. I twist my arms around his neck. Our kisses grow more frantic.

"Sofa," I breathe into his mouth. He lifts me. My thighs lock around his waist. When I feel his erection press against me, I keen toward him in a very unladylike way.

I'm vaguely aware of us moving, but I'm too busy planting kisses over every available square inch of his face to give it my further attention.

Seconds later the room tilts, and my back hits the cool, soft fabric of his sofa. He lowers me onto the couch, then climbs over me, his body covering mine.

Connor feels so weighty like this, so solid. Our lips catch lightly, slide together and then apart, neither of us rushing. We're having a moment here. I feel like he's reading my mind and I'm reading his, somehow, communicating everything without needing a single word.

He kisses me again, deeper now, and when his tongue slides against mine, a switch flips, and then I need him. Now. Urgently. My hands go straight to his ass, pulling him into me even more firmly, and we rock against each other, both too horny to stop.

I fumble at his jeans, making it as far as the top button before he breaks the kiss and eases up onto his knees. Instead of removing them, though, he hooks a finger under the edge of my panties and drags them slowly down my legs. All I can do is watch him.

I raise up on my elbows as he slides his palm up the inside of my leg, parting me gently as he charts a course toward the top of my thighs. He stares at me heavily; I am practically panting in anticipation. I don't need to ask him if he likes the view—I can see that he does. I feel powerful. Wanton.

His eyes drop, and then he's leaning down, his mouth sinking between my thighs. I nearly buck off the sofa when I feel his tongue slide against me. My breathing is shallow. I hear myself plead his name, no idea whether I'm begging him to stop or to keep going. He looks up at me, his arm sliding up my torso and gently guiding me back.

After that, I am no longer in control of my body. My hips rise to meet his mouth with each stroke he makes, and everything is decadent, the pressure building, and building, until my body goes taut, and then snaps.

Awareness returns when I feel him press a gentle kiss on the inside of my thigh. In that moment I'm almost desperate to feel his weight on top of me, and I reach for him, pulling at his forearms. He drops down instantly, willingly, his hands framing either side of my head. He kisses across my collarbone and neck.

"Gorgeous," he murmurs into my ear, and then I turn my face toward him and our mouths collide again.

If Connor makes me wait any longer I think I might physically die. My hands roam across his body and start moving downward. He's warm and hard and moving against me the second I wrap my hand around his cock, a hum deep in his throat.

"I need you," I tell him, and judging by the heated look on Connor's face, he needs me just as badly. I drag his boxers down, and this time he helps me, sliding his pants off and dropping them onto the floor.

I lie back down, both of us completely naked now, and for

a moment we both just take in the sight of the other, before he reaches back toward his jeans. He shows the condom to me wordlessly, and I nod, both of us quiet while he rolls it on.

Then his whole body is pressed on top of mine, packed together on his sofa like two sardines. The second we make contact it's bliss, my arms and legs wrapped around him, my chest pressed up against his. He slides against me and we both groan, desperate for what's to come.

But still, he's not rushing. He nudges his nose against mine; I'm almost cross-eyed from trying to watch him this close. I can see all the flecks of green in his eyes, every individual eyelash.

"You are so special," he breathes, and then he's pushing into me, and I'm no longer a person, just a loose assortment of noise and feeling.

He's slow at first, then firmer, then harder. The feeling of Connor in me, and on me, and around me is like nothing else, and before I know it another orgasm is dancing there just beyond my reach. As soon as I've had the thought he's moving, pulling me up onto his lap. His eyes flash, one hand on my waist while the other finds my core. I tilt my hips forward to get the angle I'm looking for, then bury my head into his shoulder to fall apart again, him rocking steadily beneath me all the while. He flips us over one last time and I dig my hands into his ass as his movements become clipped, frantic, until finally, I feel him tense, then still.

For a long time afterward neither of us move, simply breathe hard against each other. When he shifts his weight and pulls away, I feel bereft. Emotion is crawling up inside of me. I feel like I urgently need to tell him something that I have no idea how to put into words.

I expected him to get up, to start gathering the clothes thrown on the floor around us, but he doesn't. He rolls onto his side, then pulls me in and wraps his arms around me and holds me there without saying a word. I burrow into his neck and give over to the feeling of his chest rising and falling, the gentle glide of his fingertips stroking up and down my back, the press of his lips against my forehead.

We lie there in the quiet, and float.

Twenty-Five

"I still haven't seen your bedroom," I tell him later, much later, after we've dozed off and cleaned up. "Are you sure you have one?"

He slides his briefs on as he stands, raising them into place with an elastic snap, then turns to offer me a hand.

"I have been a bad host," he says gravely, pulling me up. "Allow me to complete the tour."

I laugh, and stand, fishing my own panties off the floor and sliding them on. My bra, I realize, is still in the other room, so I trail behind him, arms crossed over my chest.

I didn't notice it before, but his bedroom is right off the living room—the door was beside the sofa this whole time.

He flicks on the light, then slides past me through the doorway, opening a drawer in his big wooden dresser and rummaging for a moment before fishing out a T-shirt.

In two steps he's back at my side, and he pulls it over my head, holding the hem in place while I poke my arms through. He drops a kiss on my cheek.

I look down at what I'm wearing, then burst out laughing. "Connor."

He is the portrait of innocence. "What? I thought you'd like it."

I do like it. It's an enormous white T-shirt with *DinoCode* emblazoned across the chest.

It's basically your standard-issue bedroom: there's an armchair in the corner with a couple of sweaters piled up on it, an old wooden dresser, and a bed. Which, I notice, is made. I wonder if Connor is the kind of person who always leaves his apartment tidy when he goes out for the day or if he cleaned it up hoping I'd end up here later.

Left of the bedroom is *another* doorway, and I wander through it, completely agog at what I find. It's a sort of walk-through wardrobe, with clothing rails on each side, and then a master bathroom, with a *separate* shower and bath.

"This is the big flex in this apartment," I say, pointing at the two sinks. "What could you possibly need these for?"

"Simple," he says. "You brush your teeth there. And then that sink is strictly for hand-washing."

I look at him suspiciously. "Actually?"

He shakes his head. "Nah. I only use the left one."

"How long have you lived here?" I ask, running a finger along the faucet.

"Eight years," he tells me.

"Always alone?"

I thought I was being really stealthy there. His raised eyebrow tells me I was not.

"Always alone."

I shrug like, whatever, don't care. But secretly I'm pleased to know he didn't pick this place out for him and someone else.

We wander back through to the bedroom. He goes to get us water while I continue to poke around. I look up and hit the jackpot. There's a big accordion wall hook by the door and on it hang his many hats.

"I can't believe how many hats you have," I call over my shoulder.

"Why not? Hats are great." He has returned with two glasses of water. He puts mine down on the nightstand nearest to me.

I pull down what I consider to be his signature cap—forest green, embroidered with the word *Franks*—and pop it on my head.

"How do I look?" I ask, standing in front of him.

"Like you dressed up as me for Halloween."

"The correct answer there was 'beautiful,'" I say, flinging the cap toward him. He catches it with a laugh and sets it on the dresser.

"Was it? My bad."

He moves toward me.

"I think I'll keep the T-shirt," I muse.

"In that case, I better do this," he says, and before I can ask what *this* is referring to, he's peeling the T-shirt back up over my head.

"Hey," I protest, snatching it back out of his hand. "I need that."

"You definitely don't."

I wrap my arms around his shoulders and hop up into his arms. "At least let me put it back then."

Like the living space, the bedroom faces out toward the water. The city is quieter this late, but there's still the low hum of traffic, playing like a soothing background track.

We're tucked into bed now, our heads on the same pillow. The moonlight shining through his bedroom window offers just enough light that I can see the angles of his face. Connor runs his hand up and down over the curves and dips of my waist while I trace the edge of his shoulder, both of us content to explore. He never explicitly asked me to stay. It was more like the thought of me leaving never crossed his mind.

"I like it here," I tell him.

"Yeah?"

If you had asked me before to imagine where Connor lived, I'm not sure I could have even pictured it, but now that I'm here I can't fathom anything else. It's so quietly grown up.

"You make more sense to me now. You know, it's weird. We spend all this time together, but I feel like I don't know that much about you. I'm always wondering what you're thinking."

He fights a smile. "Well, that's a coincidence, because I'm always wondering what you're thinking."

"You first."

"OK. What do you want to know?"

"Everything," I say. My mind finds its most pressing question. "What did you think of Dan?"

"He was much as I expected. Not who I'd marry, but he seems mostly harmless."

"Did they seem happy to you? My mom says yes, but I think she's wrong. I think Shannon wants to dump him."

"You think or you want?"

"*Think*," I insist. "I get the vibe she doesn't want to marry him."

"And if she does?"

"No way. I'm far too loyal to Shannon to let her ruin her life like that."

"Sometimes being loyal means knowing someone you love is probably making a mistake and being there for them anyway," he offers, gently pushing the hair back from my forehead. His bicep ripples with the movement.

I don't like where this conversation is heading. I change the subject.

"Next question," I say, my attention turning to something more fun. I don't have the finesse to go fishing for a compliment. I am about as subtle as a battering ram.

"When did you start to like me?"

"Hmm, let's see," he says, lying flat, linking his hands behind his head. He takes the time to think. "I can't say for sure, but I think it was around the time you tried to tell me SQL stands for Super Quality Leads."

"That *is* what it stands for."

"You're still sure about that?"

I shrug, refusing to incriminate myself any further.

"Are you telling me you've been trying to lure me in this whole time?"

"I wouldn't say that, exactly," he says. "I didn't think I *could* lure you, honestly. You really snuck up on me. I went from having no idea you existed, to obsessing over your every movement. I never really thought we'd end up here."

"Why not?"

"I mean, talk about not knowing what you're thinking," he says. "It was so hard to get a read on you. One minute I think you're flirting with me, the next I think I'm crazy to even take a shot with you. The day you reacted so badly to me going out with Carrie was the first time I thought I hadn't made the whole thing up. Up until then, I was convinced I was cursed to have this demented crush on the girl I sit beside. A very particular kind of torture, let me tell you."

I can't believe what I'm hearing. Every revelation sets off a reaction inside me like candy popping on my tongue. I'm so overwhelmed I don't know what to say.

He rolls back onto his side. "And then of course, you hit on Ben."

"What? No, I didn't."

"You did."

"I have *never* hit on Ben."

He gives me a very pointed look. "You asked him if he was single."

"I wasn't hitting on him!" I say, indignant. "I wanted to set him up with Carrie."

I think back to that day, laughing out suddenly. "Oh my god. Is that why he was so weird with me in the elevator?"

Connor's smile creeps higher. "Was he?"

"Yes! He told me workplace relationships were forbidden and that you'd be mad if you knew we were even talking about it. He said we could get fired!"

"I mean—he wasn't lying. It is *technically* against company policy."

"I can see how seriously you take that."

He grins.

"So you like me."

"A lot," he confirms.

"You like me a lot." I nod. "But you don't know whether I like you. Despite the fact you've seen me naked."

"You introduced me to your sister as your boss."

I wrestle him onto his back and slide across him to straddle his waist. "I already told you, Connor. You're *so* much more than my boss."

"Do this again and you're asking for trouble," he warns, his hands sliding up my thighs.

I lean forward anyway, our noses nearly touching. "You're also . . . my team captain."

"Right, that's it," he says, flipping our positions in one swift movement. "I'm reporting you to HR."

I giggle. We're pressed right together now, one on top of the other. I wrap my arms around his shoulders. His lips find mine. Time melts.

Twenty-Six

Connor is up early to meet Ben the next morning and sends me on my way with a kiss and stern instructions to be the bigger person. I chant my mantra the whole way home, so giddy with the events of last night I feel like I'm floating.

It's a quick turnaround. I have just enough time to get back to the apartment and change before I have to meet Shannon, whirling through my bedroom like a hurricane.

Sam is here; I swear I hear her talking to someone, hear her moving around behind her bedroom door, but when I call her name softly there's no reply, and any noise I thought I heard has stopped.

Shannon's bridal shop of choice is in SoHo, tucked between two other designer stores regularly frequented by celebrities. It's the Instagram template of a wedding store, a boutique of quiet, understated luxury. The floors are distressed wood, and there's a jewel-toned sofa and an enormous changing room that's closed off with a heavy velvet curtain.

Shannon is already here, standing in front of a row of gowns with the sales associate, who is holding the hem of a dress out for her inspection. She turns back and looks at me, then resumes her conversation. I grind my molars.

"Morning," I say, infusing my tone with all the false cheer I can muster. I come to a stop beside her.

"Hi," she says absently. She shows the sales associate a picture of a dress on her phone, who nods, then asks us to wait here. Shannon returns to flicking through the rack.

There's a bit of an energy here. I'm mad at her about this weekend. She's mad at me about the last two years. When she finally turns to look at me, neither of us have much to say.

I recover first. "How was the comedy show last night?"

"We didn't go," she says, waving a hand. "We ended up just getting an Uber home."

Bigger person.

"Oh. How come?"

"Dan didn't know anyone on the lineup."

"That's kind of the point," I say testily.

"I'll pay you for them."

"It doesn't matter." And it doesn't. It definitely doesn't.

I'm annoyed. But I am *being the bigger person*, so I will drop it.

Another shop employee materializes, saving us from ourselves. "Can I offer you both a glass of champagne?"

"Absolutely," I say. "Shannon?"

"Sure." She shrugs. She could not look less interested.

Actually, now that I think of it, she seems a little unenthused about all of it. Considering a big part of the reason she came to New York was for this particular store, her whole demeanor is kind of . . . flat.

The woman pours out two flutes of champagne, passes them over, then disappears behind a partition. I wonder how many staff members are back there, quietly lurking.

I take a sip of my champagne, the bubbles pleasantly fizzing on my tongue. Shannon stares into her glass.

"Everything OK?" I ask her tentatively.

"Just hungover."

I mean—probably true. She and Dan drank a swimming pool's worth of alcohol last night. But she looks as airbrushed as always. If you put Shannon and me side by side and offered a stranger a thousand bucks to guess which one of us was hungover, they'd choose me every time.

"I can't wait to see this dress," I tell her, trying to bring the mood up. "I keep picturing the dress from *Cinderella,* but I don't know. Maybe that's a bit over the top?"

She gives me a tight-lipped smile.

The sales associate returns. "Here it is," she says to us, holding a gown over her arm.

Shannon nods. "It's perfect."

Would we go so far as to call it perfect? I'm not, I admit, an expert in the field, but it just looks like a heap of fabric to me. Maybe we just need to see it on.

My sister hands me her flute then slips off behind the dressing room curtain. I flop down on the sofa, sipping at my champagne. Shannon is giving me nothing here. But I chant my mantra. *Be the bigger person.* We will have fun at this dress appointment if it kills me.

To that end, I pop back up and start browsing the rack of dresses.

I've just identified the most elaborate one when the velvet curtain swishes open and Shannon hobbles up onto a raised platform, clinging to the woman's hand for balance.

OK, wow. That's a dress, all right. It's strapless, with a huge plume of fabric that's cinched at the waist and shoots up past the neckline, like a big pleated fan. It's sleek, and highly structured, fitted tightly over her hips and then kicking out into a wider train. The entire thing screams high fashion; I can more easily picture it on a catwalk than I can at a wedding reception.

I come to stand beside her. We stare into the mirror. "What do you think of it?"

I won't tell her I hate it until she asks.

She examines herself, tilting her head from one side to the next.

"It looks different than the picture," is all she says.

The woman who hoisted her into the dress immediately steps forward to explain why. The dress is a sample; the lighting in the photograph gives it a different sheen. If she cocks her hip to the side, *yes, like that, exactly,* you get a better sense of the *line*.

I stare at it skeptically. "Will you even be able to walk in that thing?"

It's so tight over the hips and legs that she can't do more than shuffle her feet.

"It's not about walking. This is the look I'm going for."

Um, OK. I mean sure, yes, she looks good—Shannon looks good in everything. But it can't possibly be comfortable. And she'll be wearing that thing for *hours*. Honestly, it's giving expensive flower vase.

"Hey, Shan," I say, wandering back over to the dress rack. "How about this one?"

The dress I hold up to her is the antithesis of the one she's wearing. It has a sparkly, corset-style bodice, with a big, flowing skirt made of layers of chiffon. Very suitable for moving, and dancing, and laughing, and all the other things you're supposed to do at weddings.

She flicks a glance at it from the mirror. "No."

"Come on," I wheedle. "You *know* Mom says it's always good to try a few different shapes, for comparison. Just to be sure."

Playing the mom card has its intended effect. She begrudgingly agrees to try on the dress.

A few minutes later and she's stepping back onto the plinth, gathering a huge handful of skirt as she climbs up.

Now we're talking!

She looks like she could be on the cover of a bridal magazine. Everything about this dress is softer: the fabric, the shape, the color. The skirt gently swishes when she moves, and the bodice makes her seem like a princess. It's romantic, and dreamy, and very Shannon—or at least, the Shannon she used to be.

Even the sales assistant is bowled over, telling her how gorgeous she looks. I snap dozens of pictures from every angle.

"I love it too," I tell her earnestly. "And not because I picked it."

"Liar," Shannon says, her mouth tilting up.

I laugh. "Well. Not *just* because I picked it."

The sales assistant reappears, carrying a scrap of fabric that turns out to be a detachable sleeve. She puts it on Shannon, demonstrating how she can wear this for the ceremony, and then remove it later when the dancing begins.

I hand her glass up to her. "You look like a princess."

"I feel like one, a bit," she admits.

She takes a sip and passes it back to me, her focus returning to the mirror in front of her. She moves left and then right. For a brief moment it could almost be said that we're having fun.

"OK, that's enough of that," she says briskly. "I'll take the other one."

I splutter. "What?"

She's already stepped down toward the changing room, beckoning the sales assistant to follow her.

"I did what you wanted. I tried your dress on," she says. "But I'm getting the other one."

"But—but—we still have more than an hour left," I say, my anxiety rising. "Shouldn't we try on more dresses?"

"No need," she says, disappearing behind the curtain. The sales associate follows her through with a clipboard and a measuring tape, ready to take Shannon's measurements.

I feel confused—and a little bit panicked. Did Shannon even *like* the first dress?

"Are you sure, Shannon?" I call from behind the curtain. "Why don't we come back later? You can think about it."

Her tone is clipped. "I don't need to come back later. I've decided."

Who cares what you've decided! I want to scream. *How do you feel?*

Shannon is dressed and back on the other side of the curtain, sitting down while the sales assistant runs her through the particulars of the purchase. I hover nearby, forgotten.

"Shannon," I say, trying to catch her eye.

"We'll take the full payment now," the woman is saying to her.

"Wait."

The spiel continues. "Alterations are done in-house but priced separately."

"Shannon."

"That's fine," Shannon says, nodding.

"WAIT," I screech, my voice ringing out in the quiet room, freezing both women in place.

Shannon is annoyed. "Annie, can you please—"

I look to the saleswoman, my eyes boring into hers. "Can you give us a minute?"

She looks from me, to Shannon, to me again, and then stands, saying she'll confirm the atelier's lead times, and be right back.

"Do you fucking *mind*," Shannon hisses when she's out of earshot.

"Shannon," I plead with her. "Just slow down for a minute. Are you sure about all this?"

"I told you I decided," she says, her jaw set.

"Decided *what*?" I say, exasperated. "What's the big rush all of a sudden?"

"It's time to get this done. And if the dress is going to be ready in time for December—"

"You said you didn't want a winter wedding!"

"Well, now I do! Why are you being so annoying about this? It's a wedding dress. Stop trying to get in the way."

"I'm not trying to get in the way! I'm trying to make sure you're happy!"

She laughs grimly. "OK, Annie. Whatever you say."

I reach for my mantra, but it is gone—blown away on a puff of air. I am not the bigger person. I am the littler person! The *little* sister. And I have had enough. "Oh my *god* can you just cut it out with all the passive-aggression?" I practically spit at her. "What is your problem?"

"*My* problem?"

"Yes! Your problem," I say, poking her in the chest, a move guaranteed to make her incandescent. "It's like you came all the way out here to show me you're still mad at me."

"No, I didn't!"

"Oh? Then why'd you bring Dan?"

She goes gimlet-eyed. "Oh, I don't know, maybe because

he's about to be your brother-in-law and I thought you'd want to make up with him?"

"Why would I want to make up with Dan?" I screech back at her. "I hate Dan! I will never, ever forgive him for doing that to you and I will *never* understand why you did."

"Well, here's a newsflash," my sister rages. "*You* don't need to understand it. It's none of your fucking business! I'm finally getting my life back on track after all the humiliation you caused me."

"*ME?* Dan cheated on you with Councilwoman Howard!"

"*Three* years ago! People make mistakes, Annie. Everything was moving so fast with the house and the wedding, and he freaked out."

"Oh come *on.*"

"No, *you* come on. You think you're so smart, but what the fuck do you know about relationships? Or about anything? You brought your boss to dinner!"

I'm thrown off balance. "He's not just my boss," I say lamely.

She throws her hands out.

"How wonderful for you! What a fairy tale. So when you fuck it up—and you *will*," she emphasizes, "all it means is that when you get dumped, you'll also get fired. And you're sitting here judging *me* about my life? That's really fucking priceless."

"What life, Shannon? Who are you, besides Councilman Dan's First Lady? Do you even want to marry him? Or is it easier to be his trophy wife than to face the truth that without this relationship you're nothing but a huge blank?"

She takes a sharp inhale, shocked at what I've said.

"Do you know what?" Shannon is so mad she is shaking. "I really fucking hate you."

A cold dread crawls up and over me. I feel how deeply she means it in the pit of my soul.

I'm distantly aware of a bell chiming. I feel, rather than hear, Shannon leave.

I turn to look at the sales assistant, who is nearby, wide-eyed and speechless.

"Sorry," I whisper, clearing the catch in my throat. "I think we're just going to leave the dress for now."

I pick my coat up off the sofa, walk slowly to the door, and then flee.

Twenty-Seven

I don't see Shannon again all weekend. I have no idea what they did, or when they left, or what she told Dan about what happened at the dress shop.

I barely remember the walk home. There was so much adrenaline coursing through my system, I blindly marched a full eight blocks past the apartment before I noticed and turned back around.

It couldn't last, of course. My agitation eventually gave way to a weighty despair. I hadn't been the bigger person, like I promised Connor I would be. I don't think I really even tried. Nor did I do anything to convince Shannon to shake off Demon Dan. I didn't even show her New York City. There's not a single measure by which her visit could be considered a success. It was a huge waste of time. And air miles.

I told Connor I'd text him updates about the rest of the weekend, but I don't. Typing out that you had a showdown for the ages feels even more hideous than saying it.

When I get to work on Monday morning, he's already there and waiting with an easy smile. Tears sting the back of my eyes the second I see him.

"How was the rest of the weekend?" he asks, his chair creaking on the recline.

I shuck off my jean jacket, avoiding his eye.

"Good."

"Did you manage to get through it without killing Dan?"

His voice is light, and teasing. I'm sure if I looked there'd be a twinkle in his eye.

"I did."

I sit, rolling forward to tuck myself in under my desk, finally looking at Connor, trying to project a sense of calm I don't remotely feel.

His smile is frozen, a frown building between his eyes. "Everything OK?"

"Why wouldn't it be?"

"Uh, I don't know." His tone changes from playful to uncertain.

I can't do this right now.

"I'm going to get some breakfast," I say, pushing back from my desk. "Want anything?"

He scratches his neck. "I'm good."

"Cool," I say, already turning away.

I know I'm being weird, but I can't help it. Connor will see right through me with even ten seconds of interrogation, and I'm still too keyed up to even attempt to discuss what happened with Shannon without opening the floodgates on a messy, ugly cry. I don't want to have to admit that I'm the one who started it. I'm already buried under the weight of my own shame.

I'm peeling off the wrapper of my second blueberry muffin of the day when I hear a familiar voice.

"Would you look who it is," Carrie says, wandering over from the direction of the espresso bar.

"Hey," I say. Pathetically.

She slides into the chair across from me. "Someone's cheerful this morning."

That someone would be Carrie. She looks positively glowing, especially when you factor in it's a Monday. I feel like a shriveled raisin.

"Where have you been? I phoned you Saturday."

"Yeah, sorry about that," she says, blowing on her mug. "I had a . . . date. Sort of."

"Oh?"

Could it be . . . *Ben*?

I wait for her to tell me more, but she offers nothing.

She sips on her coffee. "How was the weekend?"

"I slept with Connor and my sister told me she hated me," I say flatly.

Carrie chokes her coffee back out.

"I'm sorry, what?"

I shrug. "That. On Friday night I had sex with Connor, and then on Saturday my sister and I had a huge fight while trying on wedding dresses and I'm pretty sure she's never going to talk to me again."

Carrie's eyes are *bugging* out. It must be a full minute before she finishes processing the information.

"Start with Shannon."

I do. I tell her about Dan crashing the weekend.

"*Asshole*," she declares.

How they showed up at the office unannounced.

"The *ONE* day I'm not here," she seethes.

Me inviting Connor to dinner.

"Rogue move, even for you."

I tell her about the Palomas, the comedy tickets, Shannon's shitty dinner comments, the bad energy in the air, Shannon's joyless bridal appointment and her insistence that she wanted to buy a dress she *clearly* didn't like, and, finally, the argument that roared up out of nowhere.

Carrie makes me recount every word Shannon and I exchanged with precision. I give her as much detail as I can remember, but a lot of it is clouded by the mists of my rage.

The part I recall perfectly, of course—a crystal-clear memory in high definition—is the moment she told me she hated me.

Carrie dismisses this immediately. "She was being extremely dramatic. Let it settle. Then you two can talk."

Considering Shannon's last cooling-off period lasted over two years, this doesn't fill me with hope.

"Now," she says, "on to the good stuff. Namely, you fucking your boss."

"Can you not say it like that," I say, bristling. "Especially here, where anyone can overhear you."

She makes an exaggerated point of looking over her shoulders in both directions. "I think we're good, babe."

She is technically correct. There is no one around.

I start telling her what happened after Shannon and Dan left the bar, then realize I don't want to. What happened between Connor and me feels like it's just ours.

Instead, I sketch out the simplest version of events; him inviting me back to his place, sleeping together, staying the night. I withhold all the small, incendiary details—the dozens of tiny precious moments that make my stomach flip over just thinking about them.

She whistles. "So will this be a recurring event, or was it a one-time thing?"

I hesitate. "I'm not sure," I admit. "We didn't discuss it. Or make plans again."

"Time will tell, I guess," she shrugs.

Doubt worms through me. I think of when he kissed me in the office last week, him worrying I was going to blow up his life. Surely that means it's not casual for him? Hot on the heels of that thought is another: maybe that was him trying to tell me that's all it could be. I can't imagine Connor being like Andy, pretending nothing happened. If he did, I'd be crushed. I have no idea how we'd work together. But then again, isn't it just as complicated now?

My eyes wander down to my phone, and I check it absently, the display lighting up. "Shit," I say, pushing back immediately. "I have to go. Our weekly catch-up started a minute ago."

Connor is noticeably irritated by my tardiness when I slip into the meeting, though things have barely kicked off. He glares at me from across the room. Not a great start.

Worse is to come. Connor has just started talking when Brad sails into the meeting room, along with two of his cronies I recognize by face but not by name. I don't think their visit was planned. Formally, we're here to discuss some dashboard upgrades with Sven and a few of his software engineers. Not the sort of thing Brad would usually interest himself in. It has all the air of an ambush.

"How are my favorite data dweebs?" Brad says, clapping Ben on the back as he moves past, nodding toward the rest of us in turn.

"What do you want?" Connor asks, his eyes hard. He's standing at the front of the room, poised to kick off the meeting.

"We won't take up much of your time," Brad insists, sounding like a slimeball. "I thought we could have a quick chat about

Jotter's integrated templates ahead of Thursday. Oh good, Sven, you're here too. Perfect timing."

Sven grumbles something under his breath about his workload.

Brad laughs. "Always so funny, buddy. Now," he says, calling us all to attention with a clap. "Connor, Josh and Aiden here were really interested in your observations on the project's viability. I think you're right. We should kill it."

I sit up straighter, on high alert. Andy and his team have been pitching the next version of the template library for months; they've been working on this since even before the merger.

Integrated templates would offer a much more personal experience—the idea is we'd use machine learning to predict and pre-populate boards based on what users have done before. If a social media manager plans a content calendar every month, and always schedules a blog post on a Monday, integrated templates would automatically set out that format every time you went to create a new board, saving the user time and energy.

It's complicated and ambitious, but if they succeed, it would give Taskio a real edge against its competitors. I didn't even know Connor was looking into it. What hasn't he told me?

"I didn't say we should kill it," Connor says. His tension is apparent even from here. He's holding himself so rigidly it's like you could snap him in half.

"Not in those words," Brad concedes. "But let's cut to the chase here. If it's not going to be compatible with the free tier ad features, and we want to roll out Version 3.0 by September, it makes more sense to kill it."

Sven blinks. "3.0 won't be ready by September."

"It has to be," Brad says simply. "We promised Paul it would roll out in time for the float."

The float. Oh my god. Taskio is planning to go public. Are they *insane*?

I instinctively look to Connor, expecting him to look as shocked as I feel.

But he isn't. He knows about this, I realize. My mind is working quickly now, piecing the details together while the others go back and forth.

Brad, the layoffs, the secrecy—it all makes sense, suddenly. Taskio is preparing for an IPO. These are the mysterious conversations Connor's been having behind closed doors. He's been advising Brad which features should stay and go for Version 3.0; where the product department should focus its resources. And he wants to kill Andy's template library.

True to his word, Brad only stays for another couple of minutes, but the damage is done. The guys spend the rest of the time bitching about Version 3.0 and what it would take to have it ready by the fall, and Sven calls the meeting to a close, wearily saying that if they need to accelerate the timeline the dashboard updates will have to wait.

"Oh god," John says. His elbows are resting on the table, and he slides his hands up to his eyes, rubbing at them from behind his wireframe glasses with the palm of his hands. "This is a disaster waiting to happen."

I clear my throat. "What did Brad mean about killing the integrated templates?"

I can feel all the guys eyeing me cautiously, Connor most of all. When no one says anything, I ask again.

"Connor. Did you recommend they kill that project?"

He looks at me directly now. "No."

"Really? Because Brad there seems to think you did."

"He asked if it was ready and would be compatible with 3.0. All I told him was the truth."

I scoff. "As you see it."

"As everyone sees it, Annie. Integrated templates are still a long way off."

"Not if more people were working on it."

He starts to shake his head.

"It's a good idea," I insist. "If they kill that project now, all those people will end up losing their jobs."

"Not necessarily."

"Oh, wake up," I say. "They will, they *so* will. They're the last Jotter product squad left. If you make the recommendation to kill off integrated templates now, they'll all lose their jobs—just in time for Taskio to go public!"

Connor and I are standing at opposite ends of the conference room table, Martin's and John's heads bobbing back and forth, watching the action like a tennis match.

He softens. "I understand that these are your friends. It's not that it's a bad idea. But it doesn't fit with the direction Brad is moving in."

"That feature has huge potential to be a game-changer for the platform," I argue with him. "Ben says—"

"It's not Ben's call to make," he interrupts. "It's mine. And I'm telling you, it's not going to work."

Ben whistles under his breath.

"At least let me talk to them," I reason. "There might be a way to salvage this."

"No." His tone is firm, final. "I warned you when you joined this team our conversations were confidential, and I meant it. All we do is make the recommendations, answer the questions we're asked. We don't control the outcome."

"Bullshit," I argue. "We all know Brad will go with whatever you tell him. You're the one who told him about the integrated templates in the first place. And you only got that inside information from *me*."

The next review is on Thursday, the big all-hands meeting where product owners pitch ideas and share progress updates of what they're working on.

I see the scene play out in front of me. Brad asking Andy's team to give an update of where they're at, blissfully unaware that they're sitting ducks.

". . . Which is why it's important that none of this leaves this room . . ." Connor, it turns out, was still talking. "Annie. Do you understand?"

Standing there, he feels like a stranger.

"Yes, *boss*," I practically spit at him. "I understand."

Twenty-Eight

Understand? Yes. Care? No.

I find my old team exactly where I left them down in the product department. Alex is milling around near Andy's desk eating a yogurt while Andy points to something on his screen. The two of them look like the epitome of I-work-in-tech-guys. Alex is in his blue Patagonia half-zip. Andy's is green.

"Gentlemen."

"How's it going," Alex says around a mouthful.

Andy cranes his neck back. "Oh hey, Annie."

I'm mad, obviously, but I'm also not a fucking idiot. I don't need to tell them what Brad said to us upstairs. I just have to drop enough hints so they can connect the dots, and then my work here is done. I also need to do this quickly, before anyone from DatStrat figures out what I'm up to.

"How's progress coming along on integrated templates?"

Alex snorts. "What progress? It's sitting with the dev team going nowhere."

"So what will you present at the meeting Thursday?"

"Nothing," he shrugs. "Why would we? It's just an all-hands."

"Isn't it a good opportunity to show proof of concept, though? Get some buy-in from the other product owners?"

This catches Andy's attention. He swivels his chair around, his eyes narrowed on me. "What do you know?"

Just that they're going to kill your project and then you'll all lose your jobs.

Alex and Andy both look at me expectantly. Alex is leaning back against the desk now, one leg crossed over the other. Andy is perched forward in his chair, his elbows resting on his knees.

I look from one, to the other, and back again.

"I know the exec team is thinking a lot about Version 3.0 right now."

Alex's attention returns to his yogurt. "So what? They've been thinking about that since we merged."

I give Andy my best level stare. "There's a rumor going around that they want it launched by the fall. If that's true, they'll probably be making decisions about any new product features they want to prioritize. And which ones they want to kill."

He raises his eyebrows. "Why 3.0 in the fall?"

"There's . . . another rumor . . . about a possible float. But. Who knows if that's true."

"I haven't heard that rumor," Andy says slowly.

"That would explain the layoffs, I guess," Alex says, his spoon scraping around the bottom of the pot. "I still think they're dreaming."

A world of information is silently passing between Andy and me.

"Have they already decided about the features?" he asks finally.

"Like I said. It's just a rumor. I can't even remember where I heard it."

"Right."

"If they're going to make the target, though, it makes sense that they'll be thinking about which features are most compatible. Can integrated templates run with the in-app ads they're working on?"

"No," Alex says.

"It could," Andy argues.

"By Thursday?" I ask.

He lifts a shoulder. "In theory. A single prototype, anyway."

"It might be worth it. In theory."

Andy nods. He understands what I'm telling him.

"I guess we'll see you then."

"You two are being weird," Alex says, pointing his spoon from Andy to me.

Andy swivels back toward his monitor. I only shrug and tell them I'll catch up with them later. My warning has been delivered. My work here is done.

Twenty-Nine

By the end of the day I'm not the only one feeling the tension. I don't think I've ever seen Connor this grumpy. Even the guys seem beyond trying to lift him out of whatever mood he's in, and since he doesn't say a word to me, I don't say a word back. Every agonizing minute of this silence plays out with him and me sitting side by side.

Ben has been stealing furtive glances at me all afternoon, but when I look back at him his eyes dart away again. Eventually, I can take it no longer.

ANNIE: Do I have something on my face, Benjamin?

He shoots a crooked smile in my direction, then starts typing.

BEN: Hah, sorry.
BEN: I'm being weird aren't I
ANNIE: A little
BEN: Just wanted to see if everything is OK?
ANNIE: Why wouldn't it be
BEN: Pretty quiet over on your side of the table today, that's all
ANNIE: Think you might need to direct your comments to the bridge troll on my left

He types and then stops three times. It feels like he's choosing his words carefully. I can hear the tap of the delete key from here. All I can see is the very top of his fiery-red mop, bobbing up and down.

> **BEN:** Did you guys have a fight or something?
> **BEN:** Before the meeting I mean
> **BEN:** I was there for that part
> **ANNIE:** Maybe he's just in a bad mood today
> **BEN:** He wasn't before

It's like Connor senses we're talking about him. He pulls his headphones off and directs a question at Ben, effectively bringing our furtive conversation to a close. He's turned away from me completely—his back may as well be a brick wall. It really brings new meaning to the phrase *giving the cold shoulder*. I can feel none of his usual warmth.

I scroll back through my conversation with Ben, which feels weirder the more I think about it, even for the fact that he had it with me and not Connor. My mind snags on Ben's suggestion that Connor wasn't in a bad mood before, which, if I really think about it, I guess seems true. I'm just not exactly sure why Ben's first thought is that it has something to do with me. Why doesn't he just ask him?

Uncharacteristically, Connor is the first one to leave. This *never* happens.

He stands from his chair, and I look up at him, waiting.

"See you tomorrow?" I ask cautiously.

"Going to work from home, I think," he says, addressing this to the button on his coat rather than to me.

"Oh."

"See you guys."

I watch the back of his head retreat toward the elevators, my frown growing. Connor never works from home. What's going on?

I look over at Ben. He raises his eyebrows like *are you going to deal with that?*

And you know what? Yes I am. I can't handle both him and Shannon being mad at me at the same time, it's too much. If Connor wants to be annoyed with me about something, he will have to get in line.

He's already gone by the time I reach the elevators, which means he's also no longer in the lobby when I finally hit the ground floor. I push through the doors and scan the plaza around me, craning my neck to see around all the people coming and going.

There's no sign of him. It's like he's disappeared. I can only guess the direction he's going in. If I get this wrong I'll never find him now, and will have no choice but to follow him all the way back home. Like a weirdo. Or a stalker.

My luck holds—I pick the right direction and catch sight of the back of his head on the corner right before he cuts across the street. I want to dramatically call his name, but even if he did hear me, he'd turn around right in the middle of the crosswalk and then be flattened by a taxi. Which Ben would probably also blame me for, cryptically, over messenger.

By the time I race across the street it's me who is almost hit by a taxi, but I don't let this stop me. I jog the extra ten seconds until I am right behind him. Connor jolts when I reach forward and grab his arm, turning with a noise that sounds something like *wargh!*

He frowns when he realizes it's just me, looking back toward the office like *what are you doing I thought I left you back there*.

For my part, I've been so busy catching up to him that I forgot to really work through what it is I'm catching up to him *for*, and now that we're face-to-face, in addition to being out of breath (and lightly sweating) I also can't think of a single word to say. I go with Ben's thing.

"Is everything OK?"

"Sorry?"

His face is a picture-perfect translation of: ?????

"You seem like you're in a bad mood."

"I—OK?"

"If you're mad at me about something, you should just *say*."

I admit: my tone is accusing. I am rapidly losing sight of what it is I'm doing here. Meanwhile, the power of speech has totally deserted Connor. He is standing there gaping, his eyes roaming all over my face.

"You think I'm mad at you?"

"Well, yeah. Maybe. You're being weird."

"*I'M* being weird?!"

"Yes!" I say, indignant. "You are. You've been weird all day."

Retrospectively, maybe he wasn't mad before. But he's *definitely* mad now. He rubs at his temples, weighing up what he wants to say to me. Or possibly praying for patience.

"You never got in touch this weekend."

"So you are mad at me."

"I'm not *mad*," he says. "I'm—I don't know, disappointed, I guess. You said you were going to call me, and when I didn't hear from you all weekend, I thought, that's fine, you're busy with your sister. But then you came in this morning and you wouldn't even look at me."

He glares at me, but it's not angry. It's wounded. It all clicks into place.

"You thought I was blowing you off."

His hands are in his pockets, and he gives me the smallest little shrug imaginable. "What was I supposed to think?"

"Not that."

Instead of looking at me, he's looking at the ground, toeing at a pebble beneath him. My heart clenches. He's not convinced.

"The truth is—" I take a deep breath, hating that I have to tell him this. "The weekend was a disaster."

He looks up at me then, his head tilting to the side. A silent invitation to continue.

"I was not the bigger person," I say pathetically. My hands dangle uselessly at my sides. "After I left your place, I went to meet my sister at the wedding dress shop for her appointment and we got into a huge fight."

I trail off, my voice cracking on the word *fight* and I can feel my mouth twisting, my chin scrunching up under the pressure not to cry. Whenever this happens, I completely lose control of my nostrils. They're flaring in and out while I work to calm myself down.

One more deep breath and I manage to swallow back the tears that are threatening.

"I said something really mean, which I am way too embarrassed to repeat to you, and then she, well, she told me she hated me."

"Annie—"

"I was really disappointed in myself," I continue, cutting off any attempt at sympathy. "And worried you were going to be disappointed in me too. That's why I didn't text. And this morning when you asked me, I knew you'd see right through me if I even attempted to talk about it, and I just panicked."

He doesn't say anything, just gently steps forward, tucking a strand of hair behind my ear.

"So I guess in a way I was avoiding you, but not because of that. I want—" My fingers tingle with nervousness. Strange that something I feel so strongly is also so hard to put into words. "I want to do the exact opposite of avoid you, basically."

I hold my breath, waiting to see if he believes me. He catches my hand in his, raising it gently to his lips.

"OK," he says. "Then let's go. I'm starving."

He marches us across the street and to the taco spot on the corner, ordering us both a mountain of food and instructing me to elbow my way into a spot by the window. It's standing room only, so I hover, stretching my palms along the white tile countertop in front of me, claiming as much space as I dare.

He really wasn't lying when he said he was hungry. By the time he's inhaled his first taco, his whole demeanor has changed. His shoulders drop, his posture relaxes. He's back to the calm, easygoing Connor who somehow never seems to have a care in the world.

"I thought you were going to give me hell about the meeting," he says, wiping at his fingers with a crumpled napkin.

"I am," I tell him. "As soon as I finish eating."

He huffs a laugh. "That's allowed. I owe you an apology. I'm sorry."

Connor's apologies disarm me every time—I'm powerless to resist the simple honesty with which he delivers them.

I take a swig of my orange soda. "Not even going to attempt to defend yourself?"

"If I was," he says casually, "I'd say that I had just been dumped and then bamboozled by the boss in front of my whole team, and was feeling testy."

"You hadn't been dumped."

"I didn't know that at the time."

I tug on his sleeve. "I know you're joking. But—I don't like that you thought that."

He doesn't say anything. Just ducks his head into my shoulder and plants a kiss on the side of my neck. Heat blooms from the spot where he touched me.

He straightens. "I'm reluctant to repeat my opinion on the templates since it made you so mad this morning."

"I can feel the 'but' coming."

"I don't think it's going to work," he admits. "But I swear I didn't tell Brad I think he should kill it."

"OK."

"I will talk to him again," he promises me. "The thing is, though, he's really on one with the whole free tier thing. Even if the integrated templates were ready, I'm honestly not sure he'd go for it—he wants to push the software in a completely different direction. There's nothing I can do to change that."

"Of course."

"But Annie," Connor says, searching my face. "Don't repeat anything from that meeting this morning. The stuff about rolling out 3.0 ahead of schedule and plans for a float are lockdown confidential. Now would not be the time to fall foul of Brad."

Now *would* be the time to admit I'd already gone downstairs and strongly hinted at all this, but I don't want to ruin this moment. Instead, I make a mental note to remind Andy to play it cool, then banish the subject from my mind.

Thirty

The next two days with Connor pass in a happy bubble of stolen kisses and secret glances. We're busy on all the opposite days, but make plans for the weekend, texting back and forth through the evenings until we're back together each morning to pick the conversation up where we left off.

By the time the product department's all-hands comes around on Thursday, I'd forgotten all about it. When the calendar reminder pops up in the morning, I remember with a jolt that I'd meant to follow up with Andy. He's been suspiciously silent since we spoke on Monday, working, I hope, on a prototype that will help people understand how great the integrated templates could be.

I fire him off a quick message.

ANNIE: Hey. Good luck at the AH today. Please be careful not to give away that you know anything about Brad's potential plans—it's really confidential!!

It's fully forty-five minutes before he replies.

ANDY: All good

I breathe a sigh of relief. Everything is under control. Connor won't be happy if he knows I tipped them off, but when the alternative is doing nothing and watching more of my friends get laid off, I tell myself it was worth the risk. Andy will do what Andy does best, and Connor will be none the wiser.

The product department's all-hands meeting is a quarterly get-together where the entire department (plus a few interlopers) meet to brainstorm and share updates about what they're working on. In theory, this leads to innovation. In reality, this leads to mudslinging.

When you put a bunch of spoiled, competitive product managers in a room, only chaos can follow. Product squads are tribal by nature—we spend all our time working in little pods, after all—but it feels particularly toxic at Taskio. All-hands meetings have the air of a *Real Housewives* reunion, except worse, because none of these people are being paid to generate this level of drama.

It feels particularly charged when I get to the pit today. The hum of conversation has an edge to it, somehow. I wonder how much of this is because the last round of layoffs is still fresh in everyone's minds, or if it's just the fact that we all know Brad will be in attendance. The man is a panic attack on legs.

Martin, John, and I all walk down together, and I leave them near the front to say hello to some of my old Jotter crew. Connor is on the opposite side of the room, leaning against the wall and chatting away with Sven, no doubt about their two favorite subjects, software and data. Ben already warned us he'd be late—I watch him slip in at the back just as Brad goes up front to deliver a ridiculously self-important introduction to the session, telling the crowd it's time for us to *operate in our zone of genius* and that *we are all just fireworks, giving off sparks.*

The session follows its predictable format—an endless stream of product managers talking about the features they're working on, some exciting (a new calendar view), and some not (a green button will be reverting to its original blue).

Though Brad promised to let the product squads "do their thing," he has not been a passive spectator—he interrupts frequently. I don't know how anyone can stand it. I never paid him much attention when I worked in Product. I've really come to hate him since joining DatStrat.

Next is Andy. I cross my fingers behind my back, willing him to do well. I expected him to launch straight into the use case for the integrated template library, but he takes things in a different direction, mostly talking about the ethos of Jotter, instead, and some of the big-picture ideas Jotter's product team had before the companies merged.

These updates are supposed to be a couple of minutes apiece. Andy has held the floor for over five minutes now and doesn't look like he's slowing down. It gradually dawns on me that he's doing something much bigger than trying to save his product squad. Too late, I realize he's probably going for the shock factor.

"As you're all well aware, most of Jotter's product teams disbanded and joined existing squads when we merged. Except for three squads, who continued to work on existing projects that, though very different for Taskio, would, to borrow Mr. Pincer's phrasing, make a *tangible impact* when brought to market. Two of those projects were effectively killed last month when their squads got laid off. Here's why it would be a mistake to kill the integrated templates too . . ."

Oh, shit. It can only be seconds until the other guys realize what I've done.

Connor figures it out first. He looks up at me slowly, his eyes boring into mine in an absolute death stare from all the way across the room. I can't bear it; I duck my head like the chicken that I am.

Sixty seconds later I see Ben's head snap up when Andy mentions the rollout of Version 3.0. The longer he speaks, the bigger Ben's frown grows. Then his eyes roam, seeking out Connor. The two of them exchange a look. My skin prickles.

John is third to piece it together. He gently whacks Martin, the back of his arm connecting to his chest. Martin leans in, then nods at whatever John has whispered. They both look queasy.

I am in trouble, I am in so much trouble.

It feels like the temperature of the room has plummeted by about four hundred degrees, but I am panicked, and warm, and desperately trying not to show it.

The mention of Version 3.0 sends a wave of murmurs flying around the room, and Brad is quick to try and cut Andy off at the pass, saying product decisions for V3 have yet to be made.

"Really? I've heard you want to roll it out as early as September. Is this incorrect?"

Shit. Shit shit shit.

Brad has no choice but to acknowledge that it's something the leadership team is considering. Andy responds by asking if the accelerated timeline has anything to do with rumors of an upcoming flotation.

Brad says he doesn't know where Andy would have heard that. Andy looks him dead in the eye and says he has it on good authority it was under discussion with Data Strategy as recently as this week.

OK. Now I'm fucked.

The room *explodes*. Andy's update is completely forgotten as product managers shoot question after question in Brad's direction, and it takes him several minutes to get the room back under control. Brad turns his head toward Connor at one point. The look he gives him is absolutely lethal. My stomach drops when I realize that Connor has probably been petitioning Brad behind the scenes already. He's probably assuming Andy's coup is also Connor's doing.

The questions keep coming. Andy has clearly given a heads-up to some of the more senior squad leaders—several push Brad on strategies and timelines for V3. He could get fired for this. I don't think he cares.

The general consensus is much the same as Sven and Connor's from last week: they're dreaming if they want V3 to roll out in September with a whole host of new features. Brad finally gets so exasperated that he just shuts the session down with an ominous warning that any updates will always come through official channels.

I lose Connor in the crowd, but find Andy as he's being patted on the back by another Jotter product manager.

"Andy, what the hell was that," I hiss at him, drawing him away from the others.

"I thought about what you said. It was time to expose Brad's hypocrisy."

"I did not say any of that!"

"Why tell me, then?"

"I was trying to warn you to get your ass in gear before Brad got any big ideas about more layoffs, not giving you the detonator to blow up Version 3.0. Don't you realize how serious this is? Connor could get fired. So could you."

"Relax," Andy says. "Your big-deal boss is practically a founder of the company, he has equity coming out of his asshole. He's not going to get fired. And they can't fire me. It will look too shady."

"OK, then what about me?" I snap. "I wasn't supposed to share *any* of that with you. I'm going to be in so much trouble! I try to help you and this is the thanks I get? How could you not tell me? What happened to sticking together?"

"Look, I'm sorry," he says, sounding anything but. "It was a risk I had to take. You'll talk yourself out of it. You always do."

"And if I can't? Brad is not just going to let this go."

"He won't have a choice. Listen, I've got to go, I'll catch up with you later, OK?"

Connor is waiting for me outside the elevator bays. He's leaning against the wall, his arms crossed and his jaw set.

He straightens when I step out of the elevator, then turns without a word. I follow. It feels like I'm off to my execution.

He walks only as far as the first available conference room, a huge space with an enormous boardroom table as its centerpiece. It's soundproofed and encased on all sides by glass walls. Connor pulls the sliding door shut as soon as I step past him. I wonder if one of us will soon be screaming.

That might actually be preferable. Connor's deadly, silent calm is extremely unnerving. I squirm under his stare.

"I can explain."

"What were you thinking, Annie? Did you honestly just try and stage a coup in the middle of an all-hands?"

"*No*. Connor, I swear, I had no idea he was going to do that. I even messaged him before the meeting reminding him not to let on that he knew anything."

Wrong thing to say. His nostrils flare. "Is that supposed to make it *better*?"

I'm really flapping now. "No. I messed up, OK? But I swear to you, Connor, I never thought it would get this out of hand."

"What the hell did you do?"

"Nothing! Or, not that much. I told him I'd heard a rumor about the rollout of Version 3.0 and . . . encouraged them to present something at the all-hands. I wasn't specific! I dropped a few hints."

"That worked out well, didn't it," he says, his voice hard.

"You don't need to be a dick about this," I say, my own temper flaring to life. "Look, I'm sorry I went around you, and that Andy took the nuclear option and pissed Brad off, but what was I supposed to do? Leave them there like sitting ducks? When one tiny little heads-up could potentially save all their jobs?"

"Considering I specifically told you not to repeat that information, yes, that's exactly what I expected you to do."

"But you were *wrong*."

"Guess what, Annie? I don't give a shit. You can't just hit the override button on every little thing that happens in your life that you don't agree with. I've told you again and again, our work is confidential."

"Connor, just two months ago I watched half my old product team get laid off. *I* got laid off, remember? And you didn't want to hear it!"

"Yeah? Tell me something, Annie, when did you share this information with your best friend Andy?"

I hesitate. "Why does that matter?"

"It matters. When?"

Does anyone have a shovel? I am about to be digging my own grave.

"Monday. Right after the meeting."

His laugh is hollow. "Of course. And you never thought to—I don't know—talk to me about it? Or maybe give any of us the same heads-up you gave him?"

"I forgot," I say lamely.

"That's convenient, isn't it?"

"I'll fix it," I promise him. "I'll tell Brad it was—"

"Don't even finish that thought," he warns me. "You turning yourself in is the last thing that will fix this. Did you even take *one* minute to think about what the consequences of leaking that information might be? How I might feel about it? Or did none of that matter, because you wanted to teach me a lesson?"

"Is that what you think I was doing?"

"No, I think you had a tantrum the second your will was crossed and that was the last you thought about it. A bit of a pattern, I'm noticing."

I reel back. "What is *that* supposed to mean? Do you know what, fine. You're right. Maybe I didn't think it through enough and I could have handled it better, but at least I *did something* instead of just sitting around following the rules! And at least *Andy* tried to put a stop to Brad's nonsense instead of doing what you're doing, lying down dead and letting him walk all over you. You have so much power here, and all you seem to want to use it for is to help enforce a bunch of decisions made by a cowboy in a suit who you don't even agree with anyway!"

By the time I get to the end of my impassioned speech, I am panting. Connor looks like he's just taken a gut punch. I watch as he processes all the information, pulling his cap off and scratching at his hair the way he does when he's stuck on some code he can't wrap his head around. He puts it back on, then rubs at his eyes. The silence is agony. It just stretches on and on.

A rap on the glass door makes both of us jump, and we turn toward the sound. Brad is on the other side of the door, sliding it open.

"There you are," he says to Connor. "I need to speak to you in my office."

Connor swallows. "Sure."

Brad is so visibly pissed off he looks menacing; like his temper is on a tight leash and any second he could set it loose. And he will. On Connor.

I quail. Connor is right—I didn't stop to think about my actions. It wasn't until Andy was up there that I realized it's him, not me, who would suffer the consequences.

"Mr. Pincer," I call, halting both Brad and Connor in their tracks.

I can tell by the look on his face that he hadn't even noticed me in the room. His next words confirm it. "Who is this?" Brad says to Connor, rather than me.

"I'm on the data strategy team," I tell him, knowing full well he won't care what my name is. "I just wanted to say I'm so sorry about the all-hands. It was my fault."

"*Don't*," Connor warns me urgently under his breath.

Brad says nothing, but turns toward me more fully. At least I know he's listening.

"I was the one who shared the information with the product team about Version 3.0 and the possibility of the flotation. I spoke without thinking. I apologize."

Brad's lip curls. He flicks his gaze toward Connor. "My office."

He walks away. Connor shakes his head at me, then follows him.

Thirty-One

"How much trouble are you in?" Ben asks me when I get back to my desk.

"A lot."

"Where's Connor?"

"Talking to Brad."

He cringes. "Ouch."

It strikes me that Ben is looking incredibly relaxed as he leans back in his desk chair. His hand is resting on the armrest, his elbow poking away from his side.

"You don't seem that stressed about it."

He shrugs. "I'm not."

"You're not worried I like, ruined the company or something?"

He laughs. "No. I mean, it's a mess and Brad's going to make our lives a nightmare. But you want my honest opinion?"

"Badly."

"I kind of like the drama."

This pulls a reluctant laugh from me. There's something very incongruous about stoic, watchful Ben saying the word *drama*.

Ever the double act, Martin and John glide around the corner, both carrying plates piled high with food.

"Oh shit," Martin says when he sees me. "It's the traitor!"

"Wow, so we're all just . . . certain it was me?"

"It was obviously you," John says.

"Hey, have you been undercover for Product this whole time?" Martin asks me.

"What could I have possibly been undercover for?"

"I don't know, but I'm sleeping with one eye open from now on."

I roll my eyes. "Very funny."

"Not as funny as that squad lead calling out Brad in the middle of the all-hands," Martin says, tucking into a huge bite of sandwich.

"I'm never going to live this down, am I?"

"Oh, never," he says through a mouthful of food. "You will live on in infamy."

"Great," I mutter.

Ben gives me a sympathetic smile. "What did Connor say about it?"

"Not a lot," I admit. "Brad wanted to see him. He's really angry at me, obviously."

"Don't worry," he tells me. "He'll sort it out."

"Yeah," I say weakly, not remotely believing it.

The longer Connor is away from his desk, the more anxious I feel. My panic is contagious. All three of the guys look increasingly uneasy as the minutes pass, and I try not to read too much into the fact I can hear their keyboards clicking away around me, the very obvious theme song of a group chat that is absolutely on fire right now.

I try and message Carrie, but there's no reply. Trust her to be busy working at the exact moment I need her.

She finally pops up, two hours later.

CARRIE: Hey. Can you come up to my office?

I tap on the office door with a knuckle, then gently open it. If my first clue that something is very wrong was the strained smile she gives me, my second is that Connor is sitting in the chair opposite her desk.

He was hidden from view when I first opened the door, but now that I see him, I know this is ominous.

The chair beside him is empty. I take a seat. The three of us form a perfect triangle of doom.

"Thank you for coming, Annie," Carrie says, straightening her shoulders and folding her hands in front of her.

"What's going on?" I ask, looking from her to Connor, who is carefully avoiding eye contact. He is stone-faced, a hand gripping each of his knees. Unbelievable. Is he so pissed off that he's reported me to HR?

Carrie takes a deep breath. "After a serious breach of confidential information on Monday, you're found to be in violation of company practices. After consultation with your line manager"—she waves a hand toward Connor—"the company has made the difficult decision to terminate your employment contract, effective immediately."

Carrie's words hit me like an anvil. I stare at her in shock.

"Access to your emails and any shared company drives has been revoked as of five minutes ago. We ask that you arrange to return any company property you may currently hold off-site within thirty days.

"You can of course return to your desk to gather your personal belongings, but due to the nature of the policy violation, a member of HR will escort you there and then off the premises."

This is like a nightmare playing out in slow motion: the

most humiliating moment of my life unfolding in front of two of the people I'd least like to see it.

Connor is staring at the floor like he's trying to drill a hole in it with his eyes.

I chance a look at Carrie, who gives me such a pained expression I almost can't bear it.

"OK," I say, standing. My legs feel like putty. My voice sounds like shards of glass. "You don't need to escort me. I just need to get my coat."

"It's company policy," she says, rising from her desk and gesturing toward the door.

I look back over my shoulder one last time. If I didn't know better, I'd think Connor was a waxwork. He is completely and utterly motionless. Good. I have nothing to say to him anyway.

Carrie and I walk down the hall in silence. She reaches for my arm.

"Don't," I say sharply. "What the fuck was that?"

"I'm really sorry, Annie. I hated having to do that."

"Some warning would have been nice, Carrie."

"I couldn't."

"Oh fuck off," I snap.

When we get to my floor she hangs back by the elevators. "I'll wait for you here."

Ben notices me first, his eyes flicking up briefly when I'm in his peripheral vision and then doing a double take when he sees the shell-shocked look on my face. He gets up from his desk immediately. I must look an absolute fright.

"What's going on?"

"I got fired."

His eyes bug out. "You're not serious."

"I'm literally being escorted out."

"We need to find Connor. Does he know?"

"He's the one who fired me."

"*What?*" Ben says, completely incredulous. "I don't understand."

Both John and Martin pull off their headphones, asking what's going on, and I repeat the news that I've been fired. They're instantly in a state of complete confusion.

"I can't believe this," John says. "This has to be a mistake."

"It's not," I say. "I violated company policy."

"This is bullshit!" John says.

"They can't do this," Martin argues, ready to take up my defense. "We'll go on strike!"

I smile, but shake my head. "I'm sorry, guys. I hope I don't get you all into any more trouble."

"Aw man, this sucks," John says.

I fight the urge to cry.

"I'll miss you boys," I tell them. "I liked being on your team. I feel like you'll probably all hate me now, but, you know, if anyone's ever in the Village or anything . . ."

I trail off, unsure of what I'm trying to say, and knowing deep down no one will want to stay in touch with me anyway.

Ben steps forward and wraps me in a hug, and a second later Martin and John pile in, until I'm completely crushed between them.

"Don't be a stranger," Ben says when he steps back.

I nod, draping my coat over my arm.

"Bye, Annie," John says, one of his corkscrew curls flopping into his eye. Beside him, Martin gives a pathetic little wave.

"Bye," I whisper.

. . .

Carrie meets me at the elevators but decides physically walking me out of the building is probably overkill. It's very clear I want to leave. She tells me she'll stop by the apartment after work. I waspishly tell her not to bother.

I know it's not fair. I *know* she's just the messenger. But I'm still pissed off. There were a hundred different ways she could have done her job that didn't include hauling me into her office and reading out the company textbook. The thought of what the two of them must have been talking about before I got there makes me want to bleach my eyeballs.

It's those dead hours between lunch and home time, so the lobby is quiet, but still, I keep my head down, hoping to avoid bumping into anyone and having to explain that I am currently in the process of leaving the building for the last time.

I'm right near the doors when I hear Connor shout from somewhere behind me.

I stop and turn.

"Where are you going?"

"In case you missed the memo," I say bitterly, "I don't work here anymore."

"So you're just leaving? Don't you think we should talk about this?"

I give a pitiful laugh. "Sure, Connor. What do you want to talk about?"

"Frankly? I want to ask you what the hell you were thinking."

"What was *I* thinking?" I gasp.

"Yes! You had to have known Brad was going to make an example out of you. What good could have *possibly* come from telling him you were the source of the leak?"

"I was *trying* to help you!"

He looks at me like I've just said the stupidest thing he's ever heard in his life. "And I'm supposed to thank you for that?"

"Yes, you idiot! If I hadn't said anything he would have blamed you."

"So what, Annie? Even if he did, he never would have been able to prove that we put that information out on purpose."

"I can't believe this. You're standing here acting like you're the one who should be mad. *I'm* the one who just got fired!"

"And that's your own fault!" He seethes.

"Oh, thanks—really nice, Connor."

"After your heroics with Brad there was only one way that could end. I *told* you that info was confidential. I *told* you not to say anything. But of course," he says, smacking his palm against his forehead. "How could I forget? Annie knows everything."

"You know what," I snap. "Fine. Maybe that was the wrong call. But I did it for the right reasons. When did you become such a fucking Taskio robot, Connor? Brad sucks. This is wrong. You know it's wrong! And you won't do *anything* about it. You're taking the easy way out. Just like you did with *DinoCode*."

My words land between us with a dull thud. There's a difference in the way we've been arguing. Everything he said was true. Everything I said was mean. The hurt and disappointment is etched all over his face.

He swallows, looks away. Swallows again. "So that's what you really think of me. I'd been wondering."

"Connor, I—"

He shakes his head. "Forget it."

I watch him turn and walk away.

Thirty-Two

Sam is waiting for me when I push through the apartment door, my tote bag tangled around my wrist and dangling at my side. I made a detour to Citarella on the way, thinking I'd bake something—good to have a hobby when you don't have a job—but then saw they had pre-made cookies and thought, you know what? This seems faster.

Sam follows me into the kitchen, hovering over my shoulder while I hoist my bag up onto the countertop. It's hours before I usually get home, yet Sam seems totally unsurprised that I've appeared here mid-afternoon. If I didn't know better, I'd say she was waiting for me.

I take a cookie and then slide the box onto the shelf above me, but then: what's the point? I'm going to eat them all now anyway. I scoop it under my arm instead, and turn toward my bedroom.

"How was your day?" she asks, her voice rising on a note of extremely manufactured concern. Samantha is not a comforting person by nature. Need a hug? Don't go to Sam. Need someone to give you an honest opinion about your bad haircut when it feels like everyone else is lying? Sam is your girl.

"It was fine."

I try to shuffle past her, but she blocks the entrance to the kitchen. "Are you sure?" she says, trying again. "You didn't get fired or anything, did you?"

I stop. Turn.

"I did, actually," I say, my eyes narrowing. "How did you know?"

"I might have heard something through the grapevine."

There's only one way Sam could have heard, and that's through Carrie, who must have messaged her to give her a warning. I am incensed by this.

"Since *Carrie* is such a stickler for the rules this afternoon," I seethe, "why don't you remind her that sharing my employment status with someone outside the company is *also* a violation of Taskio's confidentiality rules. She needs to be careful. I wouldn't want her to get fired."

I push past Sam and into my bedroom, slamming the door behind me. It's a move so satisfying I consider opening my door just to slam it again, and again, and again.

I sit down on my bed, then stand back up. My entire system is humming. I pace in a circuit from one end of the room to the other, there and back again, until I'm dizzy.

The cookies, I find, hold no appeal. I have no appetite. I check my phone. No messages. I check again. Nothing.

I type out a text to Andy. *Got fired hope you're happy.*

I watch as three little dots bounce across my phone screen, then stop. He doesn't finish his reply.

Instead, Sam leaves, hours pass, and I don't hear a word from anyone. Not Carrie, not Andy, definitely not Connor, and not any of my old teammates, who are probably together in a bar right now, laughing at me.

I can't bear it.

Forty-five minutes and one panicky transaction later, I'm scribbling a note to Sam as I race out the door. *Gone back to Canada. Eat the cookies.*

I catch the last flight of the day from New York to Toronto with minutes to spare.

Dad is understandably very surprised when I phone home to tell him not to lock the door, and when my taxi pulls up in the driveway around midnight, both my parents are waiting in the front hall, my dad in a navy house coat, my mom in a peach fleece.

They take the news I lost my job with surprising calm.

"And you flew all the way here to tell us that?" Dad jokes, disengaging the suitcase from my hand.

Mom and I both watch in silence from the foot of the stairs as he carries it up.

I start to crack a joke. She raises an eyebrow like *nice-try-I'm-your-mother*.

There's no fooling her; she's already gleaned everything she needs to know with one look at me.

She sighs, then flicks off the light switch. "We'll discuss it in the morning."

I thought maybe I'd have a message waiting from Connor when I released my phone from airplane mode, but there is nothing, and when I wake up in my childhood bed and there is still nothing, I start to worry that yesterday when he said *forget it* he meant *forget about you and me*.

At the breakfast table Mom is not interested in any of my dramatics. When I tell her my life is ruined, she scrapes her butter knife across a piece of toast and tells me *you must not have had a very good life then*. There are plenty of jobs in New

York, she reasons, and if I don't want to live there anymore then it's about time I moved home anyway.

Dad is equally philosophical. He admits he never really understood *that tech stuff,* and recommends I speak to Dan, who can probably get me a job with the town. If nothing else, the school holidays are only another month away, and the day camps are hiring. No, he doesn't think thirty is too old to be a camp counselor.

"In fact," he says, "they'd probably value your experience."

"She can't do that, Carl," Mom says. "We're just about to do up Annie's bedroom."

I'm outraged by this. "What? No."

"You don't live here anymore," she says, unable to comprehend my objection. "You don't need a bedroom."

What is very clear is that neither of them know Shannon and I aren't on speaking terms. She hasn't told them. I'm not even sure they knew Dan crashed our girls' weekend. It's a total black hole of information, and I can't go fishing for the details without alerting them that something is up.

Shannon is aware I'm in town, that I know at least. Mom informs me she's working all weekend—something about a big open house—but that she's promised to come by for dinner sometime in the week. Sometime meaning never.

I'm allowed the weekend to wallow, and I spend most of it mad at Andy, furious every time I think about how I trusted him and how horrible it felt to have the rug pulled out from under me like that.

When it dawns on me that that's exactly what I did to Connor, I feel even worse. When I remember it's also more or less what I did to Shannon at her engagement party, I hit rock bottom on the self-pity, turning any resentment I felt at Andy in on myself.

But by Monday, my time is up. Mom is totally unimpressed with my intention to lie on the sofa for the rest of my life, telling me pragmatically that if I'm going to be here, I might as well get my appointments done. She's appalled to learn I don't have a doctor or a dentist of my own in New York—*what, don't they have them there?*—and am still registered at my home practice.

"Well then, for heaven's sake, call Dr. Lang," she tells me. "She'll probably see you this morning."

In fact, I have to wait. The receptionist regretfully tells me when I phone that Dr. Lang doesn't see patients on Mondays, but that she'll squeeze me in tomorrow at 3 P.M. I tell her this suits me fine. It's not like I have anything else to do.

Now that I'm on a roll, I decide to keep going—I book in to see the dentist in the morning, and then for a haircut over lunch. I relay my progress back to my mother.

"And then you can drop in and see your sister," she concludes for me. "She lives just behind the doctor's office."

I agree, promising her I'll text Shannon, knowing all the while that I won't.

If living in the city is swimming against the current, living in the suburbs is swimming with it, getting swept gently along, no additional effort required.

I think of Connor and how he told me he always wanted to live in the suburbs as a kid, and wonder at what point he abandoned that ambition, or if he still secretly harbors it. Then I resolve not to wonder about him at all.

My strategy for visiting home, insofar as I have one, is to go as incognito as possible, avoid direct eye contact, and keep my head down. But some interactions aren't so easily avoided. Like, for example, when a girl from my grade twelve history class is my dental hygienist.

We make polite small talk about our lives since we last saw each other—a nauseating twelve years ago—until she finally gets down to work, to my immense relief. It's unnerving running into someone you know at the best of times, but there's something extra uncomfortable about our little tableau: me, reclining in a dental chair, and her, hovering over me holding a miniature ice pick.

Say what you will about going to the dentist, but at least by necessity you can't do much talking.

"You could floss more," she tells me, and sends me on my way.

By the time I glide across town to the doctor's office I'm almost looking forward to the appointment.

Having known me since the day I was born (literally: she was there), Dr. Lang's authority is undeniable, her presence comforting in a way that's hard to explain. This woman has seen me through every vaccination, every broken bone, every mystery rash I've ever had. She knows me more intimately than almost anyone else in my life.

I sit on the bench in the examination room, feeling like a small child, while she takes me through the basics. She listens to my lungs, shines a light in my eyes, looks in my ears, checks my blood pressure. It strikes me that it's all just an elaborate warm-up: going through the motions to offset the embarrassment of doing all this while wearing a piece of glorified paper towel with sleeves that hangs open at the back.

She nods her head in approval when I confirm that I still

don't smoke, then tells me briskly *that's fine* when I get weirdly specific about how much and how often I'm drinking, and with whom.

Next she says: "And are you sexually active?"

The pang of longing for Connor is sharp and unexpected. It vibrates through me like a gong.

"No," I say, my voice shrinking down to a whisper. "I mean, yes—I am, or I was. But I'm not now."

"We'll do a standard check for STDs with your pap smear. Is there any chance you could be pregnant?"

I shake my head no, but imagine it anyway: a vision of a little kid terrorizing the playground, a perfect blend of my bossy sass and Connor's laid-back smarts.

"Why don't you lie down and we'll do your exam."

I do as she tells me while she swivels away from her laptop, dragging herself on her little rolling stool to the counter on the other side of the room. Her brown slacks are ever so slightly too short, her patterned socks on full display in her clogs.

I will myself to calm down, to not think of Connor, or being sexually active, or how we never will be again. It fails miserably.

"Sorry," I say, when she catches me trying to erase the evidence of a stray tear rolling down my cheek with the back of my wrist.

"Were you seeing someone back in the city?"

I nod again, biting hard into my bottom lip, desperately trying to suppress the sob I can feel bubbling up inside me.

"He was really nice," is all I manage to say before the tears spill over in earnest, streaming down the side of my face and down my neck. "I ruined it."

There's no stopping them now, and it seems pointless to try and stem the flow, so I grip my hands tightly on my stomach and stare up at the ceiling, begging the moment to pass.

All the while, Dr. Lang stands calmly at my side. Her hand rests gently on my shoulder. The only sound in the room is the jagged hitch of my breath as I gulp for air.

"We don't have to continue," she offers, but I insist it's fine, mostly managing to regain my composure after a few deep breaths.

For the rest of the appointment, she distracts me with easy, meaningless small talk. She tells me valiantly that I'm in perfect health—broken heart notwithstanding—then silently rubs my back for a second, before handing me a lollipop.

I make it all the way out of the building and to the parking lot, but the second I'm in the car my sadness is a wave so powerful that I drop my head onto the steering wheel and let it crash. I cry so hard and so long that by the time I sit up the stitching from the leather is imprinted on my forehead.

After our fight I was mad, then indignant, and by the time I'd been home for a couple of days, mostly just feeling incredibly sorry for myself. But I can no longer fend off the real emotions that have been lurking below the surface. Sadness, and disappointment, and regret at all the things I could have done differently.

I always thought that if I found true love I'd recognize it, and cherish it, and it would feel bulletproof. What a blow to realize that none of that was true. When the thing I'd waited for for so long finally came along I barely noticed, and then fucked it all up, and for what? I can get a new job. I can't get a new Connor.

Thirty-Three

It's a little after five when I pull up outside Shannon's house. I'm not sure I make the conscious decision so much as I just start driving.

I have never been here before. All I've seen of this house are the pictures from the listing—sent to me by Mom—after they first bought it. Shannon's car in the driveway is the only reason I'm confident I'm at the right place.

The house is an old-ish split-level covered in a sandy red brick that's common in our part of the world. Like everything in Shannon's life, it has been chosen meticulously. It's on the older, more historic side of town, facing out over the park. There's a path cutting through it which you could follow all the way to town hall, if you wanted to—perfect for an aspiring mayor—and the leafy, tree-lined street is quiet, the houses all charmingly well-groomed.

I take a deep breath and ring the doorbell, listening to her footsteps approach.

The door swings open.

I give her a perky *"Hey!,"* wildly overcompensating for how I actually feel, which is like there's an elephant sitting on my chest. I've stopped crying but the evidence of it is still all over my face. My eyes are swollen and glassy, red splotches on my cheeks and neck.

She's just home from work, I think. She's barefoot, her black silk blouse untucked from her pencil skirt. Still *so* many bangles. What a tragedy it would be if she never forgives me—I'll never be able to tease her about the fact she's turning into Mom.

Shannon has yet to say a word. She inspects me, her arm poised over the door, ready to slam it shut in my face at a moment's notice.

"I've come to apologize," I say, shakily thrusting a bottle of wine toward her.

Bringing a bottle of wine is a thing people just *do* in the suburbs, and I thought, maybe naively, that it would be better to show up here with something to offer her. It feels pathetic now. The longer she stands there without taking it, the dumber I feel.

If she's going to leave me on her doorstep, fine. I came here to apologize. I don't need to be inside to do it.

"I'm sorry," I say, taking a leaf out of Connor's book, thinking of the sweet, unfussy apology he gave me after I kissed him. Sometimes simplest really is best.

"I'm sorry for what I said to you at the dress shop. You were right that it's none of my business, and that I don't get it. And . . ." I hesitate, tucking a strand of hair behind my ear. "Worse than that, I didn't even try to get it. Not just that weekend, but before. I thought I knew better than you about what's best for you, and I was wrong, and I'm sorry. I won't make that mistake again. I know you said you hate me, and after how shitty I've been that's fair enough. But if you ever want to be sisters again . . ." The word quivers, shaking with my tears. I swallow, then give her a pitiful smile, like *no need to worry, I'm not crying, it's fine.* "If you ever want to be sisters again," I continue, stronger now, "I miss you all the time. Now would you please at least just take this wine?"

I wag the bottle in her direction, and *finally* she takes it, stepping aside to wave me in as she does. It's as close to forgiveness as she's going to offer me. I grab it with both hands.

Her house—as expected, it's Shannon—is beautifully high-spec. The inside is a lot more modern than the exterior suggests, with sparkling granite countertops and engineered wood floors. It's somewhere between a showroom and a living Pinterest board; the entire place is done in neutrals, and though there's more "live, laugh, love"–style quotes on distressed wooden boards than I'd recommend to anyone, it's also comfortable, and modern, and very on trend.

After a tour of the bedrooms, she steers me back to the main living space and opens a door leading down to the basement, flicking on the light as she descends the wooden stairs.

"The basement is mostly Dan's space," she tells me. "He calls it his man cave, or whatever."

Now I understand why the rest of the house is so nice. She's managed to sequester Dan to the basement, where he's clearly taken full advantage of his design liberties.

If you took a teenage boy and gave him a work placement at an interior design firm, this is what he'd come up with. Ridiculous leather furniture; a fully stocked bar tray on top of a mini fridge for his beers. A guitar hanging on the wall. I know for a fact he can't play, so he's bought that just to make him look cool. It's so quintessentially Dan I almost laugh.

"Where is he, anyway?" I ask as we return upstairs and into the sunny living room.

"Out, don't worry."

I try to say something like *oh I'm not worried* or *that's too bad,* but I don't want to upset our fragile truce with a blatant lie.

I expect her to walk me back toward the front door, but instead, she leads me out onto the back deck and orders me to sit. Seconds later she joins me, the bottle of wine slung under her arm. She pours herself a glass, hands me a can of beer, and then pours a bag of chips out in a bowl between us, her signature chive and onion dip in a container beside.

"How long are you here for?"

I look out across the lawn. "Permanently, I think."

"How come?"

"I got fired."

She digests this piece of information, swiping a chip across the bowl of dip.

"What about Connor?"

I knew we'd get to him eventually. Besides Dr. Lang, she's the only person outside of New York who even knows he exists. Still, I try and dodge it.

"What about him?"

"I thought he was nice," she says carefully.

I trace a finger along a bead of condensation rolling down the side of my beer can. "Me too."

"So?"

"What do you want me to say? It was exactly as you predicted."

"Tell me what happened."

"I don't really want to—"

"From the beginning," she orders. It's the tone of the Big Sister. It brooks no argument.

I take a deep breath and tell her all of it: realizing I'd been laid off, Carrie's underhand HR dealings, my mistaking Connor for an intern rather than my new boss. I tell her about Data

Strategy, and the dashboard, and all the dumb little things that have been filling up my days these last few months. I tell her about losing the wager, and hanging out with Connor, and kissing him, and him rejecting me, and then not rejecting me, and then spending the night at his place after they left, and how it all felt like the start of something big.

It all sounds so stupid saying it out loud. How do I explain the little universe of inside jokes we'd created with each other and how much they meant to me? I simply can't.

As the story goes on, it morphs into a full-on exorcism. Like at Dr. Lang's, now that I've acknowledged it, it's impossible to deny the truth of what happened and my own role in it, and I'm desperate to release all the shame and regret that's been festering inside me.

I repeat what Connor said about me doing it to teach him a lesson, admitting how close that was to the truth, and how given the choice, I accidentally chose Andy, lying and then betraying Connor's trust in the process and ruining the thing between us that might have been perfect.

By the time I come to my sorry end, she's retrieved a pack of hot dogs from the kitchen and turned on the barbecue.

She lights the grill, then closes the lid. "So what's your plan now?"

Think about him every waking moment until I die?

"I don't know. Find a new job, I guess? At some point I'll need to pack up my apartment."

"No, stupid, I meant what's your plan with Connor?"

"It's over, I told you."

"He broke up with you?"

"Trust me, it's finished. There's no coming back from that."

She rolls her eyes. "Oh my god, so *dramatic*. Did he say the words *it's over*?"

"Well . . . no," I say, frowning. "The last thing he said was *forget it*."

"Ah-ha!" she says, triumphant. "Exactly."

"*Don't* give me that look. He didn't break up with me because—because—we weren't even formally dating. That's what happens in relationships now, they just . . . dissolve."

"I doubt that's true."

"Try Hinge and get back to me," I say dryly. Then: "It's not like he's been in touch."

She hums, nodding her head. "Interesting. Have you contacted him?"

I shrug. "He won't reply."

"I think you should call him RIGHT NOW," she says in her bossiest tone. "Just apologize!"

"It's not that simple."

"Are you sure? Are you sure you can't just call him and say *Connor, I was an idiot, please will you give me a second chance?*"

"It won't work."

"It will," she says, sitting forward. She's adamant. "I had dinner with you two. That guy is in *deep*. He's probably sitting around moping, waiting for you to call."

"I don't know what about that story would make you think that."

"It's what *you're* doing, isn't it? That's what people do when they're in love, they just mope around all day."

"That's not—he isn't . . . " I splutter through a denial. Shannon is oblivious to my inner turmoil.

"Annie, guys are like . . . really simple. Like, missing brain cells simple. Just text him."

The appeal of what she's offering is undeniable.

She hands me the spatula while she goes in search of more drinks. I flip the hot dogs, then place the buns on the grill to toast, then imagine Connor coming here, and hanging out on the deck, and bonding with my sister. I will even graciously allow Dan to be there, though I draw the line at adding him to the daydream.

I've just plated the hot dogs when Shannon returns with more drinks, dumping a selection of Ontario's finest craft beers on the patio table, raided from the fridge in Dan's man cave. I'm touched by the invitation implicit in this gesture; she wants me to stay.

We eat our hot dogs in companionable silence, watching the sun leave a trail of vivid pinks in its wake as it slowly inches out of view.

"While we're on the topic of idiots . . . " She trails off, lets the words hang there. "I don't hate you. I didn't mean that."

"Oh," I say, surprised she went there. "Thanks. It . . . seemed like you did."

"OK, in the *moment* I did," she admits. "You really piss me off at times. But I didn't mean it overall."

"You didn't talk to me for two years."

"Yeah, well, you ruined my wedding," she fires back.

"Fair," I concede. "Very fair."

The corners of her mouth twitch. That we're joking about this feels like a good sign.

She hesitates. "You said something, earlier. About how if I ever want to be sisters again. You were *always* my sister, Annie. How else could I have been so mad at you?"

She reaches over and squeezes my hand, and I cling to her until tears are pooling in my eyes, and in hers. That's the thing about sisters, I guess. The love and rage both get blasted at you with full force.

She squeezes one last time, then lets go. Runs two fingers under her lashes.

"So . . . we're OK?" I clarify.

"We're OK," she agrees.

We sit quietly, both sipping our drinks. I want to ask her to put our truce in writing. I need it to be official.

"I feel like we need closure," I tell her. "You know how in the olden days, when people had a disagreement, they fought a duel?"

Shannon is confused. "When?"

"Just like, olden times. Ages ago! That's how they settled things. I think we need something like that. To clear the air."

"If you want, I could punch you?" Shannon offers.

"What? No. Why did you have that on the tip of your tongue?"

"Like a boxing match," she clarifies. "That's basically a duel, isn't it?"

"Um," I say, confused about what does and doesn't constitute a duel, even though I'm the one who brought it up. "I'm not sure. Do you have boxing gloves?"

She shakes her head. "No. We could punch each other with oven mitts?"

The tone of her voice is so openly hopeful, I laugh. She's had just enough wine to think this is a great idea.

Behind us, the patio door slides open, and out steps Dan. He stops short when he sees me.

"Hey, Dan," I say, smiling. Not even his presence can ruin this moment.

"This is a surprise," he says, not unkindly. "I didn't know you were coming to town."

"Unscheduled visit," I say vaguely.

Shannon is still workshopping the problem. "What about, like . . . two broomsticks? That's basically swords."

"What are you two talking about?"

"Annie wants to have a sword fight," Shannon tells him.

"For closure," I clarify. "Like in the olden days."

"I think if you used broomsticks you'd kill each other," he says frankly. "We could probably find a couple of tree branches around here somewhere."

It's a testament to Dan's tenure in the family that he doesn't bat an eyelid at the idea.

"No. No branches. I don't want to get my skirt dirty."

"We don't need to duel," I tell them. "It was just an idea."

"The oven gloves could work," Shannon insists. "I think I've got spares somewhere."

"Why oven gloves?" he asks.

"For boxing." She says it like *duh*.

Dan snaps a finger. "I've got it."

He takes off running. Not thirty seconds later he's back, holding two inflatable tubes that say *Go Tigers!*

"Here," he says, handing one to each of us. "Duel each other with these."

"Where did you get these?"

"They're cheering sticks," Dan says. "From the town hockey tournament."

Shannon is underwhelmed. "I'm not going to—"

I whack her on the shoulder. "These are perfect!"

Dan grins.

"Oh, it is *on*," Shannon says, fired up now. I squeal, bouncing out of my chair.

Dan takes charge from here, arranging us across from each other on the deck.

"I'll give you thirty seconds to whip each other senseless, and then your time is up."

"I want a minute," Shannon says, staring me dead in the eye.

"You have thirty seconds."

"Is that how long duels usually last?" I ask Dan.

"That's how long they last here."

"Fine," Shannon says. She straightens her shoulders. "That's all I need. I am going to win this duel."

"We'll see," I say, shaking out my arms. "I am about to duel you within an inch of your life."

She raises the stupid cheer stick like a baseball bat. My sister is nothing if not competitive.

"Let's duel clean, everyone," Dan says, really stepping into his role. "I count to three, you both move at the same time. When the buzzer goes off, the duel is over. Take your positions."

We line up facing each other, both holding our inflatable makeshift swords in our right hands.

"Three . . . two . . . one . . . and go!" he shouts.

We move for each other at the same time, her swing blocking mine twice before I aim lower, whacking her on the hip, which has all the impact of being lightly smacked with a beach ball.

Though I get the first hit in, she has the advantage now, and I spend the rest of the thirty seconds doubled over laughing at the absurdity of it all while she hits me on the back with a glorified air balloon.

It's physically ineffective, but cathartic. Like we're batting away every single irritation we've ever had.

"TIME!" Dan shouts, plucking the inflatables out of our hands. "Shannon wins."

She circles the two of us, arms up in triumph. She's Rocky Balboa in a silk blouse and a pencil skirt, taking off like a dog with the zoomies. I'm laughing so hard I'm wheezing.

"I was robbed," I huff, dropping back into my chair.

My sister does a victory lap around the lawn, then glides

back toward us, her arms still up in celebration, and jumps into Dan's arms. He spins her and sets her back down, laughing as he does. I can't remember the last time I saw anything like tenderness between them, or Shannon so relaxed, like she doesn't have a care in the world. I feel a twinge of guilt. Watching them together like this, she doesn't seem unhappy.

Mom was right. I'm not here. I don't see everything.

Connor was right too.

"What a rush!" Shannon declares, returning to her seat. She pulls at her shirt, trying to get air between the layer of silk and her skin underneath. "I fucking love dueling."

Dan cracks a beer of his own and picks up a leftover hot dog.

"So what's the deal, then?" he asks me. "Did you come all the way back here so you could duel Shannon?"

"She got fired!" Shannon hoots. "I can't *wait* to tell Principal Morris."

I point a finger at her. "You wouldn't dare."

"She lives the next street over, you know. I can tell her right now," Shannon says, then stands, and shouts out: "PRINCIPAL MORRIS!"

"Whoa there," Dan says, tugging Shannon back down to sit. "Let's try not to get you two booked for being drunk and disorderly on a Tuesday. It won't be good for Annie's résumé."

"Are you even allowed to call her Principal Morris now that she's retired?"

"What else would I call her?" Shannon says. Her eyeliner has been migrating farther from her eyes with each glass of wine. She's like a hot raccoon.

"Just Mrs. Morris, maybe? What's her first name?"

"I think it's Patricia," Dan says.

I think about it for a second. "That feels wrong. Could it be Patty?"

"Yes!" Shannon hollers. "It's definitely Patty!"

". . . So Patricia, then," Dan concludes. "I'm getting out of here before the cops show up. I'll be in the basement. You two enjoy your rager."

We do. We really, really do.

By midnight we've emptied the house of its alcohol and are almost falling-down drunk, cackling at ourselves and each other over every little thing one of us says. We attempt to duel each other three more times. I don't think I've ever had so much fun with Shannon, *ever*. I haven't felt this light in days.

She shows me to the guest bedroom, making special note of the *guest towels,* which she assures me I am eligible to use, and I thank her, then ask what time she needs to get up for work in the morning.

"I should get up by seven," she concludes. "Or at the latest, seven."

"Ironclad logic," I tell her.

Sleep mostly eludes me. As soon as I'm tucked up in bed my mind wanders back to its true interest, replaying my last conversation with Connor on a loop as if my brain is a DVD menu.

Over and over again I see his look of hurt and disappointment in my mind's eye, and with it comes a visceral full-body cringe. I feel like I'm being electrocuted by my own shame.

I squeeze my eyes shut tightly, trying to block out the images, forcing myself to think about something else, anything else. My brain helpfully offers up an image of Connor in bed, his head propped up on his elbow as he traces a path across the freckles on my stomach. *Perfect,* he'd said, dropping a kiss on the mole beside my belly button. It's a memory so sharp I can practically feel the ghost of his warmth.

It's the sound of the coffee grinder that gets me out of bed. I can hear Shannon and Dan in the kitchen, though their voices are muffled from this far away. The room tilts when I sit up, and it takes me a minute to get my jeans on again and shuffle down the hall.

"Morning," I croak, my voice gravelly. I pull out a chair at the breakfast bar, the legs scraping against the floor.

"She lives," Dan says, turning around to face me. "Glad to see you survived the night."

I give a halfhearted laugh. "Barely."

He retrieves the milk from the fridge, pours it, leaves it on the counter. A quick glance toward my sister confirms this is still a major pet peeve of hers—she's always been weird about milk, living in constant expectation of it going sour. I've never met someone who pours more of it down the drain.

She eyes the milk. Crosses her arms.

Oblivious, Dan packs up his bag.

Another thirty seconds. The milk is still on the counter. She can stand it no longer. She breaks.

"The milk?"

Annoyance crosses Dan's features; I can tell the words *who the fuck cares* are on the tip of his tongue, but he doesn't say it, just puts the milk back. Slams the fridge shut.

"Well, I'm off," he says, heading toward the garage. "Good to see you, Annie. Bring Connor with you next time."

"I will," I promise, though it's more wishful thinking than a guarantee.

"Coffee?" Shannon asks, reaching for a mug as soon as we hear the sound of the garage closing.

"Sure."

I have no idea what to make of these two. Was last night the anomaly, or is this? I fear I may never know. She pours the coffee, adds the milk. The carton is in and out of the fridge in seconds.

"How much did we drink last night?" I ask.

"Let's put it this way, the recycling box is now full," she says. "Have you texted your boyfriend yet?"

"No. Especially because he's definitely not that anymore, if he ever was. I don't even know what to say."

"I'm not even sure you need to say anything," she muses. "Just send him a picture of your tits."

I spit my coffee back into my mug.

"What? I'm just saying, men are simple creatures. Don't underestimate the value of a good blowjob."

"I'll . . . keep that in mind."

"Do." She nods. Then checks her watch. "I have to get going."

"Thanks for last night," I say, following her out of the kitchen. "It was really fun."

"It was," she says. "I'm glad you came over."

"Me too."

She walks me to the door, then folds me into a hug. I squeeze extra hard, hoping it tells her all the things I dare not say out loud.

I want so much for my sister to be happy. I'm so scared she isn't. But I have to trust that she knows what she's doing. And like Connor said: even if she doesn't, I'll be there.

Thirty-Four

I shout hello as I kick off my shoes at the front door, and when no reply is forthcoming, head straight upstairs to my room. I stop short on the threshold. I blink, then blink again. It is completely, utterly, empty. Everything is gone.

I hear my mother's footsteps approach. I whirl on her. "Mom, what the hell?"

It's clear she is feeling *very* pleased with herself.

"I told you, sweetie," she says, her tone saintly. "We're doing up your bedroom."

"Where did all the furniture go?"

"We had to move it for the painter coming."

OK, yes. She did mention the painter coming, now that I think about it. But this is extreme, surely. Waiting until I've left the house to return my bedroom to its factory settings is hardly subtle behavior. Where did she hide everything?

I have a brief vision of my parents scrambling to clear all the furniture and nearly giggle. I wonder how long she's been waiting in the wings for me to come home and see this.

"Where am I supposed to sleep?"

She taps a finger against her chin, considers the options.

"Back in your own apartment? Just an idea," she says airily, like she's tossing out a crazy suggestion on the spot.

I glance at her sideways. She raises an eyebrow.

"*Or,*" I say, calling her bluff, "I could just stay at Shannon's? Problem solved."

"Your sister won't help you. She thinks you need to go back to New York and apologize to this boyfriend I'm only just hearing about."

Shannon! Traitor. She must have called Mom the second I pulled out of her driveway to tell her I was on the way home.

I want to argue about it, but you know what? Maybe they're right. Hiding out in Canada isn't doing anything. Connor's not coming after me. If I want to fix this, I'm going to have to go to him. What am I waiting for?

"Let me look up the flight times," I sigh. "Maybe I can go this afternoon."

"Would you look at that, I have them right here," she says, unfolding a sheet of paper she's torn from her notepad. Four flight times are neatly listed. 11:45 is circled in red.

"Wow, you really have thought of everything," I muse, staring down at the paper. "11:45 might be too soon, though, even if I can get a ticket. I need to pack my suitcase."

"I've taken care of everything," she says grandly. "And don't worry about your suitcase. Your father already put it in the car."

At this I do laugh. "Oh my god, Mom. You're insane."

"An insanely good mother," she quips, then leans over the banister and shouts downstairs. "*CARL—*"

His voice drifts up from the basement. She informs him in shrill tones that we'll be leaving in ten minutes.

I don't even bother with outrage, just go with it. Now that it's decided I'm leaving, I want to get going as soon as possible. I feel an almost desperate urgency to get back and make things right.

My parents both accompany me on the drive to the airport.

Dad is pleased; we've timed the journey perfectly, missing rush hour and gliding down the highway at record speed.

Mom holds court from the passenger seat, reading out her favorite inspirational nothings from her Quote A Day desk calendar. She's saved about thirty of them in an envelope she keeps in her purse for exactly this kind of pep talk, and flicks through them one by one.

Since she doesn't know the nature of my relationship crisis, and I refuse to share any more details with her, she's riffing on a range of uplifting themes, covering all her bases.

"*Nothing* is impossible," she says grandly. "The word itself says I'M possible. Isn't that nice?"

"That's very nice." Dad nods. "Something to think about, sweetheart."

"And this one from February: 'If you don't like the road you're walking, start walking another one.'" She pauses to look over her shoulder. "Now what do you think of that?"

"Yeah, wow," I say absently. I'm already texting Shannon.

> **ANNIE:** I can't BELIEVE you tattled on me to mom!!!
> **SHANNON:** What are you going to do, duel me?
> **ANNIE:** She's reading from the Quote A Day!
> **SHANNON:** Here's a good one…A picture is worth a thousand words, so don't forget your secret weapon (your tits)
> **ANNIE:** Wow, what month is that from?
> **SHANNON:** It's the quote from today
> **SHANNON:** Good luck. Say hi to your boyfriend for me xo

I think about Connor the entire flight. How nice he is, and how fun, and how smart. How he hasn't even taught me how to play chess yet.

I keep returning to the last thing he said to me. *So this is what you think of me. I'd been wondering.* Out of every mistake I made, that's the worst. That he could believe I think he's anything other than perfect chills me to the bone.

I text him when I land, asking to talk after work. I tell him I can meet him at the office. I keep it light. I watch the message go from sent to delivered.

And then a big fat nothing.

I guess that answers the question about whether or not he's still mad at me.

But so what? Shannon was mad at me for years. I can survive it. I can wait it out. If it takes Connor two years to get over this, then I only have one year and fifty-one weeks to go.

I'm distracted while dragging my bag behind me up the stairs, mostly staring at my phone screen in case Connor decides to show some proof of life.

When I turn the key in the door, an unexpected sight greets me: it's Carrie, wearing a T shirt (and only that), her arm frozen midway through eating a raspberry.

I can hear the shower running down the hall.

We stare at each other, neither of us moving. Then slowly, I tilt my chin down and check the time on my phone. As if I should note it. In case I'm later called to make a statement about why she's here in the middle of the workday and not at her job.

I raise my eyes back to her. She clears her throat.

"I guess this would be a good time to tell you we're fucking?"

The inflection of her voice is so high that I burst out laughing. She laughs too, expelling the breath that she'd been holding.

Questions fly through my mind like a high-speed ticker tape. I don't even know where to begin.

"When did this happen? *How* did this happen? What IS happening?"

Her eyes dart toward the closed bathroom door. She looks guilty, like she's been caught red-handed.

"OK. Remember the night of the rave?"

"You had sex at the rave?!"

"*Quiet,*" she orders, grabbing my arm and dragging me into my bedroom. She turns after she shuts the door. "Obviously we didn't have sex *at* the rave."

"But something happened," I say suspiciously, remembering wandering round and round looking for them both, and that they were nowhere to be found.

"Er—yes."

"I *knew* it. That's why you took your bra off. You were advertising the merchandise!"

Carrie's cheeks flame violently—all the confirmation I need.

"It wasn't planned," she says carefully. "But she's been . . . pursuing me . . . for a while now."

I wonder how long this has been brewing between them before I noticed, and if Sam ever wanted to ask me about Carrie, or Carrie wanted to ask me about Sam. I'm surely the leading expert on them both.

"Why didn't you tell me?"

She flaps her arms in the universal signal for *I don't know*. "At first, I wasn't really sure what was happening. I could never tell if she was really flirting with me or being mean."

"Probably both," I say.

"Definitely both. But then she got more . . . focused, I guess. Like, brushing up behind me at the gallery and stuff. This is really embarrassing to say out loud."

"It isn't," I insist. "Keep going."

"I was really confused. I have *never* been with a woman before, or even considered it, or anything. But I was drawn to her, I guess," she tells me. "I felt like a snow globe all shaken up."

"Aww."

"That night after you went to bed, she—I mean, we . . ."

Carrie is self-conscious in a way I've never seen her before. Her eyes dart between me and the floor, pinging back and forth.

"Were together. I got it. Then what happened?"

She shoots me a grateful look. "Then you went out all day with Connor and we . . . *got together* again. I thought that was that, but it's just . . . kept going. I don't even really know what we're doing. Or what this means," she says, her distress rising. "Am I gay now?"

"OK, one thing at a time here," I say, squeezing her arm. "How about for now you just focus on you and Sam."

"Yeah," she says, her shoulders dropping back into resting position. "OK. You're right. I'm just freaking the fuck out a little bit."

"Not surprising, Sam is intense," I tease. "But I think sexual awakenings are supposed to be fun, you know. In general. You could just enjoy it?"

She gives me a mischievous grin. "It *is* pretty exciting. I feel sexy, and dangerous. Like now that I've had sex with a woman, what other unexpected thing can I do?"

It strikes me that in all the years I've known Carrie and had a front row seat to her dating adventures, I've never really seen her anything other than completely composed. She rarely gets excited about the guys she's seeing, and almost always maintains the upper hand. This is new for her.

"I thought for sure you knew," Carrie admits. "You've been so obsessed with my love life recently."

I think back over the last couple of months, how wrong I

was about everything. She's never going to let me live this down. But one confession deserves another.

"I've . . . been trying to set you up with Ben."

She bursts out laughing.

"I get it—you're dating a computer nerd, so we all should too, is that it?"

"Something like that," I mumble.

She hesitates. "You're not mad that I didn't tell you?"

I shake my head. "I mean, if anything, this works out better for me than anyone. But fair warning, if you two go down in flames and she kicks me out of the apartment, you're taking me in."

"That's fair. If me and Sam get serious, it'll be me kicking you out."

I pull Carrie into a hug. "Bitch," I say into her shoulder.

"Love you too." She squeezes back.

It's unexpected, but I can see it. Sam is not who I'd have pictured Carrie with, but something about it just makes sense. I send up a silent wish for this to somehow just work between them, for theirs to be that against-the-odds love story that bolts from the blue.

It might actually be me who's the most bashful when the three of us reconvene in the living room. It feels like I've just caught my parents kissing. We've hung out like this a million times before, but there's a new vibe now, and we're all settling into it.

Sam is surprised, then indignant, when she emerges from the shower and sees that I've come home. Her hair is wrapped up in a towel, her skin all pink, no sign of the sharp eyeliner that's part of her uniform when she's dressed to go out for the day.

She looks the way I felt after that night at Connor's—shiny, and happy, and like the world is a brand-new place and she's visiting it for the first time. It's so rare to see Sam without her armor. The fact that she was comfortable enough to reveal herself tells me all I need to know.

"So," Sam says a few minutes later, re-emerging from her room looking like a goth therapist. "Are we ready to discuss the fact Carrie fired you?"

I look up. Her entire face is a dare.

Fine.

"You suck for that," I say, turning toward Carrie.

She's racing to apologize before I've even finished the sentence.

"I know," she says. "I'm sorry. I'm really, really sorry. It was such a mess, honestly. Brad wanted to fire you personally, he was so, so pissed off, and Connor was trying to salvage it, I think, and said it had to be done by HR because of company policy, and they were both in my office arguing about it *forever* and there was no way I could warn you without him seeing, and then I finally got rid of Brad but he said Connor had to stay and I just wanted to get it over with as quickly as possible before he showed back up with security."

God. That is a mess.

"OK," I sigh.

"Don't be mad," she begs, throwing her arms around my shoulders.

"I'm not anymore," I promise. I don't have the energy to be. "That does sound shitty."

"It was," she says, still squeezing me.

"Good. Next," Sam says. "What's going on with Conrad?"

"*Connor*, Sam, Jesus," Carrie whines, pulling away from me. "*Every* time."

"Whatever," she says. Connor's name is of no interest to her. "What's happening there?"

"Currently? Nothing. I haven't heard from him," I tell them.

Carrie's face speaks volumes. "At all?"

"Not since I got fired. He ignored my last message."

I watch as Carrie and Sam both quietly work to put a positive spin on this, but they're both grasping at straws.

"Maybe he's really sick," Carrie suggests. "I haven't seen him in a few days."

"Or maybe I ruined everything and he doesn't want to talk to me?"

"I don't know," she says uncertainly. "He was really upset about firing you. He honestly seemed devastated."

"Read me the text," Sam orders. "What's the last thing you said to him?"

I pull out my phone and read it to her. She makes a face.

"I wouldn't reply to that either."

"Sam."

"What? It's true. And if he doesn't want to talk to you, why give him warning? Just go now. *Make* him talk to you."

"Oh yeah, like you made me talk to you?" Carrie says, raising an eyebrow at her.

"It worked, didn't it?" Sam fires back.

I am forgotten while some shared memory passes between them. The way they're looking at each other is lascivious.

But maybe Sam has a point. Why leave it to chance? I know exactly where he'll be right now.

I glance at my phone, then stand, an idea forming.

"Carrie," I tell her. "I need to borrow your keycard."

Thirty-Five

What seemed like a brilliant idea twenty minutes ago feels like an act of absolute insanity now that I'm in the Taskio lobby. What exactly is my plan here?

I briefly imagine it, letting the scene play out in my mind's eye. I approach his desk and say *hello here I am, I have turned up without an invitation to tell you I love you,* only for him to look through me and go: *sorry, I'm just about to get on a call.*

I quake at the thought, but don't stop moving. If Connor wants to send me away, fine. But he's going to have to look me in the eye to do it.

I swipe Carrie's keycard and slip through the barriers with my sunglasses on and my head down. I feel like a fugitive on the run. It's a completely unnecessary precaution, as it turns out. I ride the elevators alone and make it all the way to Data Strategy without a single person even looking up as I pass.

My heart sinks when I round the corner. Connor's desk is empty. The only two people here are Martin and John, side by side with their backs to me, living in their own little universe, as per usual.

Martin jumps when I place a hand on his shoulder.

"Jesus, Annie! Always with the jump scare."

My lips twitch. "Sorry."

"Hey, Annie," John says, greeting me like a long-lost friend. His brain catches up with him a few beats later. "Hold on. What are you doing here?"

"Uh, looking for Connor," I say, scanning the horizon, just in case he's hovering nearby. Maybe he saw me coming and ducked. "Do you know where he is?"

They both go completely silent, blinking at me, then blinking at each other.

"I guess you haven't heard, then."

Oh god. "Heard what?"

"Connor quit."

I goggle at them both. "I—for real?"

"Yeah. He sent out an email to the whole company telling everyone to go fuck themselves and then stormed out, middle fingers in the air."

I'm struck dumb. "You're not serious."

"No, I'm not," Marty says, smiling. "I'm surprised you fell for that."

I give a little halfhearted *hah*. It speaks to my incredibly agitated mental state that I didn't even question it.

"He did quit, though, that part he wasn't kidding about," John adds.

"So Connor's not here?"

John shakes his head. "They put him on leave straightaway." Then adds darkly, "He knows too much."

I turn on my heel. "OK. Gotta go."

"But you just got here," he says, incredulous.

Marty says something else, but I don't catch it. I'm already jogging away.

• • •

I puzzle over the bewildering news that he's quit all the way to Brooklyn, the subway car screeching and churning on the tracks beneath me. Connor worried I was going to blow his life up, and it's hard to deny now that that's exactly what I did. I *never* thought I'd see the day he left Taskio. What could have happened between then and now? Whatever it is, I'll fix it.

I surprise even myself with the lengths I am willing to go to to get to Connor, slipping past the doorman behind a delivery guy and into the elevators before I'm seen. But outside his apartment door, my courage fails me. Showing up at my ex (colleague? boyfriend?)'s work is one thing (insane), but showing up at his home is another altogether (extra insane).

It's too late to do anything about it now. I steel myself, force a smile onto my face, and then knock.

The door swings open—but it's not Connor I come face-to-face with.

It's Ben.

That's weird.

"Well," he says, his smile mischievous. "What do we have here?"

"Hey, Ben."

"Could you hear your ears ringing, Annie?"

So they've been talking about me. By way of signs I can't tell if this is good or bad.

"Uh, no," I say, my stomach hollowing out. "I just came to talk to Connor."

"Right this way," he says, turning down the hallway. I shut the door behind me and follow a few steps behind. I make it into the living room just in time to hear Connor absently ask Ben what got delivered.

A week away from Connor has done nothing to dim his appeal. He looks so impossibly handsome I feel like crying. He's sitting on the sofa in a gray T-shirt, practically folded over the computer resting on his lap. His hair is wildly disheveled. With one hand, he scrolls along the touchpad. His chin rests on the other.

"Nothing," Ben tells him. "We have a visitor."

He glances up at this, clocking my presence and then reeling back.

Not a great start.

I give a pointless little wave. "Hey."

He turns accusing eyes on Ben. "You can't be serious."

Ben holds up his hands. "I had nothing to do with this, I swear."

My heart sinks through the floorboards. Connor does not want to see me.

"He didn't," I confirm. "I went by the office to talk to you and the guys said you quit. So I came here."

"Right," Connor says, dazed.

Beside me, Ben is what I'd describe as an extremely not-passive observer; all the man needs is a bowl of popcorn. I look at him like *want to chime in here?* His smile only grows. Freak.

"Anyway," I say, my eyes darting back to Connor, "I can see this is probably not a great time, so I'll just . . ." I trail off, pointing back toward the door.

"No, you stay," Ben insists. "It's me who was just leaving."

Connor shuts his computer and stands. "I thought we were going to—"

"Nope. We're not. Ask her," Ben says cryptically, swiping his own computer off the coffee table and slinging it under his arm. "Annie, I will see you very soon."

"Uh, OK? Bye, Ben."

His footsteps retreat down the hall, and then there's the click of the door shutting.

It's even quieter now that we're alone.

Neither of us says anything. Connor has always been so friendly, so open, so endlessly willing to put up with my shit. Am I on the other side of that now? He feels closed off in a way that scares me. I'm worried it's already too late.

I clear my throat. "Ask me what?"

I watch him weigh it up, then decide against. "Why are you here?"

Right. It was never going to be that easy.

"I came to say sorry," I tell him. "And to tell you I've learned my lesson, the hard way. And to promise you I'll never, ever interfere with anything ever again."

He shakes his head. "I'm not sure I want this apology."

I don't get it. "Why not?"

"You interfering is a *good* thing, Annie," he says. "Or, it is when you don't go straight for the nuclear option. You always fight to fix things. I wouldn't change any of that about you. I love how much you care about your people. I just wished I was one of them."

My heart clenches.

"OK," I say. "Then let me rephrase. That's not actually what I'm apologizing for."

"OK . . ."

"I'm not sorry about leaking the news to Product, or that Andy made Brad look like a dickwad in front of everyone. He *is* a dickwad. We don't even know for sure if he has a computer! I think Andy was right to give him hell." He opens his mouth, then closes it.

"This is a weird apology."

"It hasn't started yet," I insist. "Like I said, I'm not sorry for trying to save my friends from losing their jobs when Brad was going to pull the rug out from under them. I'd do all that again.

"What I *am* sorry for is how I handled things. With you. Losing my job and losing you: those two things don't even compare. That you could think for one second that I don't care about you, that you're not the number one thing I care about, just tells me how badly I fucked everything up."

I'm rushing to get the words out now, like I'm a podcast on 2x speed.

"I love you, Connor. I love you at can't-sleep-at-night levels. It was not supposed to be like this. Falling in love at work is a bad idea! But I couldn't stop it even if I wanted to. I know I made a huge mess of things, and I understand if after this conversation you never want to see me again, and that would be fair, but just in case there's a chance that you do, then I just want you to know that I think you're amazing. Like so, so special. The best person I've ever met, actually. And if you ever want to give me the chance to make it up to you, I would really like to do that. I already have a few ideas."

Connor doesn't react at all. It's silent except for the roaring in my ears.

He clears his throat.

"What are the ideas?"

My heart soars. I hold out.

"No. Your turn. What did Ben want you to ask me?"

He shrugs. "If you wanted a job."

"Oh," I say, disappointed. "Um, that's sweet of him. But I think my Taskio days are done."

"Oh, not at Taskio. Sorry, didn't I mention? He quit too."

"*BEN QUIT TOO?*"

His mouth twists. "Why is it that whenever I tell you something, you're way more surprised about Ben?"

I could cry with the relief of Connor's gentle teasing, the dumb way he razzes me up about everything. I want to get down on my knees and beg him to make fun of me every day, forever.

"Sorry," I say, trying to keep it together, to see this conversation through, when all I really want to do is launch myself at his chest. But I don't know my rights; he hasn't said I'm forgiven. There's no mention of him loving me.

"Here I was thinking you'd be surprised that *I* quit."

"I'm more than surprised. I couldn't believe it when Marty told me. I thought—or I don't know, I was worried it had something to do with me."

"It did," he says simply.

I close my eyes, and swallow. How much trouble did I get him into?

"I'm sorry, Connor. But whatever it is, it's probably not too late to undo it. They're going to fall to pieces without you there. You can call them and negotiate, make it better."

"Can I say something now?"

What I see in his eyes when I finally open mine sends my heartbeat into a gallop. He steps in closer, gently reaching forward to catch my hand.

"After the all-hands last Thursday, I was mad at you. And then I was just really mad at myself," he tells me.

"I wasn't trying to be on the wrong side. Or to give you shit about trying to help your friends. I fucking hate Brad just as much as everyone else does. I was angry because as soon as I realized what you'd set in motion at the all-hands I knew one way or another I was about to lose you. And hurt that you didn't trust me to fix it.

"After Brad ordered me to fire you, it all just felt so *pointless*. The thought of having to continue on day after day without you at Taskio was unbearable, and not just because of your coding skills," he adds, with a goofy smile.

My laugh is watery. Hearing him say all this is overwhelming.

He keeps going.

"The truth is, I was unhappy there. I had been for a long time. I was toeing the line because I didn't have the energy to do anything else. As soon as you left, I realized what Ben had been banging his head against the wall trying to tell me for months. I was so ground down by the politics of it all, I forgot I could choose something different. Turns out you were right when you said I was a Taskio bot," he adds, his smile crooked.

"Connor," I say, squeezing his hand. "I never really thought that. I was just running my mouth."

He looks at me and I look back at him. I can feel the dust starting to settle on this misunderstanding, and with it the glimmering hope that maybe we'll be OK.

"So what happens now?" I ask him.

"We do our own thing," Connor says. "I told you before that Ben and I have always stayed in touch with the company that bought *DinoCode*. They liked an idea we pitched a while back, so we could try that, see where it goes. If Taskio floats later this year, we'll have enough cash to fund ourselves for a little while. And you," he adds. "I wasn't kidding when I said Ben really wants to offer you a job."

"But—you never called."

He hesitates. "I wasn't sure if you wanted to hear from me. I expected you to show up and ream me out for being such an idiot. When you didn't, I worried you were done with me. And I don't know. I guess before I came after you, I wanted to prove I could be different."

"I'm not done with you, Connor," I tell him, surprised to realize Shannon was right. He was waiting for me to come to him. "I just didn't think you wanted to talk."

He moves in closer. "I did, for the record."

"I-I went back to Canada. But it was good. I spent time with my sister. We cleared the air."

"That's good, Annie," he murmurs, closer than he was a minute ago. It feels like he's leaning in. To kiss me.

"You know," I tell him, my hands tentatively coming up to rest on his hips. He doesn't stop me. "It was actually her who suggested one of the ways I could make it up to you."

"Oh yeah? What did she advise?"

I can hear the warmth in his voice, the affection. Feel the heat of his skin through his T-shirt.

Mischief dances across my face. "She suggested I text saying *Connor I'm sorry here is a picture of my tits.*"

His responding smile lights up the entire room.

"Wow. That's—that's pretty good, actually. Maybe try it? I'm still kind of mad."

I burst out laughing, then smack him on the arm.

"You're right, too complicated. Just show them to me. In fact, let's take your top off."

"*Connor!*" I squeal when he reaches for my T-shirt, and he laughs at my feigned outrage, crushing me to him. He plants a huge kiss on the side of my forehead, the only part of my face not hiding in his chest. I cling to him tightly; if I didn't, I would float.

"This is serious," I mumble.

"You're right," he says, his voice full of laughter. "I'm seriously happy to see you."

I pull back slightly and look up at his shining, perfect face. The best face in the world.

"You can't just take my top off."

The corners of his mouth move. "Why not?"

"Because we broke up."

"Did we? When?"

I look at him sternly. "In the lobby, after I got fired. You said *forget it*. Remember?"

"No," he says. A bold-faced lie.

"You don't want to go out with me," I tell him, lacing my fingers together on the small of his back.

"Obviously. Why not, again?"

"Well, I blew your life up, for starters."

"It needed to be blown up, a bit. Once is good, though. Please don't do it again."

All the way back to New York I fretted that it was too late—that I'd had a chance at something and I'd ruined it. I'd apologize to Connor, and he'd probably even accept my apology, but there would be no going back to the way things were. He'd seen me for what I truly am. Why? He could always see it. It seems so obvious now.

"What if we work together and then you want to break up with me again?"

"Annie," he says, reaching up to cup my jaw. The way he says my name makes it seem like that alone explains everything. "You must be the last person in the world to notice this but . . . I love you. I'm literally never going to break up with you."

In that moment our faces are two mirror images, one staring back at the other, smiling the same way at the same time.

"Careful," I warn him. "I might hold you to that."

"Go ahead," he says, moving in closer. "I dare you."

Epilogue

One year later

Shannon's wedding sucked, by the way.

Last October, after months of stalling, Shannon finally made the request I'd been dreading—she sent me diving back into Thomas's DMs, kicking off the wedding planning in earnest. I moped for a week, then got over it. If getting married is what she wants, then the least I could do was keep my Danimosity in check.

Well. Connor kept it in check.

I'd describe their nuptials as one of the great bad weddings of our generation. Shannon looked picture-perfect but all wrong in the dress she insisted on buying. Dan's groom speech was a nauseating twenty-eight minutes long. And the bridesmaids wore black. Which was nice, because to me it felt more like a funeral.

I will never understand why my sister married him; but I very reluctantly accept that I don't have to. Really all I can hope for now is that they truly do live happily ever after. Or failing that, get divorced.

What *was* very fun was having an excuse to bring my boyfriend home for the first time, driving him all over the town and pointing out all the local landmarks, like my high school, and the ice cream shop where I won the flavor competition. That fun fact now lives on CAB Lab's new website, underneath the picture of the three cofounders it's named after: Connor, Ben, and me.

We land back in New York early Sunday evening, and decide to stop at my apartment first before going back to Connor's so I can pick up some more clothes.

When we get there, Carrie is lying prone on the couch, watching TV.

"How was it?" she asks, her hand hovering above her head, twirling a lock of hair.

"Terrible," I say, dropping my keys in the bowl beside the door.

"Dramatic," Connor comments, coming in just behind me. "It was great."

"Speak for yourself," I say. Carrie draws her knees up, vacating a spot for me to sink into. "It was painful to watch."

Her palm is already face up in expectation of my phone. I open to the photo app and hand it to her to flick through.

"Did you not have a good time?" she asks.

"No."

"Liar," Connor drawls.

He's leaning up against the wall, arms crossed, eyes shining with laughter. OK, maybe we did have a good time. What can I say? Connor looks extremely hot in a suit.

At the sound of our voices, Sam emerges somewhere from the depths of the apartment, today wearing a denim miniskirt (mine) and—inexplicably—a pair of white cowboy boots. It's like she's so happy she forgot to goth.

"Oh good, you're here." She addresses this to Connor, rather than me.

"Hi, Sam." Connor nods.

One of the more surprising developments of the last year is Sam and Connor forming an alliance—you get the impression that if they really joined forces, they could do great and terrible things.

Perhaps luckily, Sam is way too busy being head over heels in love with Carrie at the moment to do any scheming.

Sam claps. "Attention, everyone. I have an announcement."

I look up from my spot beside Carrie on the sofa. She passes the phone back to me when Sam pointedly clears her throat.

"Carrie will be moving into the apartment."

Carrie sits up. "What?"

"Aww," I say with a big dopey grin. "You *guys*."

"Annie, you're evicted."

Now I'm the one at attention. "Wait—what?"

"You're moving out."

I turn toward Carrie, mutinous.

"First I'm hearing of this," she says, holding up her hands. But I can tell by the moony look on her face; she doesn't hate the idea.

"You can't just decide this without telling anyone," I tell Sam.

"Yes, I can. It's my apartment. And we need the bedroom. It's going to be our sex den," Sam says, joking. I think she's joking.

"But then where will I live?"

Sam stares at me like I'm the biggest idiot to ever walk the face of the earth. "Um, with your boyfriend? Where you basically already live anyway."

Connor has said nothing during this conversation. When I look at him now, he's biting back a laugh.

Carrie thinks it all over. "No sex den. I want my own bedroom. I can't keep up with your crazy hours."

Sam nods. "Done."

"Hey!" I say, outraged.

"I'm hungry. Should we go out?" she asks, changing the subject.

Carrie perks up at this suggestion. "Let's go back to that dumpling spot."

Connor approves. "I'll message Ben," he says, pulling his phone from the back pocket of his jeans. "He can meet us there."

"Excuse me! This conversation isn't over!" I'm trying to sound stern. Everyone is ignoring me.

"It definitely is," Sam says, exiting the apartment first. Carrie looks at me and shrugs, then follows Sam out the door.

It's only Connor who hangs back, peeling off the wall when I stand. He pulls me toward him, his arms around my waist.

"Sorry," I mumble into his chest. "I didn't know she was going to do that."

"Really? She informed me a while ago." I can hear the laughter in his voice.

I peek at him. "And what did you think?"

"I was surprised," he says, solemn. "I thought you were already living with me. Your stuff is absolutely everywhere."

I gasp. "No it isn't."

"Seriously, there can't be much left to pack up."

"Well there is," I insist, haughty.

He chuckles, then drops a warm kiss on my cheek. He's not wrong: I am spending more time sleeping at his place than mine these days.

"So—does that mean you want to live with me?" My stomach flutters.

"Not really," he deadpans. "But how else can I be sure you start work on time?"

"CAB Labs does *flexible hours*," I remind him.

Yes, OK. I am not a huge morning person. Usually by the time I emerge from his bedroom, Connor and Ben have already been tapping away at their computers for an hour. Next month that all changes—with two new employees starting, we needed an office space that wasn't a coffee shop or Connor's dining room table. Our first project is launching soon: a coding academy geared at adults and teens. I was its first graduate.

He takes hold of my hand, dropping a kiss on the back of it. "Annabelle, love of my life. Will you please move in with me?"

Honestly, I can't imagine anything better. There isn't a single moment I don't love being in Connor's company.

"I don't know," I say, pretending to really mull it over. "I'll have to think about it."

He laughs, pulling me toward the door.

He knows the answer already. We both do.

Acknowledgments

When I first started writing this book, I could never have anticipated what an adventure it would take me on. I can honestly say it's been one of the most fun and joyful experiences of my life—like a big group project I never want to end. It's brought so many smart and interesting people into my orbit, and I'm thrilled to have an opportunity to thank them here.

From the top, to my amazing agent, Suzannah Ball: working with you is a joy. There is no person's name I'd rather see in my inbox. Thank you for everything you did to turn *Annie Knows Everything* from a word document into a finished book, including introducing me to the wonderful Caitlin Mahony, Florence Dodd, and Sanjana Seelam. I'd be hard-pressed to find a sharper, more impressive bunch of women. You make an amazing team, and I'm so grateful to have you all in my corner, along with everyone at WME whose work takes place behind the scenes.

To anyone who read and enjoyed this book, you have my two wonderful editors, Melissa Cox and Emma Caruso, to thank for that. Melissa and Emma, it's impossible to put into words how meaningful it's been to work with you both on this project, or how much fun I had, or how much I learned. Thank you for your vision, your insights, for your very funny and perceptive comments in our word docx, and for each writing me an offer letter I'll cherish for the rest of my life.

In the UK, the team at Zaffre make up some of the most creative, tenacious people I've ever encountered, and I'm so proud to publish this book with you. To Sarah Benton, Georgia Marshall, Melissa Kelly, Enisha Samra, Natalia Cacciatore, Clare Kelly, Chelsea Graham, Jenny Richards, Stuart Finglass, Evie Kettlewell, Kate Griffiths, Stacey Hamilton, Kim Evans, Alex May, Anna Perkins, Gilly Dean, and the many others behind the scenes at Bonnier, thank you for everything. It's been a dream.

In the US, I can't imagine a better home than The Dial Press. I love your mission and am so proud to join your ranks. To Whitney Frick, Talia Cieslinski, Avideh Bashirrad, Michelle Jasmine, Corina Diez, Debbie Aroff, Cindy Berman, Rebecca Berlant, Donna Cheng, Cassie Vu, and everyone else who helped make this book happen, you are a truly inspiring team. It's been an absolute blast.

Which brings me to the people who, without their support, I would not have been able to write this. To Rox and Flo, for our many writing days, and to Amanda and my amazing team at Rare Birds who helped me free up the time to finish this thing; you are all the best. Thank you to early readers Niamh Hargan and Carolyn Jess-Cooke for your feedback and enthusiasm. To the friends and family who have known how long I dreamed of doing this, thank you for believing in me and for reading all the way to the end of the acknowledgments to check if you got a mention—you did. And to Janice, Jamie, Christine, Michael, Katelyn, Taylor and especially to MJ: I love you.

Annie Knows *Everything*

Rachel Wood

Dial Delights

*Love Stories
for the
Open-Hearted*

A Note from the Author

Something you should know about me is that I've always wanted to write a romcom.

Another fact, also relevant, is that I own a bookstore in Edinburgh, Scotland, called Rare Birds. Running it has been one of the most exciting, strange, surprising things I've ever done; a constant source of joy in my life.

So much of my professional life is about encouraging people to read for fun, and to put books in their hands that will help them do that, whatever the subject may be. As the store's resident romcom reader, I spend a lot of time thinking about what makes these books tick, and if I ever wrote my own romantic comedy, how I'd want it to be. *Annie Knows Everything* is the answer to that question.

Falling in love, to me, is an act of optimism. Whether you intend to or not, when you fall in love you start to imagine new possibilities for your life you hadn't considered before. I think that's part of why romcoms make us feel good—we get to experience those moments of optimism through the characters we're reading or watching on screen. And though it's obviously true that falling in love entails moments of uncertainty (and when things are going terribly, despair), when I think back over my ghosts of relationships past, what I mostly remember is how fun and exciting and surprising and expansive it feels to meet someone you like and who likes you back.

I wanted to capture as much of *that* as I possibly could, and to write a book where the reader could feel the same, and to do it in a setting that also holds a lot of happy memories for me. I met many of the best, most special people I know through work, and it was a blast to write about the friends we make at our jobs—and about Annie and Connor flirting their way through the workday when they probably had other, more pressing tasks to be getting on with. Not to mention I loved poking fun at the tech industry and productivity culture, and writing about how much fun can be had in and around stressful meetings and emails.

Over the course of my life, I've read romcoms from beach chairs and hospital waiting rooms; books have been with me during my highest highs and the lowest lows. My deepest wish for this book is that you enjoyed yourself, whatever moment of life this book found you in. Writing it was a joy. I hope reading it was too.

Love from,

Rachel

GROUP CHAT:
The Dash Lords

CONNOR: J can you check if there's a connection error re: that missing dataset sales is chasing?
JOHN: Yea
JOHN: 504 Gateway timeout. Looks like it died mid-transfer
MARTIN: It choked again??? whyyyy
CONNOR: Too many records per request?
JOHN: Maybe
JOHN: It times out and quits instead of retrying
CONNOR: Try incremental loads to see if that stops timing out? Then cache the last successful record ID. Script can resume where it left off
JOHN: K
MARTIN: Is Ben power walking
MARTIN: I think he's power walking
MARTIN: Look how fast he's going
JOHN: Flustered for sure. Bet it's about Brad
BEN: `zx`xcv
JOHN: ???
BEN: Sorry
BEN: We have a problem
CONNOR: Say it's not 3.0
BEN: Worse
BEN: Connor, you're screwed
BEN: Annie just hit on me
MARTIN: OH SHIT
CONNOR: ...
JOHN: Can't tell if this is a joke or not
BEN: Not a joke
BEN: She hit on me big time

MARTIN: Wtf

JOHN: When???

MARTIN: Does this mean Ben's the hot one

BEN: I was always the hot one what are you talking about

CONNOR: What happened

BEN: She pounced on me in the elevator

CONNOR: Are you sure? Elevators are small

BEN: She asked if I was single!

MARTIN: Absolute gong show. Did she try to kiss you

BEN: Not specifically

BEN: But the energy was there

CONNOR: Not sure this qualifies as hitting on you

BEN: I'm telling you, she was all over me!

BEN: It really freaked me out

JOHN: That does seem bad. Sorry Connor

CONNOR: Why sorry Connor

MARTIN: Are you kidding

JOHN: Because you like her

CONNOR: According to who?

JOHN: Just seems like you do

BEN: You guys are way off

BEN: He doesn't like her

CONNOR: See. Thank u

BEN: He LOVES her

CONNOR: …for nothing

JOHN: I thought that

BEN: He's just acting tough because she's hot for big red

CONNOR: Never call yourself that again

BEN: 😏

MARTIN: We need to do some damage control

MARTIN: Ben might have to work from home for a bit

JOHN: Just Ben?

MARTIN: Too right J dog…I'm super hot as well

MARTIN: We should all work from home to be safe

BEN: This is good. I like this

BEN: What else?

MARTIN: Connor needs to dial it up BIG TIME. His strategy is not working

CONNOR: I don't have a strategy

MARTIN: Exactly. This is the problem

MARTIN: Now she likes Ben

JOHN: You could tell her she looks really pretty

MARTIN: Nowhere near enough. You need to take charge

MARTIN: Be the alpha

CONNOR: The what

JOHN: You could…show her your backend

BEN: lol

MARTIN: Look it's EASY. Just ask her to stay late then put the moves on her

CONNOR: I think I'm good

MARTIN: Cool.

MARTIN: Have fun at Ben and Annie's wedding

BEN: You're all invited btw. We're thinking summer

JOHN: Ok but seriously. How long should we work from home for?

MARTIN: As long as it takes to lead her off the scent. Could be at least a month

BEN: Could be longer

JOHN: Maybe Ben should tell her she's not his type??

MARTIN: That's genius

BEN: And it's not even a lie

BEN: I don't want to hurt her feelings tho

MARTIN: Let her down gently. Just say heyyy I was thinking about

what you said in the elevator and the truth is…you're not my type
CONNOR: Begging you not to do that
BEN: Not ruling anything in or out at this stage
MARTIN: What's your big idea then Con?
MARTIN: Work here forever and hope she notices you???
BEN: Roasted
CONNOR: Time to stop talking about this
CONNOR: She's about to walk past you
JOHN: Now's the time Connor!!! Swoop in and make your move
MARTIN: WOW
MARTIN: Ben she just looked at you AGAIN
MARTIN: It's so obvious
BEN: WHAT DID I TELL YOU
MARTIN: She's practically drooling
BEN: That's what I'm saying! She's been doing it all day
JOHN: To be fair she looks at Connor a lot too
MARTIN: Oh shiiiiit. Throuple
BEN: Do you think it's my hair? I swear she never looked at me before today
MARTIN: 100% it's the hair. You should take a walk past Receivables. Major cuties over in that department
BEN: I can't wait to tell Jim the people love his fire haircut. He really needs this win
JOHN: Maybe Connor should get a haircut?
BEN: Not a bad idea. I could hook you up with Jim? He works late on Thursdays
BEN: Earth to Connor
JOHN: I think he's gone
MARTIN: Did he seriously close the chat
MARTIN: Connor
MARTIN: Connor

MARTIN: If you don't reply in ten seconds I'm riding the elevator with Annie
BEN: lol
MARTIN: I can SEE him typing. Who's he talking to
BEN: Who do you think
JOHN: He does love her. I knew it.

PHOTO: MICHAEL WOOD

RACHEL WOOD is the founder of Rare Birds, a thriving independent bookstore in the heart of Edinburgh that was named "one of the coolest new bookshops" by the *Sunday Times*. As a former theater kid, Wood's love of storytelling began on stage, but by the time she was a teenager she'd figured out it was much easier to write the lines rather than to learn them. Born and raised in Toronto, Canada, Rachel first moved to Edinburgh to pursue a masters in creative writing and has lived there ever since.

Instagram: @rachelwouldnt and @rarebirdsbooks

About the Type

This book was set in Fairfield, the first typeface from the hand of the distinguished American artist and engraver Rudolph Ruzicka (1883–1978). Ruzicka was born in Bohemia (in the present-day Czech Republic) and came to America in 1894. He set up his own shop, devoted to wood engraving and printing, in New York in 1913 after a varied career working as a wood engraver, in photoengraving and banknote printing plants, and as an art director and freelance artist. He designed and illustrated many books, and was the creator of a considerable list of individual prints wood engravings, line engravings on copper, and aquatints.

DIAL DELIGHTS

Love Stories for the Open-Hearted

Discover more joyful romances that celebrate all kinds of happily-ever-afters:

dialdelights.com

◉ @THEDIALPRESS
▶ @THEDIALPRESS

Penguin Random House collects and processes your personal information. See our Notice at Collection and Privacy Policy at prh.com/notice.